MW01178163

COBBLED *Life*

HM FLATH

ISBN: 978-1-4669-8747-0 (sc)
ISBN: 978-1-4669-8746-3 (e)

Trafford rev. 04/04/2013

 www.trafford.com

North America & international
toll-free: 1 888 232 4444 (USA & Canada)
phone: 250 383 6864 ♦ fax: 812 355 4082

CONTENTS

DEDICATION

To Barbea who would not let me rest
until I completed this story.

ACKNOWLEDGEMENTS

To my immediate family for support, encouragement, interest in the story and their patience in ensuring that I continued in the process.

To my siblings, nieces, nephews and cousins for their willingness and integrity in orally sharing information regarding events, incidents, and authenticity of dates.

To my many friends, for their encouragement, inquiries and constructive criticism as they read, reflected and constructively criticized. Also, for listening to countless stories told over a glass of wine.

To my many teachers, university professors and educator colleagues who encouraged and inspired my interest in history.

Dear Readers

This story is based on my family's background through war, immigration and hardship where historical events shaped the relationships, the directions and the destiny of real people. While many of the names, dates, places and events are indeed factual, several are not and some of the thread that pulls the story together, is fictional and intended only to give the story a sense of reality and authenticity. Resemblances to actual incidents, events and persons, living or dead, have been altered to enhance the saga.

My hope for members of the younger generation, which includes my grandchildren, is that in reading this story, they will come to know and reflect upon their ancestors' challenges and experiences with greater understanding, compassion and appreciation.

The author,
HM Flath

PROLOGUE

The graveyard lay one mile west of the town; on the north side of the old highway number five. More than three hundred gravestones, the oldest dating back to the early twentieth century, marked the plots of those community members that had at one time or another called this community "home". There was an orderly manner in which the plots were arranged, with the oldest located at the very southwest corner of the first row of graves. Over the years the number of rows had worked its way to the east so that by 1983 the newest grave dug lay approximately in the center of the graveyard one third of the way up.

Many years prior to 1983, the town had planted spruce seedlings around the whole perimeter of the graveyard as well as surrounding the site with a five foot high page wire fence.

The seedlings had thrived, so that by 1983 they provided shelter from the fierce northwest winds, as well as providing a comforting backdrop for the graves. Even with the protection of the spruces, the winds that blew, the rains that fell, the hail that hammered, the ice that cracked, the frost that heaved the earth and the lichens that grew on the stones, had worn down the inscriptions chiseled and cut into the tombstones of those who came before.

He came to inspect the newly dug grave and to assure himself that all was in order and that the graveyard was ready to accept another member into its ever expanding community. Following his inspection of the grave he wandered among the graves and eventually found himself gazing at those that occupied the southwest corner. He noted that there existed a difference in the kind of care and attention given to those graves near the center of the graveyard and to those in the southwest corner. Whereas the graves near the center of the graveyard, that were marked by glossy marble, whose headstones stood erect and straight, whose epitaphs could easily be read and where no weeds adorned the grave, those located in the southwest corner were characterized by the effects of time and harsh conditions. Upon close inspection, however, many of the epitaphs which read, "Fondly loved—Deeply mourned", "Gone but not forgotten", "Forever remembered", "Always missed", among other inscriptions, remained visible. As he stepped over the sunken graves and as he went from one headstone to another, he was struck by the irony of the messages inscribed. The promises etched in stone, that those in the ground would always "be remembered, always missed and deeply mourned", were indeed often not kept. It saddened him to think that the bones that lay six feet below the surface, all at one time were living humans; who as people were loved, were held dear, who housed a wealth of stories and information and like the flesh that once covered those bones, now gone forever, the stories and memories—gone and forgotten.

It was November of 1983 and by the month of November, the Saskatchewan prairie had readied itself for the cold, the snow and the storms that were sure to follow. There were no fresh cut flowers laying on any of the graves, the green grass of summer had turned to brown dormancy; everything except the evergreen spruce looked as dead as the people buried there. In November, along with the cold arctic air making its way south, come grey skies. Low hanging, sad looking clouds hovered above the graveyard as if they too were in mourning.

The grave lay open . . . . green artificial grass mats lay scattered around the open six foot deep hole. The mound of extricated dirt too, was covered and the backhoe that the town man had used to dig the hole also sat near by. The operator of the backhoe sat, smoking a cigarette sipping coffee in the cab of his pickup truck where he would wait until the burial service and the internment of the casket came to completion. Following the internment he would cover, not only the casket and the body in it, but also the memories, the experiences and the knowledge of the man inside the box.

The funeral procession which began at St. Paul's Lutheran Church made its way slowly along the dry dusty gravel road. The procession was led by two long black limousines. The hearse which was in the lead carried the casket. The second limousine carried the pall bearers and close members of the family. A variety of sedans, station wagons, coupes and pickup trucks, all with their head lights on and with hazard lights flashing, completed the cavalcade. More than one hundred family members, friends and acquaintances came to gather around the hole to witness the final stage of Otto's ninety-three years of life. Slowly and solemnly the mourners gathered round to pay their last respects and to share in the message of the pastor.

He tried his best to listen to the pastor as the words of internment were offered but, as he scanned the scene and observed the sincerity of the pastor and those gathered, he wondered how long it would be before the promises to remember, to continue to love and to always miss, would evaporate like the promises made to those buried on the west side of the graveyard.

CHAPTER 1

POLAND

It was 8:30 a.m., September 12, 1909 when the knock came on the door of Martin and Paulina Flath's home in Moszczenica, Poland. That knock would forever seal the fate of, not only Otto, but the rest of his family as well.

The morning began as it usually did on a regular work day. Martin and his son, seventeen year old Hugo, had already gone to begin the day's grinding of flour in the flour mill owned by Martin. Nineteen year old Otto, the eldest son, was off to work in a textile mill in Piotrkow. Twelve year old Adolph was off to school in Jarosty with eight year old Teofil in tow. Only Paulina and two year old Olga remained in the house. Olga was sitting on the floor, playing with pots, pans and a spoon while Paulina was busy at the stove stoking the fire and heating water in order to do the weekly clothes washing for her husband, sons and daughter. There was an old wooden tub with a washboard sitting on the kitchen table waiting for hot water, soap and laundry. The clothes would be scrubbed by hand, an all day job. It was hard work but not begrudged by Paulina. Her family was together and Martin brought in enough income from his flour mill to provide a reasonably comfortable life. There was enough money to live on and a house big enough and warm enough to live in. The future looked good. The boys had all gone or were still going to school and they could all read and write in three languages: German, because both Otto and Paulina Flath (nee Hajt) were of German origin and German was their native tongue; Polish because they attended a Polish school which was the language that was used for everyday instruction; and Russian, because Russia occupied that part of Poland in 1909 and the Tsar had decreed it mandatory for all school children to learn to read and write Russian.

The knock was loud and abrupt. Paulina put down Martin's underwear that she had been scrubbing and after wiping her hands on her apron, she opened the door. There before her stood two Russian army officers with sabers by their sides and grim expressions on their faces. One held an envelope. With few spoken words, the officer handed Paulina the envelope and ordered her to open it. With nervous, still wet shaking hands, Paulina opened the envelope, removed the piece of paper and read:

> "**Otto Gustav Flath** of **Moszczenica, Poland**
> *is required to report to the army headquarters*
> *in **Piotrkow** to begin basic training in*

> Tsar Nicholas II's Russian army.
> **Duration of Service:** Two year compulsory
> **Location of Service:** To be determined."

With that, the soldiers left and with that, the Flath family's life would change forever.

With trembling hands, Paulina closed the door, placed the letter on a side table, sat down on a kitchen chair, buried her head in her still wet soapy hands and began to cry. What was going to happen to her handsome, beloved, oldest son? All of a sudden, the house which a few hours earlier buzzed with activity and good humor, became dark, lonely and empty. Only Olga's cheerful banging on the pots and pans with a wooden spoon brought slight comfort to her. She knew that now her life and the life of the rest of the family, would change and she was convinced the changes coming would not be for the better. Slowly, she raised her head, brushed back her hair and began to wipe the tears away with her apron and even more slowly took the envelope from the table, held it close to her breast, looked heavenward and prayed to God. She decided that she would not break the news contained in the letter until the whole family had gathered round the supper table for the evening meal. After making this decision, she hurriedly completed the wash, hung it out to dry and began preparing a special meal.

The last person to sit down at the supper table was Martin and when he sat down, Paulina placed the family bible on the table and began to read.

"Yea, though I walk through the valley of the shadow of death, I will fear no evil, for thou art with me, ... Surely goodness and mercy shall follow me all the days of my life . . . ." (Psalm 23)

And with that, she handed the envelope to Otto. Bewilderment covered Otto's face as he took the envelope, opened it and read the orders out loud for the rest of the family to hear.

There was mixed reaction from the others, ranging from pride on Martin's face, anguish on Paulina's face, excitement on Hugo's and Adolph's faces to obliviousness on Olga's face. Color drained from Otto's face as the realization of the contents sunk in and what it might mean to him and his future. He, Otto, was going to be a soldier in Tsar Nicholas II's army.

Two days later, Otto, with a rucksack containing the few clothes he had and his order papers, said a tearful farewell to his family and began his journey into the unknown.

The road to Piotrkow was very familiar to him, as he walked it every day, to and from work; but on this day, rather than ending his walk at the factory, he would take a different fork in the road and end up at the army recruiting station. From there an army vehicle would transport him and several other recruits to the military basic training camp which was located a few miles outside of Lodz. However, before the trip to the camp there were a few matters that had to be settled at the recruiting station.

The intake corporal greeted Otto, checked his papers, sent him to the recording secretary and from there, he was pointed in the direction of the recruitment nurse and doctor where his physical condition would be examined.

Following the physical examination, he made his way to the army barber. He sat on a stool, the barber clasped his hand clippers and chewed off every hair on Otto's head. He was then ushered to the quarter master stores where he was issued the standard Russian army recruit issue: one pair of boots, a battle dress uniform, one combat tunic, one pair of combat fatigues, two wool shirts, two pairs of wool stockings, two pairs of body underwear, one helmet, one rifle, one bedroll, one rucksack, one belt, one pair of mitts, one tin cup, one spoon and one razor.

After being outfitted, Otto was steered to the overnight barracks from where he would be transported to the basic training camp the following morning. Once at the camp, he would be assigned his bunk, his platoon and his company.

Approaching the camp, Otto could see the camp's fence, guard house and barracks. As he gazed at the complex, he convinced himself that being a soldier for two years would be a good experience. The buildings were new as were his clothes and his rifle. This was going to be exciting . . . . not ever having to march or obey army commands, would bring new experiences to him. After all, this was 1909: this was a time of relative peace. Russia was not at war; the last war prior to 1909, was in 1905 where Russia was humiliated by the Japanese and there did not seem to be any serious conflicts looming on the horizon. In addition, following the Russian/Japanese war, the Tsar embarked on the rebuilding and the modernization of his army . . . . never again would he be embarrassed by a defeat at the hands of a minor world power. With the buildup of the army there might be good opportunities for a soldier such as him.

The drill sergeant barked out his orders to the new recruits. There they stood. All were at attention. They all looked peculiarly similar: all were young, all were fit, all wore the same standard issue uniform. All had their shoes polished, all were white, all were bald and all were of Polish, Russian or German descent. All carried the same standard issue army rifle. All were very similar but there was one very basic difference which was not evident at first glance. The difference was that, among them some could read and write—others could not.

Standing there lined up in front of the sergeant, Otto was filled with excitement but also with some dread. Within a few moments, someone else was going to make a choice for him over which he had no control. This choice would dictate his future. Was he staying in Poland? Would he be sent to Russia or the Ukraine? Was he going to be placed in the infantry, the artillery, the cavalry? Would it be in Siberia? St. Petersburg? Moscow? Poland? The alternatives were many. He would soon know his fate.

The Sergeant lifted up his clipboard, gazed at the printing before him and began to speak,

"Metro Ostrinski, Yuri Symchuck, Nestor Shimilov, Demitre Vakewsov, Vasil Yuminski, Otto Flath. Otto Flath??"

What kind of name was that? It didn't quite fit! A German among the Poles and Russians?

Otto was just one of a thousand new recruits brought to this basic training camp. The Tsar's determination not to be embarrassed in war again was the reason for the massive build up of the Russian Army. In addition to heavy recruiting, the Tsar also was determined to improve the quality of the fighting soldier. He, therefore, enlisted numerous Prussian officers who would be in charge of molding and shaping the largest fighting force in all of Europe. Basic training would last four weeks, at which time the men would be deployed to their respective companies and regiment. Training followed the Prussian model—rigorous, harsh, tough, exhausting—all bordering on being cruel and as such, these methods of training created a highly disciplined, tough, cohesive army. The Tsar's pre WWI army was a proud, well-trained group.

The training was going well for Otto. He was young and strong, and he fit in well with most other members of his platoon. In spite of the high levels of fitness among the men, the early morning conditioning drills were brutal and beginning to take their toll. After two weeks of training, the recruits, though accustomed to the routine, were often fatigued and neared exhaustion. On one particular morning the drills had been exceptionally strenuous. The recruits had been put through their paces of the obstacle course three times before 10:00 a.m., followed by a three kilometer cross country run. Covered with mud mixed with sweat, fatigues ripped from crawling under barbed wire, muscles aching from climbing the rope ladder and from hundreds of push-ups, and with the constant verbal abuse showered on them by the drill sergeant, their tempers became very short. Finally at noon, the exhausted recruits lined up, tin cups in hand, and waited for their daily cup of gruel. Tired and weary Otto stood in line, head down, eyes fixed on the ground staring at nothing in particular. The line inched forward but Otto was slow to move ahead in step with the recruit ahead of him. He glanced up and was about to take a step forward when he felt a great push from behind and felt himself being shoved to the ground. With his cup half filled with dirt and with hands and feet caked, he shifted his eyes upward to see what had happened to him. There above him with hands on his hips and a scowl on his face stood Vasil, one of the men in his platoon that he could barely tolerate. Upon seeing who was responsible, Otto's body began to be consumed by rage; he knew that he was no match for the bigger, stronger Vasil, but he also knew that if he did nothing and backed down from a fight, he would lose face and be branded a coward. Once branded, he would become the target for every other bully in the platoon.

There are times when emotions and blind temper override our common sense and dictate our actions . . . . sometimes with regrettable results.

Without a word, Otto put down his cup, wiped the dust out of his eyes with his sleeve, leapt from the ground and flung himself at Vasil. The fight was on. Very quickly, the combatants were surrounded by other recruits who enjoyed witnessing a good scrap. The combatants did not disappoint and as they wrestled, punched, kicked and yelled, the crowd grew bigger, the volume of dust created grew larger and the cheering increased as the crowd urged their favorite on to victory . . . . or defeat.

Pokovnik Constantine Vasiletvich Zaharoh, the officer second in command of the regiment, came this day to do his weekly inspection of the training camp. Hearing the yelling and cheering at the slop kitchen, he wandered over to see what the commotion was all about. He pushed his way through the crowd of onlookers and calmly watched the scrap for a few moments. When he had seen enough, he strode into the open, barked out an order to stop, reached down and grabbed Otto by the collar and yanked him to his feet. Sheer terror consumed Otto when he realized who it was that had stopped the fight . . . . he was fully aware of the consequences of being a participant in a fight . . . . fighting was forbidden and he would be punished harshly for it. So with fear, pain and trepidation, Otto unsteady and trembling tried to stand erect. He saluted the Pokovnik.

"What is your name?"

"Otto Gustav Flath", came the barely audible reply.

"Say your name again. I can't hear you," commanded the Pokovnik.

Having had a second to compose himself, Otto stood erect, saluted the Pokovnik again and repeated, "Otto Gustav Flath, sir."

"Report to my office immediately!"

With that, Otto scraped as much dirt and blood as he could from his face, hands and uniform. He found his cup and spoon and after emptying the dirt from it, he slowly made his way to the Pokovnik's office. He knew he was in deep trouble and as a cold sweat began to break out on his face, his mind raced through the possible punishments he might receive. Would he be placed in solitary confinement? Would he be placed in the guard house for a week? Would he have to clean latrines for the rest of his training period? Would he have to sleep outside with only a blanket or perhaps on a bed of rifles? Would he have to dig holes? Would he have to put up targets at the shooting range? The army had effective ways to deal with those who did not conform and strictly obey.

Slowly and deliberately, Otto opened the door to the Pokovnik's office. He had never had to face disciplinary action before. He did not know what to expect and as he continued forward, he felt the palms of his hands become clammy, felt his stomach churn and hot burning bile began to fill his throat and mouth. Here he was . . . . he had no choice . . . . running was not an option . . . . he had to face the consequences. The army did not offer the rule breakers any options. The army made decisions for you. You obeyed, period! Otto was not in control of his destiny . . . . the Pokovnik was!

CHAPTER 2

Otto closed the door behind him, stood at attention, saluted the Pokovnik and with the bravest face he could muster and with his voice cracking, barked,

"Private Otto Flath reporting, Sir."

"Stand at ease and come, come closer to my desk, private."

"Yes, Sir."

As Otto approached the desk, he saw a handsome man, aged about forty, before him. He was broad shouldered, clean shaven (except for a handlebar mustache), clean shaven head, neatly pressed brownish khaki uniform, tunic emblazoned with medals and bars representing many commendations for past service and military achievements. He was obviously a career military man.

His eyes were blue, his eyebrows dark but showed signs of greying, his hands looked strong, as did his forearms. His fifty-six inch chest rose and fell slightly as he breathed and carefully reviewed the report before him. Grimly, his eyes rose from the paper in front of him and then focussing them on Otto, he said,

"You know, son, that fighting is forbidden and you must be disciplined."

"Yes, Sir."

"Tell me again. What is your name?"

"Otto Gustav Flath," came the reply.

"How old are you?"

"I will be nineteen in December, Sir."

"Flath, Flath, Flath," the Pokovnik mused with chin resting in his hand, "that is a German name, is it not?"

"Yes, Sir."

"You know, Otto, that Russia and Germany are not very friendly toward one another anymore and you being in the Russian army may be very difficult for you. I would advise you to change your name, but let me ask you some more questions. Are you able to read and write?"

"Yes, Sir. I can read and write in Russian, Polish and German, Sir."

With that, the Pokovnik's eyebrows raised slightly, his eyes opened a little wider and a frown appeared on his forehead. "Can you ride a horse?"

"Yes, Sir."

"Can you cook?"

"No, Sir."

The Pokovnik tapped his feather pen on his desk for a few moments, then he looked Otto in the eyes and said, "Otto, I am in need of a new personal valet. The one I have now has served his term and wants to return to his family, so I am thinking that you may be the man to replace him."

Otto just stood there in disbelief. Could this be real? Am I dreaming? Surely, I am not that fortunate! A thousand images raced through his mind but he merely stood there waiting for further instructions.

"You get yourself cleaned up and report back to me at sixteen hundred hours sharp . . . . here! We will talk some more, at which time I will make my decision."

In disbelief, Otto marched back to his barracks and almost trancelike, washed the crusted blood from his face and hair. He carefully shaved his face, repressed his uniform, all the while rehearsing possible responses to the inquiries which would be made by the Pokovnik. Here was his one opportunity to escape the harsh conditions of a regular soldier and he better make the best of it.

Sixteen hundred hours came quickly and he promptly reported back to the Pokovnik, still in awe and full of excitement. Once again, he opened the door to the officer's office and faced the Pokovnik.

"Otto, I have made up mind, you will be my valet for the next two years; but first, you must serve your punishment for fighting. After that you will complete your basic training and following that, I will issue your order papers as to where and when you will report to me in St. Petersburg. Relax Otto. I know you will be a trusted and faithful servant. I am posted here for another month and then I am returning to St. Petersburg for the winter."

Otto still thought he was dreaming.

So it came to be that Otto Gustav Flath was spared the wretched life of a foot soldier in the Tsar's army where he would be merely one of one million four hundred thousand. Where the life of one soldier meant nothing. Where food was scarce and where comforts were few. Where time away from family was measured in years . . . . not days or weeks. Where privacy was nonexistent. Where creativity and individualism was stifled. Where most of your comrades were illiterate and superstitious. Where surviving a battle was questionable. Where sleeping outside on maneuvers was the norm. Where life in most armies was robotic and mindless. Otto was lucky. He avoided the harsh existence of a foot soldier in Tsar Nicholas II's army.

That night, Otto lay shivering in his bed roll. He was outside, laying on six rifles, rain soaking his face and blanket. He was paying for his fight earlier in the day. Even though the discomfort was nearly killing him physically, emotionally he was ecstatic. What will it be like to serve such a high ranking officer?

"I pray to God that I will be able to meet his expectations. I pray to God that he will like me and not make me return to the misery of a foot soldier," murmured Otto.

The promise of a warm dry bed, clean sheets, clean pressed uniform, good food, hours of work that in the army could only be dreamed about, but all which was about to happen to him . . . . he could endure the present pain gladly . . . . if only he could meet the demands placed on him.

Otto knew that he had lots to learn. What did he know about the life of a high ranking officer? Protocol? What was that? Social graces? Etiquette? He knew nothing about an officer's way of life. After all, he came from a rural polish society where, at that time, travel was limited, money was scarce, communication was by letter, notes, or word of mouth. Where the main source of social etiquette was learned from your family, neighbors or church gatherings. He had a lot to learn. So much so, that it frightened him.

He knew that he would have to accompany the officer to the officer's parties. He knew that he would be responsible to keep the officer's clothes spotless, his shoes shined, his supply of socks, underwear and all toiletries well stocked, even his saddles polished and his horses brought to him. He wondered what it would be like living with the officer in his home. Surely the task would prove to be overwhelming and he would fail and be sent back to regular duty.

"Dear God in heaven. I pray that you will give me the courage and ability to carry out the officer's demands successfully."

Over and over, many imagined images of what the future might bring, flashed through his brain. Gazing at the clouds, feeling the cold droplets of rain on his face, he finally fell asleep. Tomorrow he was going to wake up and prepare for his new assignment. God help him.

Otto's years from 1909 to 1917 were spent looking after the personal needs of Constantine Vasilevich Zaharoh, Pokovnik of a cavalry regiment in Russia's 3rd army, traveling with him on maneuvers and looking after his daily needs. I wish I knew where and when these assignments occurred and what his specific routine was like during his years in St. Petersburg, but I don't. He rarely talked about this time in his life. I wonder why? Maybe he couldn't bear to compare the easy life filled with parties, good food, playing flute in an army band and little responsibility with the reality of his life in the 30's, 40's and 50's . . . . nine children to feed and clothe, with very few comforts but a great deal of responsibility. Did he harbor some secrets about those years that he dared not share? The more I reflect on this, the more I believe the latter to be true.

Occasionally, and mostly on Sundays, Otto would leave the house and go for a walk lasting several hours. I don't know where he went . . . . I didn't follow him . . . . or why he went but now I can imagine what he would be thinking during these solitary times. I know that I do the same thing now. I reflect on my past. I replay the events that led me to where I am today. I recall the stupid things I did and also the odd good and smart things I did. I suppose it was no different for him. We, as kids, never asked about his experiences and he rarely volunteered. I guess he thought we weren't interested or perhaps there were secrets he did not want to share and maybe not sharing them, was the best for all of us. The bits and pieces of information about those years came to me when my parent's friends or other family members dropped by for an afternoon or evening and we would overhear talk as they reminisced about life in the old country. His real story went with him to his grave . . . . lost forever . . . . too bad, but I guess that's the way life is. We get so caught up in the present, that the past has no interest or space in our daily routine. It is only as we get older and have more time, that we begin to realize that life isn't only about the present or the future. The past also has a hold on us whether we want to admit it or not. That is why history books are written, that is why billions of dollars are spent exploring the universe, digging up pots, unearthing ancient civilizations, musing about our origin. We all have a deep desire to know who we are, where we came from and how we got here . . . . I suppose that is why searching out our family trees has become big business.

CHAPTER 3

RUSSIA

Otto was leaving the home he grew up in. He knew where he was going and to some degree what his future held in store. He had completed his basic training and was off to St. Petersburg, Russia. The journey would carry him from Piotrkow, Poland, north and east to the shores of the Baltic Sea where St. Petersburg lay, the Venice of the North. The trek stretched from Piotrkow, Poland to Warsaw, and on to Vilnus, Lithuania, through Latvia, and onward to Pskow, Russia. Then finally, on to St Petersburg. In total, a distance of approximately 1850 kilometers. The journey would take five to six days. Otto had time to think.

The countryside between Warsaw and St. Petersburg consisted of mostly the northern European plain which was generally flat and monotonous. The train travelled slowly stopping at every hamlet, village or town along the way . . . . top speed was thirty-five kilometers an hour. The train track had been recently completed and the trains that serviced the route were relatively modern and comfortable. It seemed peculiar to Otto that the clientele on board did not conform to the modernization of the train. The villages and the towns along the way were very similar . . . . the houses were built on both sides of a single dirt road. Every house was built of logs covered with a mixture of mud, manure and straw. The roofs were all thatched and most of the barns were attached to the houses. Most of the stops consisted of only a small platform. Poverty was on display everywhere . . . . from the buildings to the way the people dressed. Otto congratulated himself that he would not have to spend his life in the manner in which he viewed the people boarding and departing the train. He was off to the jewel of the north . . . . the envy of most cities . . . . even Paris. He lost interest in watching the countryside pass by and as one day became the next, he became increasingly anxious to begin his new life. What would it be like? Would he be able to go to the ballet? Would he meet beautiful girls? Would he have to work hard? Would he get along with the Pokovnik's family? A thousand thoughts filled his head. Soon these questions would be answered.

As the train came ever closer to St. Petersburg, the villages were spaced farther and farther apart. The farmland was turning into a spruce and birch forest. Mile after mile of nothing but bush and swamp. He knew he must be nearing his destination. On the morning of the seventh day of travel, St. Petersburg displayed itself in all its splendor. Narrow dirt roads turned into wide cobbled boulevards; mud houses turned into bricks homes with big well-manicured lawns and gardens. The scrubby spruce trees became large firs and the people's dress turned into fine fur hats, wool coats and white shirts. Barren landscape became a hub of activity. Everywhere he looked he saw people bustling about, fine carriages transporting men, women and children from somewhere to somewhere else. On the outer edge of the city, he passed huge factories; then, as he neared the railroad station, he passed by fine buildings . . . . the likes of which he had never seen before.

The train began to slow down and suddenly there it was . . . . the end of his journey by train and the beginning of a new human journey. Otto grabbed his rucksack, slung it over his shoulder, stepped off the train and onto the station platform. The station itself was a marvel . . . . marble floors and columns . . . . the roof, made of glass, seemed to stretch forever. He could hardly believe his eyes. Moszczenica, Poland . . . . St. Petersburg, Russia . . . . worlds apart! How would he fit in?

The Moscow Train Station was located near the terminus of Nevsky Prospect, St. Petersburg's main boulevard. The boulevard was built by Peter the Great and he built it to rival the finest streets in all of Europe. It was wide and straight, beginning across the Neva River from the winter palace, stretching three kilometers in distance and lined with more than 1000 shops. The buildings erected on both sides were in themselves works of art. All designed by the best known neoclassical architects from all of Europe but mainly from France, Italy and Germany. In order to build the boulevard and erect the buildings, Peter the Great enlisted serfs from across Russia and paid them nothing. Thousands died during the construction but that did not matter . . . . it was a wonder!

As Otto stood there in wonderment, a taxi pulled up beside him and he heard a voice call his name. He shook his head, blinked his eyes and turned his attention to where the voice originated. The voice came from the taxi driver. He introduced himself to Otto,

"My name is Oleg and I am Pokovnik Constantine's chauffeur. He has sent me to bring you and your belongings to his quarters."

The taxi was a two seater which could carry four passengers plus the driver. It ran on wooden wheels capped by solid rubber bands. The seats were cushioned black leather, the canopy was a black shellac canvas, the body was painted black and was adorned by the double headed eagle . . . . **the property of the Tsar.** It was pulled by two matching, shiny, sturdy black geldings. Not a speck of dirt was seen anywhere.

Otto took it all in as he stepped on the running board and plopped himself onto the luxurious back seat. This was going to be wonderful! He could sense it all now! The grandeur of the city and the life style of the military officers in St. Petersburg were his to embrace, experience and enjoy. What an opportunity . . . . he was not going to waste it. He was nineteen years old and in a city of 2,000,000 inhabitants.

Oleg gently slapped the reins on the horses rumps and the team responded by quickly establishing a steady quick trot.

Their shod hooves making a rhythmic clop, clop on the smooth cobble stones of the street. The sound from the wheels passing over the cobbles was muffled by the rubber rims. It was fall, the air was crisp and clean, the streets were clean, the trees were losing their leaves and the smell of decaying leaves mixed with the odor of freshly deposited horse droppings peaked his senses.

The carriage traveled from the station towards the army barracks which lay on the northeast bank of the Neva River along with other installations. Traveling along these roads, unlike traveling through the Russian countryside, was most interesting and exciting. The thirty minute ride went by in a flash. The carriage crossed a sturdy, stone built bridge across the 500 meter Neva, turned left off of the first cross street and 400 meters later, stopped at the guard house at the entrance to what was going to be Otto's new home . . . . home for at least two years.

The military police at the guard house ordered Otto to step down from the carriage and called him into the guard house to check his credentials and order papers before he would let Otto proceed into the camp. The inspection did not take long, his papers were stamped and off he went to meet his new co-workers and Constantine Vasiletvich's family.

I often wondered what a nineteen year old man from a tiny polish village would be thinking when he was suddenly exposed to a city of two million people. Coming from a place where you knew everyone by first name; where your family lived to give you comfort and safety; where your friends were; where your house was rustic having no electricity, no running water, heated by a wood burning stove; where the best dressed lady, maybe had two good dresses; where your social life may have centered on two or three evening community dances at the local school in a year; where life was simple. Then suddenly being thrust into a complex sophisticated maze of social diversity, contrast of wealth and extreme poverty, social and political unrest, unparalleled architecture, wide paved streets with side walks. Homes that were lit by electricity and had indoor running water. Where your bathroom was self-contained. Where you could listen to a radio. The contrast between village life and life in the metropolis is staggering and surely the big city would be totally intimidating.

Life would begin anew for Otto. If he was going to have any life outside of his job, he was going to have to make new friendships, become involved in new spare time activities, adjust to a completely different way of life. There were no brothers to talk to, no close boyhood friends to hang out with, no community gatherings, no Sunday family dinners. Life in the big city and in his new surroundings, could be a lonely one. He did not even know the Pokovnik beyond his name, rank and place of residence. What he did know was that the conduct of the officers, the officer's families, and their servants was proper, strictly ruled, dignified and where failure, inefficiency and tardiness were totally unacceptable. One could be dismissed from a position for the slightest of mishaps. He would do his job, do it well and keep his mouth shut.

The officers and their families were housed in separate sections within the larger army compound. The front doors of the unit faced the street and the rear entrances faced the inner court yard. The horse barns used by the officers were located on the opposite side of the houses.

Oleg steered the horses and carriage through the gate to the complex, stopped the team in front of the Pokovnik's residence, tied the reins, stepped down from the carriage, unloaded Otto's rucksack . . . . then knocked on the door. Within a minute, the door opened and a woman wearing a black dress, white apron and a white babushka appeared. Oleg said a few words to her and she responded by approaching Otto and saying,

"Dybozcha. I was told that you would be coming today. Come in, come in; I will show you to your room."

The entrance to the rear of the apartment was small as was the rest of the apartment. He had anticipated being welcomed by a larger dwelling; however, he was to learn later, that since the build up of the army which began two years previously, housing was at a shortage and even the officers had to put up with smaller residences than they had been accustomed to. However, comparing it to what he had been used to, it was a castle. The building was constructed of stone and brick. It contained a kitchen, dining room, parlor and a small den on the main floor and four bedrooms and a bathroom on the second floor with a couple of smaller rooms in the attic where he would sleep. The bathroom was shared by all. The apartment seemed to be furnished with only the basic furniture; there seemed to be a lack of personal touches to the decorating, however he did notice a piano in the parlor.

Otto was led up the two flights of stairs and was shown the door behind which his room was located. The doorway was low and as he entered the room, he had to duck his head to pass through it. The room contained a single cot, a small bedside table, a cupboard for his clothes and two chairs. One small window opened up to the courtyard which was surrounded by other buildings, identical to the one in which he was to live. A coal oil lamp sat on the bedside table . . . . apparently the attic was not wired for electricity.

Nothing more was said between Otto and the servant. He closed the door and surveyed the room that was to be his for at least two years, unless something went wrong and he would be dismissed only to serve his time as a regular soldier. Another possibility would be that the Pokovnik would be transferred to another regiment or get killed in battle. He would be called when the Pokovnik returned from his day duty and would inform Otto of the details of his new position.

At 1600 hours sharp, Otto heard the back door open and heard the sound of a strong male voice. By this time Otto had put away the few civilian clothes that he owned, had found a place for his shaving razor, razor strap, shaving brush and comb (which he did not need). He had placed his bed roll on the cot and hung his army great coat in the closet. Lastly, he found a place for his identification papers, his writing pad, and his address book. This was the sum of his belongings: he owned nothing else.

He heard the sound of footsteps on the stairs leading to his room . . . . then a soft tapping on his door.

"Otto, the Pokovnik has asked that you come downstairs to meet him and the rest of the family."

"I'll be right down," replied Otto.

He had been waiting, ready for an hour, for this request. Finally, he would learn what his tasks would entail and he would meet the family and find out how he would be treated. He entered the parlor where the family had gathered and quickly surveyed the people who were all standing waiting for his entrance. His eyes focussed first on Constantine Vasiletvich . . . . the dominant presence in the room. Next his eye focussed on Mrs. Vasiletvich. She, like her husband, stood erect and proud. She looked to be a few years younger than Constantine. She was tall, trim and was obviously physically fit. She was wearing riding breeches, a leather jacket with a white blouse underneath. Her hair was black, shoulder length with slight curls. Her eyes were deep set, brown and her face was tanned. To Otto, she looked ravishing.

"Otto, this my wife, Tatiana." Otto stepped forward, kept his gaze on her eyes and offered his hand, which she took, clasped it gently and shook it politely. Introductions were then made with the children; Peter, fourteen, twelve year old Alexander, and seven year old Natalie. Last to be formally introduced, was the maid Olga.

Following some polite conversation about the train trip and the weather, the children were dismissed and Constantine, Tatiana and Olga sat down and listened while Constantine gave Otto a list of expectations, duties and expected remuneration.

"Tomorrow, Olga will take you to our tailor to have you fitted for your daily work clothing and your formal dress clothing. You will also be issued with two pairs of shoes, underwear, shirts, winter and summer coats as well as wool sweaters, gloves and mitts. You will be responsible for purchasing your toiletries, casual wear and writing paper."

Tatiana interrupted, "Otto, you will eat with the family but, when we have guests or are entertaining, you will have to eat in the kitchen with the rest of the servants."

"You will be free to go where you wish on your time and days off but you must not stay out later then 22 hundred hours. We will give you a key to our house as well as a general pass to get out of and back into the compound. When our regiment is on maneuvers, you will accompany me personally. I will give you a list of duties and chores for you to do while we are here as well as for when we are away. We all welcome you Otto, and hope that you will be happy here and will be of good service to us."

"Thank you very much," was all that Otto could say.

The valet that Otto was replacing stayed on for two weeks to show Otto 'the ropes' which made falling into a regular routine much easier. His time was evenly divided between work around the stables and work on Constantine's uniforms. The duties involved polishing, cleaning, washing and exercising the Pokovnik's horses, washing and ironing clothes. There was lots to do but once the routine was established, he found that he usually had two or three hours to spare in the afternoon. He began filling in the time by walking around and investigating the whole army camp. To his surprise, it was immense. The camp was divided into several sections. The administration buildings were found near the guard house. Also in the same area, the messes as well as the camp infirmary were located. The next section bordering the complex, was the married officers quarters as well as the singles quarters. Then across from the parade square, the soldiers barracks were located. It seemed like these went on for miles. Scattered among the barracks were barns, store houses and haystacks. The armories were situated at various locations. The whole complex housed 230,000 soldiers, 50,000 horses, haystacks, equipment yards, even the beginning of motorized war equipment, namely trucks, motorcycles and cars. This compound housed only the hussars, cavalry, cossack and infantry divisions. The artillery, navy and whatever air force there was, were housed elsewhere. Beyond the barracks and outlying buildings lay the exercise fields. These fields contained the simulated mock battle fields, shooting ranges and marching routes and horse pastures. Otto could only explore a small part each time he had some time to spare.

Otto did not explore any area outside the complex during the first two weeks of his new job. He polished, shined, pressed, folded, refolded, swept, organized and reorganized everything that he was responsible for. He was determined to stay. He liked the children and Tatiana was someone he could look at all day. His meals were as good as those at home and he had his own room. Life for the first two weeks was good.

On the eve of his third week, Constantine called Otto into his den and asked him to sit down as he had something to tell Otto.

"Ottto, you have been my valet for two weeks now and it is time that I gave a report on your progress".

Otto did not know what to expect . . . . he had done the best he could . . . . he knew that he was not told ever to repolish or reshine any harness brass buttons, or shoes. He thought that he was getting along well with Olga and Oleg, so he felt quite confident that his report would be positive.

"Otto, this is the Russian Army. What you see here is only a small portion of the Russian armed forces but also what you do see here is the showcase of the Russian Army. When visitors from abroad come to review our forces, this is where they are brought. I know that you have been exploring the facilities and that is why I am telling you this. We have the finest horses, the best loyal soldiers, the finest uniforms, the most modern equipment and the most trusted officers in all of Russia. Believe me, many of our other facilities are not like these. So what I am saying to you is that everyone must keep the standards extremely high. Even the Tsar comes to inspect this camp frequently. Otto, I am pleased to say that you have more than met mine and Tatiana's expectations of you. My children favor you and the servants report that you mind your own affairs, are punctual and can be trusted. Keep up the good work. As far as what is in store for the regiment, I know that we will remain in St. Petersburg for the fall and for the winter. There will be many social events in preparation for Christmas and many upcoming winter activities."

With hearing all of this, Otto ran up to his room, sat down and quickly wrote a letter to his mother, father and siblings back in Poland, informing them of his good fortune. He posted the letter which would arrive back in Poland after three to four weeks.

Each day began like the previous one. Each morning Otto would get up and prepare everything that the Pokovnik asked him to have prepared. He would usually have to have the Pokovnik's clothes laid out the previous evening. Then in the morning he would get up, go to the barn where he would feed and water the Pokovnik's horses and make sure that all the riding equipment, saddles, harnesses, halters and bridals were clean and in good repair. Following his chores, he would then go to the kitchen and eat breakfast with the rest of the maids and servants who would be on duty that day.

Domestic help was abundant in St. Petersburg and therefore the pay was low. Even Otto's pay was minimal. With his pay he was able to purchase his personal needs; he could purchase an article of clothing now and then. If he was prudent with his spending, he could have enough money to go the occasional concert, play, or circus entertainment. Even officers salaries were limited since the build up of the army. Otto's salary was paid out of the Pokovnik's own earnings. The thought of getting married, renting his own apartment and paying for an independent household was out of the question. As long as he was the Pokovnik's valet, he would have to remain a single man unless the Pokovnik came from a wealthy aristocratic family and had the means to support both himself and other families in his employ. But this was not any concern to Otto now. He had a good secure position for two years.

Often in the afternoons when the children had finished with their academic lessons for the day, Otto would be asked to spend some time with the children. Most of the time was given to music lessons, dance lessons and singing lessons.

Sometimes, he played board games with them or he would go for horseback rides with Tatiana and her children. The children's music teacher had a number of instruments available and they practiced on the piano, violin, trumpet, flute, french horn and other wind instruments. Otto soon found himself picking up music sheets and listened and learned to read notes. One day the music teacher heard him hum a tune as she was listening to the children practicing the same sheet of music.

"Otto, would you like to learn to play an instrument? Come, the children would love to have you practice with them. You do have time and it will not cost you anything. You spend a lot of time here, so you might as well enjoy learning to play."

Otto thought for a brief moment and then replied, "I would really like to learn to play the flute." It was then settled; Otto was given a flute to play and practice with and he would join the children whenever his duties would permit. Both he and the children looked forward to their practice time together. He practiced diligently, nearly every evening while he was alone in this room. Hidden in the attic, he would take out his flute and in the dim light of a coal oil lamp, he would repeat the scales, try to refine the sounds made by the flute and he tried to make sense of the clefs, largos, half notes and beats. He had had no exposure to sheet music before . . . . his only encounter was that of the notes that accompanied the hymns in church hymn books. Those he had never tried to understand. Because of the invitation to learn to play the flute, he felt more connected to the family and they to him. Although the relationship with the children was somewhat informal, his relationship with the Pokovnik and his wife remained formal.

Life in a Russian family at the turn of the century was serious business and structured. The father was the head of the household and dictated the expectations for the rest of the members of the household. There was always a certain sternness to the whole family atmosphere. Father was very strict with the children and the attitude towards dress and social conduct was very Victorian in nature. Open affection to one another was rarely displayed especially in a military family. Only the closest of friends and family would be greeted with a hug or a kiss or would be invited to participate in family gatherings. It was most unusual that Otto would be invited to participate in the family activities. He knew that he was being accepted and trusted.

"Otto, the tailor came by today and stated that your uniforms are ready and that you should go to his shop and try them on to see how they fit. You know that the Pokovnik is very fussy about these matters so I will go with you to ensure that the fit is appropriate and acceptable. We will go later today," stated Tatiana. With those instructions, Otto harnessed Tatianas's favorite driving horse, hitched it on to a single seat buggy and they went to visit the tailor, Abram Freidman.

"Come in, come in Frau Vasiletvich, sit down. Can I bring you a cup of tea? I will call David and tell him to bring the uniforms; they are just being pressed and checked over."

"Da, da," retorted Tatiana. Otto stood there and waited for David to bring his new outfits.

"Come to the back where there are mirrors for you to see yourself."

The new uniforms were brought out. One battle dress uniform made for formal occasions and two for general wear around the house or for informal trips outside of the base. First, he put on the trousers. They were made of finely woven wool with narrow bottoms so they would slide into the near knee length boots. The waist was ample and the leg length was good. The trousers were held up by a pair of white canvas suspenders. Next he put on the shirt which had no collar and fit tight against his underwear. The tunic followed. It was tailored to fit. It was made with the same material as his trousers. The tunic fell just below the hip. It featured a mid neck stand up collar and buttoned on the right side of his body. The front was adorned by two rows of brass buttons, six on each side, and a white leather belt clasped the middle. Shoulder straps were buttoned down, each with a smaller brass button. Each shoulder strap bore his rank, service branch and unit number. These shoulder straps would be the same on his gymnastiorka as on his great coat. The battle dress uniform was black but trimmed with blue piping around the collar and part way up each sleeve. He was given a pair of white cotton gloves and a military cap. He tried it on and it fit perfectly. He stood in front of the mirror proudly and admired his handsome image. Even Tatiana was impressed. Since winter would soon be upon them, he was issued a fur ushanka hat to accompany his great coat and battle dress. Abram Freidman carefully packed Otto's uniforms, handed the boxes to Otto and after paying Abram, Otto and Tatiana returned to the barracks.

On the way back from the tailors, Tatiana and Otto chatted about the upcoming winter, the festivities that were about to occur and about the children's education.

"Otto, you have been with us for over a month now and you have not gone anywhere nor have you been invited to dine with us. I will ask Constantine if he would like you to share Sunday dinner with us. I will ask him tonight. There are also many social activities planned for the up coming months, some of which I would like you to attend."

"Wow," thought Otto. "Now I know for certain that I am being accepted into the household and my position will be secure."

The world in which Otto found himself was completely alien to him. He found himself having to make adjustments at every turn. The formality and the strictness that was present was something he had not been accustomed to. At home, he did very few domestic chores as those had been left to his mother. Now he found himself laying out clothes, shining buttons, pressing uniforms. He was even occasionally called upon to help out in the kitchen. The size of the city frightened him; it was huge compared even to Lodz where he had been many times. Here, though, he knew no one . . . . he was by himself. The only other adults, males and females, within his daily contacts were the Pokovnik, his wife, the servants and the stable help. Loneliness began to get a grip on him. At times, he felt that it would have been better to stay as a regular in the cavalry, at best, life would be more exciting. There were few moments of pleasure and gaiety found in his daily routine. But he did find pleasure in practicing his flute with the children.

He even surprised himself that he was able to read the music notes and match the required sound with the flute itself. He was improving and the music teacher was most pleased with his progress.

During moments alone lying in bed, we all reflect on past events and dream and plan our future. We visualize mentally becoming rich, becoming famous, visiting exotic places and even laying out plans how we might achieve success; however, we as individuals define success. We set goals for ourselves and plan how we are best able to improve the situation we find ourselves in. We dream, we plan, we do. I am sure that Otto, during these times in his room in the attic wondered if this was the life for him. How could he make friends his own age? How could he meet some girls? He was nineteen and I know that at age nineteen, girls were very much on my mind. (At the time that I am writing this, I don't find them quite as interesting anymore, damn!)

On his meagre salary he would only occasionally be able to go to a symphony, an opera, a ballet. He could speak Russian but he was not Orthodox or Catholic so church was not attractive to him. There were a few servants and maids that he could associate with but so far had seen none that caught his eye. The realistic goals that he could set for himself were dictated by and limited to his position. He was secure but he was also a prisoner, bound by his duties and the limitations these duties placed on his ability to move freely and improve his social and financial position. Darkness came early at this latitude and the nights became longer and longer like the darkness he only saw for the future. Here no one asked for his input into decisions. The Pokovnik did not ask Otto what he should wear or how he could plan for future wars; Tatiana did not ask him which horse he should saddle for her or what should be on the menu when she would entertain other officers and their families; he was not asked what he would like to wear when he accompanied the couple on their outings; he was not asked how the household should be run. Even the decisions needed for his own personal improvement were limited. The only brightness that came into his otherwise dull life were the letters from home and his flute. He decided that he would learn to play the flute well enough that he would be able to join the base military band.

Life with the Vasiletviches was not all gloom and darkness. Constantine was a decent man, even though he was strict with his children. He did have a tender side to him. Often while Otto was preparing things for Constantine, they would chat on a personal level. Constantine understood the loneliness that would eventually set in and he liked Otto so he would engage Otto in conversation about his family background and ask Otto about his. He encouraged Otto and reminded him that given time he would love St. Petersburg. He encouraged him to explore what the city had to offer and he would insure that Otto was given time to do that. Winter though, in St Petersburg was long and harsh. Arctic storms often came blasting across the Baltic and slammed against the city, so winter was not the best time to explore St. Petersburg. However, he promised Otto that he would be asked to accompany him and his family when they would be going to a musical or some other stage production.

November was the month that featured the highest level of social activity for the military. Summer maneuvers had ended, the higher ranking officers had all returned by the end of September and plans and arrangements for the social activities were laid out and coordinated by the end of October.

"Otto, the Grand Duke Nicholas Nikolaevich is holding his annual ball, a tribute in recognition of the army and naval officers at the Yusopov Palace. It will be held in two weeks time and you will accompany my wife and myself to the ball."

CHAPTER 4

Winter comes early to lands north of the sixtieth degree parallel. By the middle of November, the cold and snow has a firm grip on the land and does not let go until April. Almost six months of continuous freezing temperatures, near total darkness, and heavy snow falls topped up with blasting north winds makes time pass slowly; winters in St. Petersburg are long and depressing.

As well as winters being long and cold, St. Petersburg was isolated from the rest of the world during the cold winter months. The harbor was completely frozen in by two or more feet of ice; there were no highways, or snowplows to clear the roads even if there was a road. The trains could travel but they too were prisoners of the cold and snow. Trains would freeze up and snow piled higher than the locomotives themselves made travel outside of St. Petersburg very risky. St. Petersburg was not in a great location for being the capitol of Russia.

Isolation, even only the feeling of isolation weighs heavily on a person's persona; depression sets in, moods become unpredictable, and sometimes violence and suicides occur. The Russian nobility and Russia high society in St. Petersburg were well aware of what darkness and coldness will do, so in order to counteract the effects of isolation, the nobility and the wealthy partied. They partied often and they partied hard. Vodka flowed freely. The parties however were not merely drinking fests but rather were highly organized first class gatherings. St. Petersburg boasted opera houses, theaters, ball rooms and concert halls which rivaled and even surpassed those found in London, Paris or Vienna. The extravaganzas displayed in St. Petersburg were paid for by the Russian peasants and by the factory workers. The Russian nobility believed in the Robin Hood mentality, but only in the reverse. That was instead of 'take from the rich and give to the poor' it was, 'take from the poor and give to the rich'. For this, the Russian upper class would pay and pay dearly.

The atmosphere in the Pokovnik's house was electric. There was a constant hustle and bustle as the maid, Otto, Oleg, Constantine and Tatiana readied themselves for the occasion. The day of, as well as several days prior to the Yusopov's ball, all were engaged in shining, polishing and primping. Tatiana had her hair done in the latest fashion. She bought a new gown, hat, gloves and shoes. Constantine had Otto give his brass buttons an extra good polishing, and Otto made sure that Constantine's best shirt, red tunic, fur cap, great coat and boots did not have a spec of dirt, dust, or anything else on them. The Vasiletviches were going to be on display along with the other Generals, Pokovniks, Princes, Princesses, city dignitaries and wealthy businessmen. The event at the Yusopov palace was considered to be one of the most prestigious gatherings of the social season; therefore, all had to be perfect, done to the highest societal and military standards.

Everyone ate early on the date of the Yusopov ball and by 1800 hours, all were ready to start the four mile trip to the palace on the banks of the Moika River.

Oleg and Otto harnessed the carriage horses. They checked the Russian horse harness bells, the reins, the bridles, the carriage itself, as well as the horses. The evening proved to be colder than expected and the moisture being wafted in from the Baltic crystallized in the air, giving the night an eerie atmosphere. Otto and Oleg had lined the carriage seats with sheep skin blankets and at the last moment, placed foot warmers in the carriage as Tatiana and Constantine were not wearing their outdoor boots. Extra wool blankets were placed in the carriage as well.

With everything in place, Oleg urged the horses forward, then stopped the carriage as near to the front door as possible. Otto, in the mean time had put on his great coat, sheepskin mitts and fur hat, mounted his horse and accompanied Oleg to the door. Otto dismounted, walked to the door and opened it. The couple was standing ready to go.

"Tatiana looks lovely," Otto thought.

Her fur hat was made of sable as was her coat. Her coat was buttoned but left a low cut collar open. Underneath the coat, a bright blue high collared satin dress could be seen. Her neck was adorned by a very expensive gold necklace below which hung several strands of pearls. Otto had never in his life seen such finery but rather than gape open mouthed, he stoically held the door open for the couple, accompanied them to the carriage, stood by the carriage as Constantine helped Tatiana into the carriage. Once inside, Otto helped Constantine tuck the wool blankets around the both of them, then mounted his horse. They were off to the ball.

Their carriage was not the sole carriage on the street that lead to Nevsky Prospect. Shortly after leaving the military compound other carriages from the compound and from the homes of the wealthy joined in a long line which resembled a parade. The night had taken hold of St. Petersburg by 1800 hours. The streets were only dimly lit. However, on this evening, the silence of the night and the darkness of the night was broken by the cheerful sounds of the multitude of harness bells, combining with the soft thumping of the horses hooves making contact with the newly fallen snow. Along with the sounds the carriages made, the streets were lit by the oil lanterns which perched themselves on every carriage. This whole procession along the streets, created an air of excitement and anticipation that could be only best appreciated by those who were part of the procession.

The horses' breaths froze each time they exhaled and soon icicles began forming around their nostrils and hoar frost formed on their muzzles and bridles. As well as frost forming on the horses, frost also built up on any mustache which curled up a little at the ends. From there, icicles too began to form. Otto did not even notice . . . . he was too enrapt in the almost eerie atmosphere of the trip to the palace. He did not know what to expect . . . . it was his first exposure to the way of life of the rich and famous.

After forty minutes of travel along the Nevsky Prospect, the carriage slowed to a walking pace and turned onto Moika Avenue. Many guests had already arrived and were patiently awaiting their turn in line. Oleg stopped the team and waited as each of the guests in front of them unloaded and entered the palace rotunda. Slowly the carriage came closer to the front of the line and Otto could now see the impressive exterior of the grand palace and could only imagine what those walls hid from the public eye. Constantine had told him that the Yusopovs were one of the wealthiest families in all of Russia and that at least four generations of Yusopovs owned and lived there. Otto could see that the palace was three stories high, surrounded by a high wrought iron fence. The portico consisted of six white marble columns. Otto did not know what style the palace followed or who the architects were that had their hand in the construction of that building. He only knew that there, brightly lit on a dark St. Petersburg night, it was magnificent. He could hardly wait to see the interior.

Otto caught a glimpse of the reception hall while the Vasiletviches were stepping off the carriage and were entering the palace. He could see the Princess Yusopov and her husband greeting the guests after they had their outer garments checked in. He saw the splendid chandeliers and the famous stairway leading to upper banquet rooms and guest quarters. Then it was time to leave the drop off area and park the horses and carriage. The driveway to the parking area led them around the side of the palace, through an archway and into the palace's plaza. Oleg and Otto tied their horses, removed the horse blankets from the carriage, placed them on the horses and secured them, at which time Otto asked,

"Where do we go from here?"

"I have been here before so I have an idea where to go and what to do."

With that Otto followed Oleg into the servant's entrance and into a smaller reception room designed especially for these occasions. Oleg immediately recognized a woman dressed in formal attire and struck up a conversation with her.

"Otto, come over here. I would like you to meet a friend of mine." Otto presented himself extending his hand to the woman. She took it and gently squeezed it.

"Otto, I would like you to meet Svetlana. Svetlana is one of the Princess Yusopov chamber maids and has served the princess for many years." Otto bowed slightly and exchanged pleasantries with her.

"Otto, you have not seen the palace before and I understand that this is your first time attending a ball of this kind."

"That is correct," replied Otto.

"I have a copy of the program for tonight and I do not have to serve the guests so I have time to show you the palace and explain the program to you as we go. Would you like to do that?"

"Yes, I would be most pleased to be able to tour the palace."

Otto could not believe the opulence that was displayed as they went from room to room. He saw various styles of architecture but he did not know one from another. Svetlana explained baroque, neoclassical, oriental moorish and empire hallways. Each room was furnished in the style of the room with beautiful inlaid floors, niches bordered by elegant marble columns and statues. There were hundreds of sculptures, paintings and tapestries from famous artists about which he knew nothing. On and on it went. It was mind boggling to him that any one family could be so wealthy.

Half way through the tour, Svetlana took out the program and explained, "Since it is winter, the guest list is only five hundred; in summer when the guests are able to be outside, the prince and princess will entertain up to two thousand guests. Tonight while the guests are arriving, caviar, hot sausages, hot chicken livers and smoked salmon will be brought on trays to the guests. They will also have the choice of drinking vodka from a shot glass or champagne. At 2000 hours, the ball room doors will open and the guests will be seated according to their social importance. Your Pokovnik and his wife will be seated near the rear. A fashion show will then take place interspersed with performances by jugglers, dancers and singers. The orchestra will feature some numbers by Tchaikovsky, Liszt, Schumann and other well known composers. The highlight will be a short performance by Anna Pavlova. She is currently the most admired ballerina in St. Petersburg. It says on the program that she will do a number from Sergei Diaghilev's dance company. The dance is from Ballet Russia, Sleeping Beauty. She is very small so she developed a ballet slipper with wood at the toes so that she would look taller. This is what is catching everyone's eyes."

It made no sense to Otto.

"Following the program there will be a short interlude during which time the chairs will be removed and the dancing will start shortly thereafter," Svetlana explained as she glanced at a clock on the wall. "It is almost that time now, so let us hurry because I have to check with the princess to see if she needs to freshen up, fix her hair, change her gown or whatever else she might require."

The dancing started at 2200 hours and would last until the last guests were either too tired or too drunk to continue. Oleg told Otto to expect to be there a long time.

With all the guests occupied in the ball room, the collection of attendants, valets, chauffeurs and guards gathered in groups scattered throughout the palace and waited for the call to return their employers safely back home. Constantine sent out his call to Oleg and Otto well before the bulk of the revelers were ready to end their festivities. Quickly Oleg fired up the foot warmers, gathered the assortment of blankets and readied the carriage for their return journey. Otto, in the mean time attended to the coats, hats, scarves, boots and mittens. Constantine and Tatiana were tucked safely in their bed well before dawn.

The following day being Sunday, the family gathered for their Sunday dinner to which Otto was invited. The discussion among Constantine, Tatiana, Oleg and Otto centered on the previous night's activity.

"Wasn't that a wonderful event!" exclaimed Tatiana.

"Very much so," replied Constantine, "but I worry that these parties will not last forever."

"Why do you say that?" Queried Tatiana.

"You know that the factory workers look upon these events as a colossal waste of money," explained Constantine. "They feel that they are being treated unfairly and need to be given better wages. Remember it was only four years ago when one hundred workers were shot to death in the palace square as they were staging a peaceful demonstration led by Father Gapon. They have not forgotten the massacre and they blame the monarchy and the wealthy for this. Bloody Sunday, they call it."*

"There is much unrest in the city, especially among the factory workers. Fortunately, there is no war going on at this time but I fear that if the Tsar needs to move the troops out of St. Petersburg there will be trouble. Mark my words. There is constant talk of revolution."

Otto listened intently.

The days passed and as they did, winter took a stronger hold on the city. Otto continued to practice his flute, wrote the occasional letter home, dutifully cared for the horses and assisted Constantine as best he could. He attended several more smaller gatherings and celebrated Christmas away from

---

* *Bloody Sunday was a massacre of over 100 Russian workers in the city of St. Petersburg, Russia on January 22, 1905. The large peaceful procession led by Father Gapon was attacked by the Tsar's Cossacks as it made its way to the winter palace armed only with a petition requesting the Tsar's influence to improve working conditions in the factories.*

his family and alone; the Vasiletviches would include him when it suited them but it was not like being at home. Once the allure of the big city and everything that went with it subsided, loneliness did set in. Constantine was right.

CHAPTER 5

Each and everyone of us, whether it is woman or man, girl or boy, old or young, is most satisfied and finds happiness when successfully facing a challenge. It is not the end result of conquering the challenge that is most satisfying; the most satisfying aspect of the achievement is in the planning and the training; the process through which we go to get to the end of our challenge. That makes us truly happy. This is most evident in athletic challenges. The euphoria of getting a gold metal at the Olympics lasts for only a short time. During the training period required to reach the pinnacle is when athletes will suffer, endure and sacrifice time, money and almost anything else in order to reach the top and that is the time when they are most motivated. Once there and if no other challenges have been accepted by them, often depression, loneliness and emptiness sets in.

I have asked myself these questions for years. Why would a millionaire who has $10,000,000 want $20,000,000? Why would a very wealthy person deny himself/herself a new coat? Why would a quilter, who has more than a dozen beautiful handmade quilts, want to make another dozen that she will never use? Why would people risk their lives climbing Mount Everest, K2 or the Matterhorn? Why would a powerful dictator want to conquer more lands? Why would a painter continue to paint masterpiece after masterpiece? There doesn't seem to be a logical reasonable answer to these questions but in reality, there is. All of these people have one thing in common (surprising that a billionaire would have something in common with a starving artist); they all are trying to determine where the limits of their abilities lie. The millionaires want to find where the limit to his ability to pile up cash lies. The mountain climber wants to see where his physical limits lie. The quilter wants to stretch to the limit of her abilities to combine sewing skills with art. The rich man won't buy himself a new coat because the money needed would lessen the pile of dollars to some degree: he does not want to see his mountain shrink. The mountain climber continues to challenge mountains until one day when the mountain beats him and he freezes or falls to his death. He has reached the limits of his abilities. I often thought people who participate in ironman contests are crazy, but I guess they too are trying to discover the limits of their endurance.

So it was with Otto during the winter of 1909-1910. He had reached the limit regarding how shiny one could polish a button or a shoe or a canvas belt or a puttee. There is a limit as to how much oil one can put on a saddle or a harness. There is a limit as to how pressed and how neat a uniform can become. He needed more and by accident he found it. He found the flute. Playing the flute has no limits. There is no ultimate goal once reached that can't be surpassed. One can never say that the flute cannot be played more beautifully. Like the painter, the perfect painting has never been painted. Like the quilter, the most beautiful quilt has not been created. There is no judge capable of defining those limits. Like the rich man, he knows no limits of how big the pile can grow.

So, Otto practiced his flute; that was the only thing during the long cold winter of 1909-1910 that brought him some measure of happiness and provided a stimulus for doing his other work and fighting the loneliness that otherwise plagued him.

Night after night, after the family had gone to bed and the house was dark. Otto would take out his flute and play. The soulful sound of the flute combined with the howling north wind could be heard throughout the house, creating a sad and mysterious atmosphere. Laying side by side in their bed at night Constantine and Tatiana would listen to these sounds until they went to sleep.

"Tatiana, I have not asked you this before but night after night we hear Otto, up in his little room, practice and play his flute. Do you find that it disturbs you or annoys you? Because if it does, I will tell him that he has to limit his practice time to daylight hours. It does not disturb me; I rather like it," said Constantine.

After a brief silence, Tatiana replied, "My love, you know that the dear boy is far away from home and as much as we have tried to make him part of our family, he is lonely. We are not his people. He is not totally comfortable here with us, or in St. Petersburg. He has no real friends . . . . only acquaintances. No, Constantine, do not ask him to stop. Let him have his flute. Even if the sounds would disturb me, I could not ask you to stop him from playing. Also Constantine, I am very pleased that you saved this boy from the hell he surely would have faced had he stayed in the regular cavalry. Our children love him and I feel that we need him to be as happy as possible. Leave him be."

With those words, Constantine placed his arms around Tatiana, held her close, kissed her forehead and whispered, "Good night, my love." Soon they drifted off to sleep with the sound of the flute and the wind filling the room.

One morning as Otto was helping the Pokovnik get ready for his day, Constantine said, "Otto, you have been practicing the flute everyday and you, with our children, have entertained us on Sundays and both Tatiana and I think that you are accomplished enough to play in the regiment's band. You know that every regiment has a band and the band is made up of soldiers from the rank and file in our regiment. You are not a regular soldier but I will talk to the band master and ask him if he would allow you to become a member of the band. Would you like to do that? You do have time in the afternoons and if the band practice schedule does not interfere with your duties here, I certainly would support and encourage you to play in the band. You need to get out and meet other people and do other things. It is obvious that you are not entirely happy here and perhaps a diversion from your routine would be good medicine for you. I would rather that music become your medicine than vodka. Think about it and let me know your decision. If the answer is yes, I will take you to the band master and he will give you an audition. I am sure that you would pass the audition requirements. There are always new members replacing those who have served their time or for other reasons have left the band. You have heard it play several times so you know how large it is, what kind of music they play and how well they play it. Give it a try . . . . you have nothing to lose."

That night, an excited Otto practiced longer and louder than ever. Also that night, Tatiana said, smiling softly, "Constantine, maybe we made a mistake."

Two weeks later Otto had another uniform to clean and press.

CHAPTER 6

This morning began the same as nearly every other morning. The Oleshenko family woke early and got themselves prepared for the day that lay ahead. Papa Oleshenko was a self made wealthy businessman. Mama Oleshenko came from a middle class family and now had become one of the 'nouveau riche' and Anya, their only child, was attending an all girls private school. Anya was sixteen, going on seventeen and was in her final year at that school. She would graduate at the end of June. Mama Oleshenko having married into the upper class of St. Petersburg took it upon herself to ensure that her husband would succeed in the business world and that her daughter would be groomed and polished enough to marry into preferably, either a family that was wealthy or influential. She used her influence whenever and however she could . . . .

always smiling on the exterior . . . . always scheming on the interior. Anya had become like putty in mama's hands. She was being molded into the form and shape created in mama's head. So far, Anya had been pliant and obedient.

Mama waltzed into Anya's bedroom more cheerful than she usually was. A cup of tea in her hand, a giddy smile on her face and a steady stream of words spewing from her mouth.

"Anya, Anya, come sit here on this chair and let me fix your hair."

The mornings always began this way. Obediently Anya sat down and mama promptly went to work removing the tiny strips of cloth that shaped each curl.

"My goodness Anya, your hair gets lovelier each day. These ringlets that reach your shoulders really highlight your beauty. Oh look, what do I see here? My goodness, I will have to reset this curl and comb it out again. You know Anya, this is your last year at school and I have some very great news for you this morning."

Hearing those words, Anya perked up and began to pay attention. All the previous accolades heaped upon her had no impact on her: she had heard them all, over and over again.

"Yes, mama, please tell me, what is the good news?" asked Anya.

"Your father and I have been preparing for this news for a very long time. Ever since you were born, I began working on your dowry, collecting fine linens, cutlery, silk pillow cases, embroidered place mats, English bone china and all sorts of things that you will need when you get married and start your own family. We have been saving money to add to your dowry and we have been searching for just the right man for you to marry."

Anya just stared at her mother and couldn't believe what she was hearing. "Mama, what are you saying? Are you telling me that you have selected a husband for me?"

"Yes, yes my love. We have found the perfect match for you. He comes from a wealthy family; his family own and run a large import/export business in St. Petersburg. They travel to America and all of Europe searching for fine goods to sell and trade."

"What is his name?" whispered Anya.

"His name is Ivan. Right now he is serving the military and will be for the next year. Once his enlisted time ends, he will become a partner in the family business and he will be ready to settle down as I am sure that you are too. Isn't that exciting?"

Mama prattled on but Anya could think of only one thing.

"I am not ready to become a wife. Mama is old fashioned; I know that most girls my age get married but now there are also many girls in my school that are not getting married as soon as they graduate. A jumble of thoughts raced through her head . . . . she would finish school . . . . she would run away . . . . many modern girls choose their own husbands. What am I going to do?"

She no longer was paying any attention to her mother. Thankfully, the marriage wouldn't take place for another year.

"Anya! It's getting time for you to go to school. Come, I'll help you get dressed. Then come and have a bowl of hot cereal before you leave. I know that this comes as a shock to you but I know that you will learn to love this man. It may take time. I didn't love your father at first either but it all works out. Ivan is stationed at this base and your father and I have invited Ivan and his parents to come and meet you."

Anya couldn't eat her cereal; she got herself bundled up for the two kilometer walk to school, grabbed her school satchel and ran out of the house. Tears streamed down her face and she felt them freezing on her cheeks as she stumbled along to school.

She fully understood what the family's plan for her was . . . . the school she was attending focussed on changing girls into ladies. They were taught how to speak and when to speak. They were taught the names of famous and modern composers, actors, ballerinas and artists so that they could engage in high society conversation. They practiced using cutlery, how to hold a champagne glass, how to smile, how to curtsy and even how to flirt. Anya loved the training; she was having fun. All the girls would giggle and make humorous comments as they were being put through their paces. The talk among them was most interesting and had become more so as the last year of training was coming to a close. They talked of going to America, traveling across Europe; some who were getting married talked about weddings, some talked about becoming actresses and singers, others about becoming teachers. To Anya, this talk was exciting and now after the morning's announcement, her hopes for a different future seemed out of reach. Her mother had decided and she knew that she would not have the strength to resist. She would do what mama says.

Every year as the sun rises a few minutes earlier than the day before and the rays regain their strength, a battle between old man winter and 'ol sol' takes place. The earth struggles to shake winter's icy grip and in the northern reaches of the earth, this struggle is dramatic. The months of minus 40 degree temperatures freeze the earth two meters below the surface. The water in lakes and streams freezes to a depth of more than a meter. The snow that comes early does not melt until April and with each storm and snowfall, the accumulation of snow piles higher and higher. Even the harbors freeze solid. When March arrives and the first signs of a thaw appear, everyone can hardly wait for spring to arrive and in these northern latitudes, the event that signals the final triumph over winter and kills it for another year is the break up of the river ice.

It was Saturday when Constantine on his return home from an early morning meeting announced that news has come from upriver. The news being that the ice on the Neva was breaking up and that the break up should arrive at St. Petersburg in a few hours.

"Papa, papa," Natalie chirped, "will you take me to see it? Remember you took me last year. Please papa!"

Constantine smiled down on little Natalie as he remembered the ice breakup last spring. They had watched the ice on the river rise and come crashing against the bridge. They had listened to the thunderous booming that occurred as the meter thick ice broke up into huge chunks; they had listened to the grinding sound as tons and tons of ice scraped against each other and along the sides of the river banks.

Natalie and her father, Constantine, were not the only ones to be amazed and mesmerized by the ice break up on the river. The ice on a river does not disappear in the same fashion as ice on a lake or pond. On a lake, the ice melts from the top and as the water on top of the ice gets deeper, it softens the ice beneath and eventually the ice rots, sinks and breaks up. On a river, the ice gets broken up from below the surface and often in dramatic fashion.

"Natalie, I would love to take you to the bridge to watch but I have another very important meeting that I must attend this afternoon. But I have an idea; maybe if you talk nicely to Otto and beg him, he might take you."

"Otto, Otto would you? Would you?"

"Of course, Natalie. I have never seen it so, yes, I will take you," replied Otto.

With that, it was decided that Otto would take Natalie to the Liteiny Bridge. Constantine told Otto and Natalie that the break up would be most dramatic at that location because it was 400 meters wide and was supported by six cast iron clad piers which, when rammed, would create a thunderous noise.

It was a sunny warm day and the walk would take under an hour even walking slowly. At that time of year, it was most prudent to walk slowly and carefully. The sky was bright and blue and the sun shone pleasantly on the city. The city itself though did not present a pretty picture. Over the past six months, a thick blanket of soot and dirt covered the whole city. The buildings showed the effects of the smog and smoke created by all the wood and coal burning stoves as well as soot from factory chimneys. The streets and sidewalks which were never cleared of snow, ice, horse turds and garbage carelessly thrown, began to display the result of the neglect. Looking down the street, the mounds of ice topped by the insulating effect of the horse turds on top, resembled an unending field of tiny mesas. Water pooled in the footprint depressions on the icy sidewalk made the walk to the bridge painfully slow.

When they arrived, a crowd had already begun to gather but Otto was able to find a spot against the rail facing the direction that the break up would occur. The view up the river was clear for about a kilometer before the river made a bend.

"Listen Natalie," Otto said, "do you hear the rumbling in the distance?"

"Yes, I can," replied Natalie.

"Look! Look! See the ice moving; it won't be long now," said Otto excitedly.

Sure enough, the warning signs of the major break up became most clear.

"Why is the ice waving, Otto?"

Otto explained. "Natalie, this happens because far away from St. Petersburg the snow begins to melt earlier in the year and as the water starts to flow into the main river, it brings with it stumps, trees, and chunks of ice. Somewhere a dam builds up and the water then, rather than flowing on top of the ice, begins to flow under the ice and this then lifts the whole thick blanket of ice and begins to carry everything with it."

Both Natalie and Otto stood mesmerized as the phenomenon continued to unfold. Thousands upon thousands of tons of ice heaved and groaned. Water churned and gushed everywhere. The break up came like a juggernaut. Nothing could stop it until its energy was lost when reaching the ocean. Huge slabs of ice came crashing against the iron clad piers amplifying the already deafening noise. Otto became so involved that he completely forgot about Natalie. Natalie, in the meantime had climbed onto the railing, half leaning over, in order to get a better look. All the spectators were standing shoulder to shoulder and were cheering and clapping as the break up made its way slowly under the bridge. Natalie, who was not taking care to secure her own safety, suddenly slipped and started to topple over the rail and onto the churning mass below. She automatically flung her arm in an effort to save herself and by only good fortune, was able to grab onto a sleeve next to her. She fell backwards onto the bridge deck and lay there. Otto only had heard a small cry for help and quickly turned his attention to Natalie who was lying on the ground. Instantly, Otto fell to his knees and peered into Natalie's face. He then sensed another presence. His eyes gazed up and not a foot away, he found his eyes locked to another set of the most beautiful soft blue eyes he had ever seen.

Moments like this, which last mere seconds, and the impact and feelings resulting from these moments last a life time. Their eyes became like magnets drawing each others faces closer together. Both bodies feeling a warmth and glow like never felt before . . . . their bodies pushing toward each other, welcoming one another. Immediately, longing for each others touch, both losing complete awareness of their surroundings. Now the thunder and the pounding felt in their heads and in their hearts became louder than the thunderous crashing of the ice against the piers. Both did not move. What was happening? Their brains pounding in an effort to respond to what their bodies were telling them.

"I'm okay Otto. I'm not hurt."

Those words broke the spell. Not a word was exchanged. Eyes became unlocked. Otto reached out and lifted Natalie to her feet. The gorgeous blue eyed girl rose, put her arm through a soldier's arm and disappeared into the crowd. The crashing of the ice faded as did the crashing in Otto's chest and stomach.

"Let's go home," he said to Natalie.

On the way back, Natalie looked up at Otto and said, "That was amazing!"

Otto replied, "Yes Natalie, it was most amazing."

She did not understand the metaphor.

A little while later, Natalie said, "Otto, don't tell mama or papa, please."

"No, Natalie, I won't tell. The secret is ours."

CHAPTER 7

After a long winter's hibernation, St. Petersburg once again sprang to life. Spring rains washed the dirt and grime off of the roads and houses. The bright long sunny spring days awakened the sleeping trees, new born grasses poked their heads through the earth to reach the sunshine, and the crocuses and tulips burst into full bloom. The whole city and countryside became invigorated by the awakening. As was the custom, the army base took full advantage of the spring air by planting flowers, trimming bushes, sweeping the parade square, painting buildings that needed it and even scheduling concerts, which featured the regiment bands in the band shell which bordered the parade square.

The military had diverted water from the Neva River by trenching a canal. Along the canal, gardens were planted, ponds were built and a maize of pathways was constructed. The canal served many purposes and the soldiers during their free time as well as citizens who lived on the base shared the space. Sundays were special. Every Sunday from early spring until late fall, the various military bands would perform. Families and soldiers would bring their blankets and picnic lunches to the grassed area around the band shell and enjoy a free concert.

Otto's regimental band was scheduled to entertain on May 23, which was the second last Sunday of May. This was special for Otto because the band leader had chosen to feature the flute in one of the pieces that would be performed. He had ample warning of this; therefore, he had practiced hard and repeated his interlude to the point where notes were not required. He was confident that he would do a good job of it.

May 23, awoke to a bright clear sky and the promise of a warm spring day. It was the kind of day that caused the cooped up residents of St. Petersburg to abandon their houses, dress up in their Sunday best, attend a church service, then stroll along the miles and miles of pathways and sidewalks that bordered the stretches of river and canal banks. There was a large community of Germans living in St. Petersburg that Otto had just learned about and he had started attending the Lutheran church of St. Peter and Paul. To his surprise, it was within walking distance from the base and was situated right on the Nevsky Prospect. He had made it his goal to attend the Sunday service on this morning.

Following service, he hurried home, quietly ate a light lunch, changed into his band uniform, picked up his flute and sheet music, quickly played his assigned interlude, glanced at himself in the mirror and strode into the bright sunshine.

As usual, when the band began their afternoon's performance, the people began to gather. Some sat on benches provided, some sat on blankets eating their picnic lunches, others stood and listened while some others just strolled by slowly. This day the band leader had chosen pieces from Schubert, Schumann, Liszt and Chopin. Otto's moment came during the third piece featuring Chopin's Mazurka but it would be broken up by a slow almost mournful interlude from Traumarie. The lively sounds of the Mazurka softened, and Otto stood and softly began to transfer notes to sound. He knew what he had to do. He could play it without looking at the notes but because he did not want to make a mistake he concentrated on the page in front of him and did not look up. He was so pleased with his effort and the longer he played, the more confident he became . . . . so confident that with three bars remaining, he lifted his head and panned the crowd. Their eyes met. Otto's heart leapt into his throat . . . . he could not continue . . . . there she was . . . . fate had brought her back to him. He sat down on his chair and did not even attempt to play the following piece. The same feeling, the same pull, the same warmth, the same rush of adrenalin, the same confusion. This time he would have to say something, give her a signal, make some contact. He could not let her go without at least an introduction. Would she stay to the end? He could not just leap up and leave the band shell: he could not cry out, "Here I am" or "Please don't go". He was stuck in the formality of the situation as was she. She was with the same soldier as on the bridge. She could not say, "Ivan, you go on, I am going to stay to the end"; or "Ivan, I must meet the man who is playing the flute"; or what she felt like saying . . . . "Ivan, go home, I would rather be here alone." Like Otto, she was trapped, but now she knew. She knew where he could be found again. The concert ended and the audience clapped politely; the girl did not link arms with the soldier beside her and as she strolled past the band stand, she turned her blond head, gazed at Otto, and smiled slightly. His image etched forever in her brain and her image etched forever in Otto's brain. Would they ever meet? He had no idea where she lived or even who she was.

The band leader confronted Otto, "What happened? Why did you not finish playing? You were doing so well. I was very pleased with your efforts. What happened?"

Otto replied, "Sir, as I was inhaling air in order to finish, a fly or a mosquito flew up my nose and I could not continue. I am sorry." Not the truth, but the band leader would not have accepted the real explanation.

She did not stay, she couldn't. Otto knew that but he was almost giddy with happiness from seeing the girl again. He did not have any way of contacting her; his only hope was that she would return to the band shell when his band was scheduled. Later that night, he decided that rather than practice in his room, he would go to the banks of the canal and practice there.

Anya had almost forgotten the meeting on the bridge. Chance momentary meetings occur to all of us . . . . a passing glance, a smile, a nod. The opportunity to begin a friendship exists briefly and whether or not the friendship will blossom and grow, depends on a quick response. Occasionally, second and third opportunities arise and with the right words and the right gestures, we are in a position to begin a long lasting relationship. The choice lies with each individual. Anya knew this. At night, lying in her bed, she wrestled with her thoughts. She knew that she could determine the path her acquaintance with the flute player would take. She was torn between the feelings harbored in her heart and the situation in which she found herself. She was going to marry Ivan. She knew that by meeting the flute player, all the plans her family had for her would be thrown into chaos. She knew nothing of the flute player. His name, his family, his dreams were all unknown to her. Was he rich? Was he poor? Where was his home? What was he like to talk to? Her heart told her that she had to find out. She could be cheating herself of a happiness otherwise unknown to her if she didn't meet him. Her head told her that the urges and desires felt would, with time, disappear and her life as was planned, could go on uninterrupted.

Anya found herself in a dilemma; one which even her classmates at school could not help her with. Some of the romantic types said, "Anya, you must follow your heart" and some of the pragmatists said, "Anya, don't be foolish. You don't throw away a solid future for an unknown. Time will make things right. You will forget the flute player and you will learn to love Ivan." Anya would not dare say anything to her mother or any other member of her family. She had to make the choice by herself and after several days and nights of wrestling with her options, she decided to follow her heart. She would, if she could, befriend the flute player. Late afternoons found her strolling past the band shell, eyes searching for the one she knew she had to meet.

Otto sat down on a park bench, took out his music and placed it on the bench beside him. He then took out his flute and began to play the notes in front of him. He would practice for one hour before he had to return to his duties. There was no one around to distract him, so he was able to engross himself entirely in the music before him. After this hour of practicing, he stood up, folded his music, placed the flute in its case and turned to go home.

"I have been watching and listening; you play very well."

Otto cleared his eyes. There, within three feet of him stood the blond, blue eyed girl he had been dreaming about for days and days. At last, at long, long last. She took a step forward, shyly looked up at Otto and said,

"Before you say anything, I have to tell you something. Ever since our meeting on the bridge, I have thought of you often. I have tried to dismiss you from my mind but I couldn't, especially following the second time I saw you. Forgive me, I know that I should not be forward but I just had to meet you."

Otto, gazing into the bottomless blue eyes, could only say, "I, too, have been dreaming about this moment. My name is Otto. Please, can we talk for a few moments. I can't let you disappear like the last two times."

He placed the music and his flute back on the bench, placed his hands in hers and held them tightly. The pent up passion, flowing like electricity from one to another, created a bond that would last for life.

"We don't have much time to talk," said Otto, "so let's meet under the Liteiny Bridge. Can you meet me there tomorrow?"

"Yes, yes, Otto. I can be there by 2:00 tomorrow afternoon."

The romance had begun; there was no turning back.

Neither wind, rain, cold, hail nor snow would have kept Anya and Otto from missing their prearranged encounter and on this day, conditions were perfect for a young romance to blossom and flourish. They talked and they walked. Both were anxious to learn of each other's past: their families, their birth place, their education, their hopes, their dreams and all else that people want to know which cement the bonds that keep people together. Time slid by much too quickly and soon it was time to return to their respective homes.

"When can we see each other again? Is it possible to meet here again?" Otto asked.

"I would love to see you on Sunday, but our family has been invited to a larger family gathering, so it cannot be Sunday," replied Anya.

"Sunday is not possible for me either," said Otto. "I have been told by the Pokovnik that he and his wife are hosting a gathering of people also. There must be many of these gatherings now that the weather is good and the days are longer. Soon the armies will be going on maneuvers and there won't be any more opportunities to meet until the fall season."

Following a hug and a light kiss on their cheeks, Otto and Anya arranged to meet again on the Monday following.

CHAPTER 8

Constantine's place hummed with activity in preparation for the last family gathering of the spring. Everyone involved with Constantine's household was hurriedly going about their responsibilities in preparation for the anticipated gathering in the afternoon. Outdoors, the street was raked and cleared of debris and horse droppings, the windows were washed and the door knobs were polished. Inside the courtyard, the cobble stones were brushed, the tables set, the flower arrangements displayed, the large tables from which the food would be served were organized and covered with fine linen. There was even a small stage set up from where an ensemble would play and entertain the guests. On this day, Constantine, as well as Otto himself, would wear their battle dress uniforms. Otto was busy making sure that Constantine's clothes were spotless.

He checked every button, every medal and every belt that would be worn. There could be no hair, no dirt, no spots, no untidy creases and no dull sheen on any article of clothing and after assuring himself that all inspected clothing would meet Constantine's standards, each article was laid out neatly on the bed.

After everything was laid out and he was satisfied with his work inside, Otto went outside to confer with Oleg to arrange their respective duties because they would be responsible for directing the guests carriages and even some guests automobiles, as well as assisting the guests as they stepped off their carriages and from their automobiles.

By noon, only the last minute final details were remaining. All was ready for the anticipated gathering of family and fellow officers and their families.

The guests began arriving shortly after the noon hour and Otto was kept busy directing the carriage drivers and assisting the ladies as they stepped from the carriages. One by one they lined up and waited their turn to unload. Otto recognized some faces and he even remembered some of the officers' names but most were strangers and therefore he concentrated solely on ensuring that the passengers unloaded safely. It seemed to Otto that the line of guests would never end as carriage after carriage stopped and he helped with the unloading. Some of the carriages were higher than others and those that were higher required an unloading step to be positioned accurately to facilitate the comfort of the passengers. When the step was required, Otto would position it correctly, then hold out his gloved hand to assist the ladies and make certain that they did not trip on the step or entangle their shoes in their floor length dresses. He found this task exhausting both physically and mentally. He was forever bending down, picking up and moving the cumbersome step. In addition, he found it mentally exhausting because he dare not make a careless move and cause injury to one of the guests. If a guest should be hurt, he would be held accountable and the consequences could be severe.

Otto gazed past what was the second last carriage, to see a gorgeously matched set of bay carriage horses pulling a two seated open carriage. At the first glance of the rig he knew that it belonged to a family with considerable wealth. He also could see that the occupants were not military personnel. He surmised that these people were either family or friends. He would take extra precaution with this group. When the unloading spot became vacant, Otto motioned for the driver of the team of bays to move forward. He noticed that there were three people in the carriage. The two facing him appeared to be husband and wife and the person with her back toward him appeared to be younger and was probably the couple's daughter. He would help the older woman first, then the daughter and the gentleman would be left to fend for himself.

The carriage driver motioned the team forward to the unloading spot and Otto, with the steps in hand waited for the horses to stop. When they did, Otto put the steps in position, smiled, and motioned for the woman to take his hand as she stepped down. He watched carefully as she made her way to the cobble stoned driveway. When he was satisfied that she was safe, he turned to look up and face the other female passenger. Immediately, he sensed that something was unusual. Normally, he would expect the passenger to be ready and perhaps even half standing in order to step down quickly. The lady was not moving. He looked up into her face and realized why this passenger was acting differently. Blood drained from his face and his body froze. Confusion engulfed him; he did not know what to do. The lady was Anya. Instinct told him to pretend they were complete strangers and that he should not acknowledge that they had previously met, let alone had seen each other privately. Anya too had stared in disbelief but only momentarily as she quickly gained her composure. She smiled, held out her hand and said,

"Well, sir, are you not going to help me from this carriage?"

"Yes, yes, of course, I am sorry," came the reply and with those words, he took her hand in his and gently helped Anya to the ground. Her father followed quickly and without turning around, all three made their way to be greeted by their hosts who had observed the incident and who were waiting to receive the last of the invited guests.

Once all the guests were inside, Otto, trembling like a leaf, sat on the portable steps, put his hands to his chin and breathed a sigh of relief. The rest of the afternoon, for Otto, would be spent attending the parked horses, cleaning up the horse droppings from the street and monitoring the street in front of the compound. He had ample time to plan his actions when it came time for the guests to leave and the loading process would begin. After mulling over the alternatives, Otto decided that in the best interests of his present position, it would be prudent to pretend that he and Anya had not previously met. So when the time came to load Anya's carriage, both he and Anya only cordially acknowledged each other and she was off to her own home. They would meet tomorrow and they would have lots to discuss.

The next morning as Otto was busy laying out Constantine's clothes for the day, the door to Constantine's chamber opened and Constantine walked into the room and said,

"Otto, sit down a while, I need to talk to you."

These were the very words Otto was dreading to hear. He wondered if Constantine had noticed the exchange between Anya and himself when the carriages were unloading. He was worried that he had raised suspicion and that he now would have to explain the situation to Constantine. Sweat began to form on his forehead and the palms of his hands began to feel cold and clammy. He sat down and quietly listened to what Constantine had to say.

"Otto, I am not going to ask you directly to explain your and Anya's actions yesterday but I need to explain something to you. Otto, both you and I are here not because of my own financial means but because of the generosity of another person. You know that the army cannot afford to pay for the kind of life that we live here in St. Petersburg. My pay would never cover the expenses so the only way that officers like myself can enjoy this kind of living is if we are independently wealthy or come from wealthy families. You know that the promotions to the rank that I have, come not from the soldier's ranks but rather from the wealthier and or politically influential people in Russia. In my case, my father was not a rich man but my sister married a self made millionaire. It is my sister that pays for our lifestyle.

She does this because her husband did not have access to the 'who is who' in St. Petersburg and through me, her family can have access to the so called better class of people. She could, at any time, deny me the money and I would be forced to leave St Petersburg for an outpost in Siberia or some other outpost. So you understand that it is very important for all of us . . . . you, me and my family, that we do nothing to provoke her. The one thing that she is most proud of is her daughter, Anya. She has, over the years, tried to mold that girl into her image of what a young lady should be. So far, Anya has obeyed and has done what has been expected of her, but now I am afraid that she will have trouble with Anya. You see, my sister has chosen the man that she would like Anya to marry and Anya has told me that she is not ready for marriage and does not want to marry Ivan. Both my wife and I witnessed the looks on your and Anya's faces yesterday and I suspect that something is going on between the two of you. I convinced my wife into believing that the reason you froze and lost your composure was because you were not expecting to see such a pretty girl. Now I must tell you, please do not pursue any private contact with Anya because if you do, and if I am told of it, I would be forced to send you to the regular army as a regular soldier in the cavalry. You are like a son to me, Otto, so do not disappoint me. There are numerous other girls in St. Petersburg, who would be more suitable for you in your position and you would not have to worry about any unpleasant consequences."

With those words, Otto was dismissed and in total bewilderment, Otto, shaking, went back to his room in total shock. He sat on his bed, completely devastated by

Constantine's words and for a long while, his brain was completely empty of any thought . . . . to him, at that moment, all that meant anything to him was ripped away and all that was left of him was an empty shell. The fullness and the joy that he was experiencing a few short hours before, had disappeared in an instant. Now, life had no meaning. Any drive or ambition to do his job well, momentarily disappeared. But after lying on his bed for a while, realizing that he had many duties to perform, he rose and mechanically finished his duties for the day.

Later at night, when he would be alone in the solitude of his room, he would be able to assess his situation better and perhaps he would be able to make some sense of the whole dilemma, come to some conclusions and let the chips fall where they may. He made no definite plan other than he would again meet Anya tomorrow under the Liteiny Bridge. She would be there, no one else knew of their meeting, so all was not yet lost.

As it often happens, the weather reflects ones mood. The day began with a strong north wind, blowing and bringing in icy cold rain from the Baltic Sea and the rain did not ease until shortly prior to Otto's and Anya's secret meeting. Because of the weather, Otto took along his ruck sack and stuffed it with a blanket, some cakes and a jar of cold tea. He made his way to the bridge long before Anya was to be there. When he arrived under the shelter of the bridge, he spread his blanket, sat down and stared hollow-eyed at the scene before him. Everything reinforced his mood; the blossoms on the flowering plants seemed to weep as they hung their heads under the weight of the rain and seemed to be crying as water dripped from their petals. The ducks on the river shivered with cold and the grey sky did not let any sunshine through. All seemed as bleak as his future. He stared at the pathway that Anya would be taking and after what seemed like an eternity, he recognized her figure happily bouncing down the pathway. She did not seem to be sharing his mood and only after coming to a halt before him did she realize that something was amiss.

"What is wrong Otto? It is me, Anya. Aren't you happy to see me?"

Otto, taking her hands in his, looked down at her and with tears in his eyes said, "Anya, please sit down beside me. I have some terrible news." With those words Otto related all that had transpired the previous day.

Shaken and saddened, Anya asked, "What are we going to do? We could run away and you could take me with you to Poland. Do you want to do that, Otto? I would happily go away with you."

"Anya, Anya, if it were only so simple. I am in the Army, Anya, and I have to serve my term. If I would desert the Army and then get caught, I could be shot. No Anya, that is not a choice. I have thought long and hard about it and you know that I want to be with you but under the circumstances, nothing that we could do would keep us together. There are too many things working against us. To start with, your mother would never approve of me . . . . a German Protestant and having little money . . . . also, you are engaged to be married and furthermore the army would not allow me to get married since I have more than a year left to serve."

Young love, passion and romance was suddenly shattered by ethnicity, religion, social status and economics.

"What did we get ourselves into?" Whispered Anya as they held each other close. "I do not love Ivan. I don't want to marry him. I love you."

"Please Anya, let's not talk about it anymore. Let us just secretly see each other when we can."

"Yes, that is all that we can do. Soon I will be going to our dacha and I know that your regiment will be leaving St. Petersburg also. We may only be able to see each other a few more times."

In silence, Anya and Otto clung to each other, their bodies responding to each others passion and there under the bridge, welcomed each other openly and became one. Their love making was more an act of defiance against those who would keep them apart and deny them the happiness that they felt they were entitled to.

CHAPTER 9

POLAND

The old heavy wooden door that opened on to the street creaked and groaned as it inched back. Pushing at it with all her might, puffing and murmuring excited words, was little five year old Olga, "Mama, mama," she yelped as she tugged at her mother's dress. "Come quick, come quick!"

"Why? What is happening Olga?"

"Quick, quick," came the response and no other explanation was forthcoming.

Paulina was in the middle of preparing the evening meal for the family and really did not want to be interrupted. Hesitatingly, she let Olga take her hand and lead her outside. It was late afternoon and the sun was about to set when Olga and Paulina stepped out of the house onto the street and looked down the way to see what all the excitement was about. The glare from the sun's rays prevented Paulina from focussing immediately on the scene before her but eventually, as she squinted and her eyes adjusted to the outdoor sunlight, she got the picture. On the street before her, was a small group of people gathered around what seemed to be a person dressed in a uniform. Because of the glare, she did not recognize the person responsible but she did recognize her sons, Hugo, Adolph and Teofil, along with some other neighborhood boys. She could hear the excited chatter among them as the whole group inched its way closer to where she and Olga were standing.

"It's Otto, it's Otto, mama," came the cry from Olga.

"Oh mien lieber Gott," ("Oh my dear God,") whispered Paulina and she jerked her hand away from Olga and ran into the middle of the gathering. Otto had come home from Russia!

That evening the whole Martin Flath family sat around the table longer than usual because every one of the six others had a thousand questions and late into the night Otto found himself answering them as best that he could. He told them in detail of his experience in boot camp and the resulting appointment to his present posting with the Pokovnik, Constantine Vasiletvich Zaharoh. He described as best he could the nature of his assignment, his work load and his responsibilities. He described in detail how the life of a high ranking officer in the Russian army differed from that of the average Russian peasant. He told them of the parties, the pageantry and of the strict protocol that accompanied this life style. He spent an hour or more describing the city of St. Petersburg; its show of wealth, as a demonstration of Peter the Great's vision for the city, its delicate architecture which seemed to deliberately defy the harshness and cruelty of the northern Russian winters, its immense size with its two million inhabitants.

Questions were asked about his personal life and he told them about his quest to learn to play the flute. He told them about the German Lutheran church that he had discovered. He told them of his role in the cavalry and he told them what life was like during military maneuvers. What he didn't tell them, was of his affair with Anya. He didn't tell them that she was Constantine's niece and how devastated and broken hearted he became when he was given that news by Constantine. He did not tell them that Anya, who was to marry Ivan in the New Year of 1911, convinced Ivan that the child she was carrying was his and hurriedly got married in early August. He did not tell them since that time, he and Anya would see each other secretly whenever they could. He did not tell them that Anya and their son were the reasons for his decision to enlist for three additional years. He did not tell them how, on the days when his band played outdoors, Anya would come with little Albert, sit down on a blanket and smile adoringly as they listened to the band play. He also did not tell them how heartbreaking it was that he could not hold Albert, cuddle him, tease him, tussle his shiny golden hair, tuck him into bed at night, read to him or do any of those things that most fathers would do with their infant sons. He did not tell them how he longed for Anya and Albert during the long months his regiment would be away from St.

Petersburg. He did not tell them how difficult it was to harbor a secret such as this and not be able to share it with anyone for fear of the reprisals that could develop. He wanted to tell them how much he loved Anya and Albert and how he had hoped to return to Poland with them when his compulsory two year stint with the army came to an end. He wanted to tell them how he and Anya had planned to break away from the clutches of her family but how these plans failed because of her father's refusal to take her and Albert with him on a business trip he had made to Lodz. He dared not tell them any of these things. Here in Poland, his own mother, father and extended members of his family would also not approve. He knew Anya and Albert would be shunned and his own relationship with Anya would be scorned. After all, she was Russian, Orthodox and married to another man. He knew that prejudice and intolerance worked both ways. There, sitting at the table with his family, came the realization that he would have to carry this secret to his grave.

When he was asked again by his father Martin, as to the reason for signing an obligation to serve willingly in the Russian army for an additional three years, his explanation was that life for him with the Pokovnik was good, work was easy, food was good, there seemed to be little danger of a war breaking out, and besides there was little work in Poland. Other than family, Poland held little appeal. As a matter of fact, many of his extended family, he explained, had already left for other lands. Many Flaths had gone overseas to the U.S.A., Brazil and Canada. They talked late into the night and it was not until the last lit candle flickered out, that they went to bed. There would be more time over the coming two weeks to reconnect.

The days of Otto's furlough were spent visiting with old friends and relatives. An electric tram going from Piotrkow to Lodz had been installed during Otto's time in Russia and Adolph talked Otto into riding it to Lodz and back. Electric trolleys were common in St Petersburg but they were a recent addition to the transportation system found in rural Poland. The distance from Piotrkow to Lodz was only fifty kilometers, the distance from Moszczenica to Lodz was even less. After walking five kilometers to the tram station, they would be in the heart of Lodz within two hours.

Otto was familiar with Lodz and the surrounding area because the Flaths had settled in several places near Lodz. Martin had four brothers and most of them, along with other relatives still resided in Pabianica, Michalov, Aleksandrow, Piotrikow and Jarosty. As a matter of fact, Otto had been born in Aleksandrow. On this day though, Otto and Adolph would not visit any of them; they would spend all day walking along Piotrowska Avenue, enjoying the hustle and bustle of a rapidly growing city, taking in a silent moving picture show and eating ice cream at one of the many sidewalk cafes.

The day went by quickly but during their time together, Adolph told Otto how he had been dreaming of leaving Poland and emigrating to Canada or elsewhere. He told Otto that there had been many discussions at home about the possibilities of leaving Poland and going to the U.S.A, Canada, or Brazil. Adolph told Otto that their father, Martin had sent inquiries to his brother already in the U.S.A. as well to as a couple of cousins living in a place in Canada, called Saskatchewan.

"Mother wanted to wait until your compulsory time in the army was completed and then all of us would go together as a family," said Adolph.

How could Otto respond to a statement like that. Here his family was counting on him to emigrate with them and now he had committed himself to another three years in the army. Guilt and confusion engulfed him.

"Oh, what a mess I have made of things!" he said to himself. "Only, if only, Anya and I had not met!"

He realized how disappointed his mother and his brothers would be because of his decision but what were his options now? He had no choice. If he deserted the army and filed for emigration, the authorities would be informed of his desertion and he would surely be caught. That night, it was with a heavy heart that he went to bed and tried to make sense of the whole mess.

The topic of emigration was discussed among Martin's family several times during Otto's stay and the conclusion was that Otto would return to Russia and the rest of the family would actively pursue emigration with or without Otto. Should sponsorship and approval be acquired sooner than Otto's release, they would go and he would then follow on this own. It was settled.

Otto would return to his position in Russia with mixed emotions . . . . and reflecting upon his decision to sign for an additional three years stint in the Russian cavalry, he boarded the train in Lodz to begin his trip back to St. Petersburg . . . . a three day trip . . . . plenty of time to think. Upon reflection, he realized that the paths of life in Russia all led to dead ends. His career in the army led nowhere; there was no chance of rising in the ranks where only in the upper echelons of the military hierarchy was the pay sufficient to raise a family. Also, his love affair with Anya would not end favorably. She was married to Ivan, her mother still dominated the family and even if she and Albert were to come to a foreign land with him, his own family would not be accepting of the situation. Besides, what work would there be for a man who for the past few years, was the valet for an army officer and before that, a man who operated a weaving machine and worked in a flour mill? He had little cash and no knowledge of what it took to be a pioneer in a foreign land. He would stay in Russia in the army for the next three years . . . . he had decided. He still loved Anya and he would see both Anya and Albert as often as was possible without raising any alarm bells. He would continue to do his duties to the best of his abilities but he regretted having obligated himself to Constantine for another three years. It was at this moment, that his heart was not in Russia, but back in Poland.

The gloomy mood that he was experiencing was reinforced by the gloomy look of the city as the train wound its way through slums and industrial neighborhoods. He rarely saw this side of the glamorous St. Petersburg. His life style did not bring him in contact with the peasants and working class but as the train slowly passed through these areas as it made its way to the Moscow station in St. Petersburg, he could plainly see the poverty and the misery that many of the people experienced in Russia. Most of the working poor lived in squalid conditions: no running water, open sewers, no electricity, no schools for the children and no hospitals for the old, the sick and the dying. As he neared his destination, the streets that he passed by widened and became cobbled. The sewers were now underground, the yards neatly kept and the people on the streets were dressed in fashionable clothes. By the time he was welcomed back by Constantine, his wife and children, Otto's mood had improved. They gathered around him and peppered him with questions about his leave and his trip back to Poland.

That evening, Otto was informed that during his absence, the army and, in particular, his regiment was going to experience several changes. He was told that in a month his regiment consisting of five thousand cavalry soldiers and four thousand horses would be leaving the barracks in St. Petersburg and would be transferred to Dubno in the Ukraine. He was told that when morning came, he would be responsible for packing everything that he and Constantine personally required and that there was no indication how long the army would be stationed at Dubno. In addition to packing the trunks with personal items, he, along with Oleg were responsible for packing the saddles, bridles, blankets, horse shoes and all else that supported the three horses that Constantine and himself would use while in the Ukraine. He and Oleg would have to look after boarding the horses on the train and Oleg would sleep on the rail car that carried their horses. He was then told by Tatiana that the family, along with others were planning a gathering prior to the departure. He was also informed that Ivan was being transferred to Rega, Latvia, and that Anya would be going there as well. This news shocked Otto but did not entirely surprise him. He had heard rumblings that additional forces were needed in the outlying regions of Russia to secure the borders. Austria/Hungary especially seemed to be flexing its muscles in an attempt to reinvigorate a crumbling empire and the Galicians in the Ukraine were showing signs of rebelling against the Tsar.

Again, as often happened before and would likely happen again and again, where Otto went and what happened to him were out of his control . . . . others were shaping his destiny.

The news was devastating to Otto. At the time that he signed for additional service, there was no indication that these new events were on the horizon. What he had believed was now totally contrary to what was going to happen. His image of three years of relative comfort in St. Petersburg was now going to be three years of what might as well be solitary confinement in the backwoods of Galicia. He knew that the Galicians were poor and lived isolated lives but he had no concept of the level of poverty and the primitive conditions with which the inhabitants had to contend. There were many questions in his mind that lay unanswered. How long would his regiment be posted there? Would they move? Would the Pokovnik return to St. Petersburg for the winter? What comforts would be afforded to him? How cold were the winters? How far away from the camp was the nearest city? Where the hell was Dubno? How would be able to keep in contact with his family and, most importantly how would be be able to keep in contact with Anya without her family or Constantine finding out their secret?

Many of the answers would come naturally in the due course of time but he and Anya would have to devise a plan whereby they could communicate to each other in secret. The army would have telegraph and perhaps telephone lines strung and railroads built to the camp but the use of those devices would be exclusive to the military. He could get some information about Anya and Albert from Constantine but he would not dare ask too many questions and too often, because they may raise suspicions in Constantine. The only alternative left to him was to devise a plan whereby no one would suspect that he and Anya were writing to each other. His most immediate problem though was getting in touch with Anya as soon as possible because they had not set a date for a meeting prior to him going on leave. He also began to experience the sinking feeling and the hollowness in the pit of his stomach that comes with the fear of losing something which one loves and holds most dear and precious. With these new events, would Anya give up hope of a continued relationship and would she completely abandon him? Separation begins to dull the senses and the passion that is present when two people in love are together physically. Does she still love him enough to take the trouble and the risk? He had to find out! He knew that she would be present at the 'going away' gathering but that was not going to happen for a week or so and in this state of panic, he would not wait that long. He decided that he would go to their favorite meeting place under their bridge every afternoon and hopefully, she still shared the deep desire to be together and would come to the conclusion that it would be there that Otto would be waiting.

He went . . . . she came . . . . with Albert by her side. Tears of joy and relief welled up in Otto's eyes as they approached. Now there was no doubt that Anya still cared for him. Her coming ever closer, erased any doubt that he had made the correct decision to reenlist. They together would work things out . . . . make a plan and follow through.

Otto was overjoyed to see Albert accompany Anya but he also became nervous. Albert was now beginning to talk and though he was accustomed to seeing Otto, he did not know who he was. Was Anya taking a risk by bringing Albert? Would Albert tell Ivan of his trip to the bridge with his mother? Wordless, Anya and Otto embraced . . . . the passion and the comfort welled up and engulfed them like a surging tide. The desire and other feelings harbored within each exploded into the open and with tears of joy and longing, they kissed and hugged while Albert looked on, totally confused and bewildered by what was happening.

"Otto, we have so much to talk about. I have missed you. I don't know what is going to happen to us. Is it over for us? What are we going to do?"

The jumble of questions, mixed with statements poured out all at the same time. Otto, still holding her in an embrace said nothing and after Anya emptied herself of all the pent-up questions and feelings, she said, "Otto, I have brought some food and drink. Let's have a picnic and we will talk."

They spread the blanket on the grass, laid out the food and drink, sat down with Albert between them. They shared the food and drink together . . . . they were a family.

"Otto, I have a very good friend here in St. Petersburg that I can trust completely. Already, I have confided in her and told her of our relationship. She is completely understanding and is willing to help us. I have also asked her if it would be possible for us to correspond with one another through her. You could write to me, address the envelope to her and she would then readdress it and send it on to me and I would do the same. What do you think of my plan?"

"If you are sure that you can trust her, it is an excellent idea. I have thought and thought about what to do, but I have not been able to come up with any kind of solution. I was ready to give up and thought that you would give up too and forget about me."

"No, Otto, never, somehow, someway, sometime we will be together as a family. It know it Otto. I have some other news . . . . I am with child again."

Happiness, joy, confusion, fear, dread and sadness dominated the rest of the time together and each went their separate way home, no more confident or clear of the direction their paths would lead them. They would take one step at a time and in three years time, perhaps the outcome would be clearer.

CHAPTER 10

Lists of items that required packing were finalized and given to Otto. There was no urgency to complete the packing as their regiment was scheduled to be one of the last ones to leave St. Petersburg. The sheer size and numbers of manpower, horses, equipment, supplies, ammunition and weapons made it impossible for the relocation to be completed quickly. It was impossible to travel in one contingent. The trains were limited in size and numbers . . . . there were no aircraft for transport . . . . there were no paved highways . . . . there were no connecting grid roads, no connecting rivers to accommodate the move . . . . the solution? Travel by train where and when possible, unload men, horses and supplies, march to the nearest railroad and start all over again. This process of forming the Russian Third Army would take months to complete but upon completion date, Otto was told that the army, without reserves, would be comprised of four army corps (one hundred, eighty thousand men) and three cavalry divisions (fifty thousand men and fifty thousand horses) for a total of 230,000 men without reserves. The plan was to eventually occupy the castle at Dubno and the barracks being constructed on the outskirts of the city. The army was also busy extending the railroad and hoped that it would be completed in time to accommodate the transfer of troops, equipment, supplies and horses.

At the moment, the logistics of the transfer to Dubno was not the most important issue with which Otto had to deal. His participation in the whole event was relatively minor in regards to the grand scheme but number one on Otto's mind was not the packing up of things, rather his main concern was that of keeping in close contact with those he loved . . . . the most important of which was Anya. When and where would they meet again? Would their plan to write to each other work? Would the mail get through? Would their letters be censored? Would he be able to keep in contact with his family in Poland? These and other questions would only be answered in time. In the meantime, Otto was kept very busy sorting, assembling and packing the items chosen by Constantine, Tatiana and himself. Since there was limited transport, the selection of personal items was kept to a minimum. After several days of choosing and packing, the trunks were labelled with identification tabs, tied securely with hemp ropes and placed conveniently for the transport. Soldiers would then load them onto the trains to begin their two thousand kilometer journey to a place that Otto had never heard of before. After they had placed the last trunk on the waiting pile, he trudged slowly back to his room. He sat down on his cot and surveyed the empty room and the emptiness of the room only intensified the feeling of emptiness in his heart.

The Pokovnik called Otto and said, "Otto, we will be leaving for Dubno tomorrow and of course you will accompany me. We will be traveling in a sleeping car along with other officers and their valets. Write your goodbye letters to your family and others that you are leaving behind; these can be mailed from here, thereby having a much better chance of being delivered. We will have to get up early to be ready to go."

"Sir?" Otto hesitatingly asked, "I was told that your family was planning to have a gathering before we had to leave . . . ."

"We were Otto, but the orders came today that there is room for us on the next series of trains so we have to cancel our family plans. It's too bad but we can only follow the orders of those higher up in rank than us," came the response.

"Sir, may I ask you a question?"

"Why of course, Otto, what is it?"

"Sir, I have never heard of Dubno before. Where is it and what is it?" asked Otto.

"Come with me. I still have a map on my desk. I will point it out to you and give you a short history and other information about the region."

In his now almost empty office, Constantine found the map that he sought and pointed to the area north and west of the Carpathian Mountains and began his oration.

"This is Galicia. It is an interesting place; the people occupying this region come from many different ethnic groups. The eastern part is mainly Ukrainian and the western part is mainly Polish. Dubno itself was started and fortified by the powerful Ostroski family . . . . they were Polish. However, there are many Jews living here as well . . . . some Belarussians, some Czechs, some Austrians and some Hungarians. The Cossacks have ruled and protected Volhynia and the eastern side for many centuries and Taris Bulba, the great Cossack leader, attacked Dubno and occupied it for several years. The land is quite productive but much of the area is swampy and forested . . . . especially in the foothills of the Carpathian Mountains which separate polish Galicia from Hungary. Most peasants are very poor and backward and not many of them are able to read or write. The reason for this is due to the way the land is owned and managed . . . . the people are steeped in religion and are guided by old tradition and superstition. You know because you have seen how many of our soldiers conduct themselves. The Cossacks, on the other hand, are very independent and can be cruel and vicious . . . . not many people wander into the territory that they control. They are proud, excellent fighters, who have no fear. There now Otto, you have had your lesson . . . . get ready to leave."

The transporting of men, materials and equipment proved to be more cumbersome than what was planned for. Even by train, the army could only travel little more than 100 kilometers a day. Horses had to be taken off the train, exercised, watered and fed, then reloaded. On occasion, the whole train of supplies had to be shifted to another train because some of the railroads were narrow gauged beds and others were a wider gauge. Otto had ample time to survey the countryside and see first hand what the life of a peasant was like. He concluded that in reality, the life of a peasant in Galicia, apart from being more isolated, really wasn't much different from the life of a peasant where he had grown up. Both seemed to be poor . . . . not yet fully understanding that being poor was a relative term and poor could mean more than lacking comforts in the home.

After days and days of watching the countryside slowly drift by, the train came to a lurching halt and with the stop came the word that this was the end of the line. They had reached their destination. Constantine called Otto and explained that because the barracks and officer quarters were not fully completed, they would be housed in the homes of several different land owners, bankers, businessmen or former army quarters. Some of the enlisted men were sent to the barracks that were completed but others lived in tents. Most of the weaponry and ammunition was stored in the fortified Dubno Castle. The army headquarters were also set up in the castle. Otto, Oleg, the soldiers and the army brass were kept busy organizing and reorganizing as more and more soldiers and cavalry were sent to get the Russian Third Army up to its assigned numbers. Fortunately, the weather had cooperated and all were settled in before the first snowflakes fell.

The winters that dominated the steppes of Galicia were often harsh . . . . temperatures remained below freezing for weeks on end . . . . snow and blowing snow swept across the nearby treeless plains and hammered everything in its path. In preparation for this annual occurrence, the peasants of this region, over the centuries, learned how to cope with and survive the brutality which cold, snow and wind can bring. The harsh conditions of their environment and their state of poverty created a tough resilient society able to survive with few physical means at its disposal. The people knew how to keep themselves warm having little fuel. They knew how to build warm homes for themselves and their livestock. They knew how to preserve food which would have to last for months. They learned all these things, not from books or from scholars; they learned from their families and from life experiences. The steppe region of Galicia boasts some of the most productive land in the world. The soil combined with ample sun and rain produces a great variety of grain crops, vegetables and hay. However, because of the harshness of the winters, food for humans and livestock had to be stored and preserved. The Galicians knew how, yet in spite of this knowledge, they were among the poorest In Europe.

The peasants developed a pattern whereby they built their homes in clusters . . . . safety in numbers. The typical house contained two rooms but quite often only one. The walls were built of logs, squared off and piled one atop the other. The cracks between the logs were plastered with a mixture of clay, straw and cow manure. A herring bone of approximately five centimeter diameter branches were attached diagonally to the logs, inside and out. Then these were plastered over with the same mixture as the chinks in the logs. If the peasants could afford it, the walls were then whitewashed with slaked lime.

The roof was thatched with wheat straw and the floor consisted of hard packed clay. The windows were small and most were shuttered rather than paned and the one door was constructed of slabs of wood held on to the door frame by leather bands which acted as hinges. Inside, the combined oven and stove was made of rocks bound together with a clay and straw mixture. These ovens also served as beds. In winter, the tops would be kept warm by the fire inside. Mattresses were made of straw and the families slept under chicken or duck feather filled duvets.

Most of the peasant's animals were housed in a leanto attached to the house. Each family plot was surrounded by wood pickets driven into the ground to keep in the cows, pigs, chickens, ducks, geese and perhaps a horse. Mounds of hay and straw could be seen piled in the corner of the yard which was food for animals in winter. In most of the clusters of homes, one would find a communal oven and well where mothers, grandmothers and children would gather on a weekly basis and bake their bread and buns. People could survive but there were no luxuries; the land owners made certain of that.

In these climes, winter's grip stalled or stopped nearly all movement. Everybody and everything hunkered down for the winter and awaited the reawakening of spring.

The winter of 1913-1914, was no exception and by November, the Russian Third Army had gathered enough food and supplies to last the approaching winter. Approximately one quarter million men and thousands of horses awaited the coming blasts of cold and readied themselves for whatever the winter would bring. The soldiers were kept busy going on winter war and survival maneuvers. They would march, eat, sleep and simulate war conditions for days at a time. Supply trains would shuttle back and forth, testing the army's ability to wage offensive and defensive battles in the foothills of the Carpathian Mountains.

Otto's cavalry regimental officers were housed in a home of a former Austrian colonel. The home contained many rooms and offered a comfortable residence and command post for the officers. Otto had to share one room with Constantine and aside from that, his duties remained much the same as they were in Russia. Each day, he would rise, dress, prepare a samovar of tea, put on his great coat and attend to his and Constantine's horses. Upon his return to the house, he would eat a breakfast of eggs and sausages. When the Pokovnik left, Otto would tidy up the room, do whatever washing was necessary and then finally have time to sit down to practice his flute, and write letters to his beloved Anya and to his parents in Poland. He wrote more often to Anya than he did to his family. He told Anya in every letter, how much he missed her . . . . holding her, touching her, smelling her breath on him, talking to her, laughing with her. He told her how much he would love to see Albert learning to talk, play, read and write. He told her of his experience traveling to the Carpathian Mountains. He told her of his dreams that he had of being with her and his dreams of taking her and Albert with him to a distant land. He told her of Martin's plans to emigrate to Canada and how Martin had contacted cousins in Canada about the possibility of sponsorship. He told her how he would dutifully serve his time in the army. He told her how he hoped that Constantine would be sent back to St. Petersburg for the winter and how much he missed St. Petersburg. He told her how isolated this place was and how it lacked any kind of cultural events that he was accustomed to. He told her how time weighed heavy on him and how much time he had to think and plan . . . . yet how he could not do anything about them . . . . only dream.

He told her many things but he couldn't tell her everything. He learned this shortly after he had moved into the same room as Constantine and because they shared the same room, Constantine was fully aware of all of Otto's activities and habits. One afternoon as Constantine sat at the table that also served as a writing desk, Constantine said,

"Otto, I need to talk to you for a few moments and I need to give you some advice."

Otto's ears perked up as he nervously sat down on his bed waiting to hear what Constantine had to say. Constantine began,

"We have been here in Dubno for two months now and I, myself, have a better understanding of our assignment. I would like to share some information with you. To start with, the third army is not the only army in this region. There are a total of six, spread along the foothills in Galicia. They are here in case of a Hungarian/Austrian invasion which may come sooner than we think. The exact location and the numbers of soldiers, horses and arms are a secret which, even I, have not been informed of. Since it is a secret, letters leaving our regiment and coming in to our regiment are censored. I don't want to tell you this but I was ordered to censor all your communications to the outside world. I am sorry, I should have told you this before and should have warned you to be careful about what you say. Others also read your mail. So far Otto, you have not said anything that would get you into trouble from the military but I have to confess that I have complete knowledge of you and my niece, Anya. I have known this for a while now but did not confront you with it until I had time to digest the news and make a decision on what I should do or would have to do about it."

Otto could barely believe what he was hearing. With great trepidation, he began to wring his hands, break out in a sweat with his face turning ashen grey. It was as if a ton of bricks had landed squarely on his stomach.

"Otto," continued Constantine, "you have been with me now for several years and as I have told you before, I regard you more than just a loyal servant, I think of you almost as my son . . . . as does my wife. I have therefore decided to try to protect you. I promise you this, I will tell no one else . . . . not my sister, not the army, not my children, certainly not Ivan, and not even my wife. Also you must not under any conditions admit that you are aware of my knowledge of the whole situation. Otto, I am very happy for you in many ways but I also worry about you. As far as I am concerned, you can continue writing to Anya but you must not mention her real name in any of your letters . . . . use Anya's friends name. That will protect both yourself and Anya, should anyone who censors your letters begin to become suspicious of who this woman is that you are writing to. I have to admit that when I first found out, my immediate thought was that I would have to follow through on my previous words to you when first Tatiana and I became suspicious that your and Anya's relationship was more than casual. Finally Otto, do not say anything in your letters that might cause the army to investigate you further. Many of the censors are paranoid regarding spies and your name alone stands out like a sore thumb. Say what you like in your letters to Anya and your family and I will read them and ask you to change anything that I feel could jeopardize your safety here with me."

With those words, the bonds between Constantine and Otto strengthened and Otto's devotion to his boss increased a thousand fold. Then, for the first time since becoming Constantine's valet four years previous, Otto stood up, reached out and spontaneously they hugged each other, like a father and a son would hug each other.

The winter passed and the snow, ice and frost gave way to rain, water and dew. The maneuvers conducted in the harsh conditions of winter were now conducted in the no less harsh conditions of mud, swamp, flies, gnats and dirt. Letters arriving from Poland and St. Petersburg did not come often but when they were delivered, they came in bunches . . . . all showing signs of having been opened and read. Some of the letters even had sentences blackened out by the censors. In spite of the censorship, Otto was very anxious to read them and find out what was happening in the outside world.

He found out that Martin had found a sponsor in Canada and was making preparations to move his family to Radisson, Saskatchewan, Canada. He was told that his cousin, Gus Flath, was there as were other Flaths. He was also told that several other families from around Lodz had gone already and more were preparing to leave. He did not know the exact day or date . . . . or even who, in total, would be going. He wrote back and told his family how he wished that he could go along and experience the new venture together. It sounded like Canada was a land flowing with milk and honey. He explained that within two years he would get his release and follow them to their new home.

He found out that Anya had given birth to a baby girl. The baby was healthy and happy but Anya stated that she did not know who the baby resembled. She told Otto that she was happy for his family and their plans to emigrate to Canada. She hoped that he would be able to follow them. The words in her letters were becoming more impersonal and Otto began to feel that their love for one another was beginning to fade. He knew that words alone from letters far away, could not keep a true loving relationship together forever. He too, felt the loosening of the ties that had previously bound them together and he began to feel the urge to entertain some other females. In Dubno, his choices were few but there were some.

CHAPTER 11

They came using various means of transportation. Some came on horseback, some on carts or in carriages, some walked, some by train from units farther afield and then by horse driven taxi. Some came escorted by camp followers, some singly, some with their temporary peasant girl friends and some even with their wives. The high ranking officers brought their valets with them as well. They came through the gates of Dubno castle to celebrate summer and the successful build up of defenses in Galicia. All was ready in case of a confrontation with the Austrian/Hungarian armed forces. Champagne, caviar, smoked salmon and several local delicacies had been ordered to be served as hors d'oeuvres. Spit-roasted piglets, mashed potatoes, cabbage rolls and cooked vegetables would be served for the main meal. Vodka would flow freely. A Cossack band comprised of squeeze boxes, mandolins and fiddles was hired to entertain the celebrants following the meal. Dancing girls and other girls that curried men's favors were brought in as well. It was going to be a great party and Otto, along with other hundreds of participants were genuinely excited. The months of isolation and celibacy had taken its toll.

Dubno castle had been built by the wealthy Ostroski family a couple of hundred years previously and had been built to accommodate large gatherings. It was not nearly as fancy as the Yusopov palace in St. Petersburg but it would more than meet the requirements for this occasion. The women, men, girls and boys who were not on the invited guest list but there to serve and accommodate the official guests were not permitted to participate in the festivities. There were however several other areas in the castle where the servants and valets could dip into the champagne, eat caviar and dance to the music that drifted out of the ballroom. Once the invited guests had been watered and fed and the music had started, the time would come for the servants and others to enjoy the celebrations as well.

Rumblings of war had been circulating for many months but on this night, the thought of going to war with Austria/Hungary was far from the minds of the party goers. Privately though, Otto could not help but reflect on its possibilities; but, like the others, he would dismiss his fears and enjoy the evening. The sounds of laughter and music that filtered from the ballroom grew louder as the evening progressed. The party was going well . . . . even for Otto. As a matter of fact, Otto was quite proud of himself. Earlier in the day, he had his hair cropped close to his skull, he had sharpened his razor so that he could have a close clean shave, he had trimmed his mustache and even waxed the ends a little. His black riding boots shone brilliantly, his black uniform highlighted with blue piping, along with his white leather belt and gloves, all placed on a five foot eleven inch, one hundred and seventy pound erect frame, resulted in quite a handsome figure. The servant girls did not disappoint him . . . . he was taking advantage of his stature and the image he presented. He flirted with them, charmed them with his good looks and his social graces. He impressed them with his graceful dance steps. He pressed the flesh teasingly and was having a carefree time. Just when they were all expecting the noise level to rise and the celebrations to become more active, sudden silence was all that emanated from the ballroom.

"I wonder why the music has stopped and all has become quiet," Otto whispered to his dancing partner as he held her close.

"I am sure I don't know," she replied, "and we cannot enter the hall now. We must wait until we are summoned. We can only wait to find out."

Within minutes, the party broke up and the guests boarded their carriages and other means of transportation and vanished into the night. The fun had come to an abrupt end. All the way back to headquarters, Otto puzzled as to why the evening had ended much too early and why the guests all wore such grim expressions on their faces.

Upon the return to their quarters, Otto prepared Constantine's bed by pulling back the covers and fluffing up the pillows. He then waited for the Pokovnik to give him further instructions, hoping for an explanation. He waited patiently as

Constantine prepared himself for the night's rest and after a few minutes, Constantine approached Otto.

"Son," he said, "I have some terrible news for you, for me, for my family, for the Tsar and for all of Russia. Germany has declared war against Russia and full mobilization is to begin immediately." **

Otto glanced at the calendar and noted the date. It was August 1, 1914. This announcement came somewhat as a surprise but not totally unexpected. The account of Austrian Archduke Ferdinand's assassination in Sarajevo was well documented. This assassination would begin a series of events that ultimately would lead to the announcement just heard. Otto, at the time, did not know nor could not even imagine the disaster which was to follow. He did not know that by the time all was said and done, humanity would suffer 35,000,000 casualties . . . . 15,000,000 of the casualties would be deaths and of those, 10,000,000 would come from the military. Russia alone would count for 2,000,000 dead soldiers . . . . not all of them due to gun fire. He did not know that after four years of battle, this war would become known as the war that would end all wars . . . . how ironic.

Otto could not fall asleep . . . . nor could Constantine and some time in the darkness of the night, Constantine finally interrupted the silence.

** *The assassination of the Austro-Hungarian heir to the throne, Archduke Ferdinand, on June 28, 1914, provided the Austro-Hungarian government the excuse to invade Serbia. The invasion of Serbia by Austro-Hungarian forces on July 28, 1914, brought Russia into the fray which then led to Germany's declaration of war on Russia on August 1, 1914.*

"Otto, I know that you are awake. I cannot sleep either. You know what keeps jumping into my head? I keep thinking . . . . what are we doing here? What is this all about? This is total madness. What is there to gain? A few pieces of land? For whom? We are going to kill each other and for what reason? Because someone else speaks a different language? Because others worship God in a different way than we do? Because others wear their clothing differently? Because others have skin and hair colors that are different from ours? It makes no sense to me, Otto. All that every one of us just wants, is to be happy . . . . to have a family . . . . to be safe . . . . to live without fear. Look at yourself and the other two million men in our army . . . . what do they want? Do they want to lose their lives just because the Tsar wants to prevent Franz-Joseph of Austria from ruling this pathetic piece of ground? Of course not! This is sheer madness. It makes me sick. I have been in battles and I know what is coming."

Otto listened intently as Constantine expounded on his views and feelings about war and finally he interrupted, "Sir, what is it really like? What can we expect? What are our chances of surviving?"

"I think that our chances of defeating the Austrian/ Hungarian forces are good. We have been here in this region for a long time. Our strength in numbers is far superior to those of the 'enemy' and our training has been excellent. The Austrians are not aware of our strength and as of now, there are no German forces in the area to assist the Austrians. The Austrian army will be coming through the mountain passes while we will be advancing from the plains. It makes a huge difference, but

Otto, I have experienced first hand the horrors of war. I fought in the Russian/Japanese war just a few years ago. There are not words that can describe the hell that occurs on the battle field. The human mind is not capable, nor designed to deal with everything that is happening around you. In a very few days, you will be in that kind of situation . . . . believe me. Otto, I am an officer and I know that I should not be talking this way but I have needed to tell someone else just how I feel."

Otto never said a word as he lay quietly listening to his chief spill his guts.

"Otto," he went on, "I have sat in on many war planning sessions over the years and I am dumbfounded as to the way generals and politicians alike describe war. For instance, they call the killing fields, a theatre . . . . imagine . . . . a theatre of war . . . . as if war was some kind of entertainment. Why don't they call it what it is . . . . a slaughter field of men and horses. They call the dead and wounded 'casualties' . . . . and treat them as if they are numbers . . . . 10,000 casualties, they will say. Why don't they say 10,000 fathers, brothers, uncles . . . . men who have souls, who have families, who have hopes, who have dreams. Maybe if they thought of it in those terms, they would not be so eager to forcefully send their fellow brothers to kill or maim other brothers in the name of victory . . . . victory or loss decided by the number of dead and wounded. It really makes no sense but I guess if you are the one sitting at a breakfast table in St. Petersburg, Paris or New York, reading the news coming from the battle fields and you read the headlines, 'Russian Troops Advance Ten Kilometers' and the article goes on to explain that only 5,000 casualties were incurred, it somehow sanitizes the horrors and makes it more acceptable. I believe that all those who, in the name of their religion, language or whatever else, would wage war, should experience the killing fields themselves and participate personally with gun and bayonet in hand. Perhaps then they would know what it feels like to stab another person, a person who you have no personal quarrel with and don't even know, and watch his eyes as he slowly realizes that he is going to die. Perhaps they should be placed in the middle of the battle and be forced to listen to the screams of agony and pain coming from wounded men and horses. They should be forced to experience the incredibly horrific screams and explosions of artillery shells as they explode around you. Perhaps they should view the battle site with guts hanging out of horses bellies, of brains spattered everywhere, of blood flowing in rivers and pooling into huge black ponds. Readers, politicians, war planners and bigots don't see these things . . . . don't know these things . . . . to them it is more like a game of chess only to be played with real live chess pieces and real live consequences."

"Otto, once this is over, you will not want to remember it, or even talk about it. You will only wish that it had never happened. I can only hope and pray that we will come out of this alive, Otto, and that the war will last for only a very short while. I pray that our forces will overwhelm the Austrians and that they will surrender without too much death."

"I have said my piece . . . . now try to get some rest, Otto. Tomorrow will be a long day."

CHAPTER 12

There would be no sleep for Otto on this particular night. Revolving images of the horrors of war, plagued him as he tried to sleep. Only the people that had directly faced the horrors of hand to hand combat and the whole culture of war, are able to describe the emotions involved. Otto's fears on this night would only escalate in the weeks and months to come and, although frightened by what lay ahead, thoughts of his family and of Anya weighed heavily on his mind as well.

He had received a letter from Poland which told him that his family had indeed emigrated and were on their way to Canada. What came as a surprise to him though, was that only some of his siblings went and some remained in Poland. The family was split up. His mother, Paulina, thought it best for the whole family, if Martin, along with their sons Adolph and Teofil, would emigrate first and the rest of the family would wait for Otto's return from Russia and then emigrate to Canada as well. Left behind were Paulina, Hugo who would help Paulina, Otto, and young Olga.

He had also received a letter from Anya informing him that Ivan was sent to East Prussia where he was to serve in Russia's First Army under Rennenkampt.[***] She also told him that she and the two children had moved back to St. Petersburg and were living with her parents. Reflecting on the situation, Otto began to realize that nearly all the people most dear to him were in danger. Only his father, Martin, and his brothers, Adolph and Teofil had gotten out of harm's way.

Only when one wants the night never to end, daybreak comes much too soon and with only a very few moments of restless sleep, Otto and Constantine rose and began sorting and packing items felt necessary for whatever lay ahead of them. Along with his uniforms, Otto was only to take a very few personal items: his shaving gear, writing materials, his pocket watch, and a handful of civilian clothing. Before the sun reached its zenith, Constantine and the whole cavalry regiment was packed up, mounted and hastily beginning the hundred kilometer move towards the Carpathian Mountains to meet up with the Austrians. The railroad from Russia only extended as far as Dubno . . . . the rest of the march would be by horse drawn wagons and carts. Even though it was midsummer, the transporting of two hundred, forty thousand men and

---

[***] *Paul von Rennenkampt (1854-1918) was given the command of Russa's First Army which participated in the invasion of East Prussia, August 1914.*

equipment would take at least two or three weeks as there were few roads and those that did exist were merely dirt tracks across the steppes leading to the passes of the Carpathian Mountains.

The usual practice of sending patrols and scouts ahead of the masses of soldiers that followed was employed and with each passing day, reports would be brought back which indicated that they were nearing the front where the initial battle would transpire.

Constantine's regiment finally met up with other regiments and the battle plans, under the leadership of General Ruzski were drawn up.**** The Russian Third Army was made up of four army corps and three cavalry corps for a total of nearly 240,000 men. There were no tanks, no aircraft, no large artillery and even only a very few large guns. The main offensive weapon to be utilized was the mass of humanity equipped only with rifles and bayonets and horses spread across the 250 kilometer front of Galicia. The plan was to send wave after wave of cavalry followed by infantry into the front lines and eventually the opponent would run out of ammunition and manpower, thereby forcing the enemy to retreat or surrender. The life of a soldier was cheap and could easily be replaced. New conscripts, who would need little training, would be thrust into spaces vacated by the dead or the wounded. Carnage was expected and the loss of lives would reach the tens of thousands.

**** *Russia's Third Army, under General Nikolai Ruzski (1854-1918) was one of several armies that comprised Russia's southwest forces. The commander-in-chief of all the forces engaged in the South West front was Nikolai Ivanov. (Source: Wikipedia)*

Constantine was confident that the third army would not suffer such losses. He was confident that the existing army had been trained sufficiently to dispatch the enemy quickly and would not require the help of newly untrained conscripts. Constantine knew that his regiment was equipped with new Mosin rifles with attached bayonets and had much ammunition at its disposal.

By August 2, 1914, the Russian Third Army had prepared itself for the first of several battles with the Austrian/Hungarian Army and later the German forces as well. The historians would later name this confrontation The Battle of Gnila-Lipa, August 26 to August 30, 1914. The Gnila and the Lipa being tributaries of the larger Dniester River.

Otto had no clue as to where he was, nor what he should be doing there.

"Otto, we have the lead Austrian Army in front of us and will be engaged in battle tomorrow morning. We are setting up our command post here as the Austrians are only a few kilometers away. The timing for the attack will come from General Ruzski and could come at any time. Our battle plans are complete. Your duty will be to keep in contact with me and run errands for me during the fighting. Our field quarters consist of a large tent plus a smaller one from where you will do your duties. These tents will move and will be kept within walking distance of the trenches should there be some. If there are no trenches, the tents will be set up at the end of the day and the necessary supplies will be brought there. You do not have to stay by my side as I ride among the troops but you must keep in touch with me in case I require something. You will be kept very busy I assure you," explained Constantine.

"Am I issued a rifle and ammunition?" asked Otto.

"No, all the rifles are needed by the infantry".

"Do I bring your food and drink on horseback?" asked Otto.

"No, you will usually be close enough to the fighting to be able to bring all I need on foot. You on a horse, make too big a target," came the reply. "The only time you will need your horse is when we are advancing or retreating quickly."

Otto had never in his life faced a situation like this before and was frightened more by not knowing how he would react once the sounds of exploding shells and agonizing screams of wounded men and horses reached his ears. He felt helpless.

The shelling began at dawn but rather than the Russian army taking the offensive, the Austrian army attacked just as the sun began to rise. From outside his tent, Otto saw thousands of Cossacks on horses gallop at full speed out of the encampment. Then he saw thousands more foot soldiers carrying only rifles and ammunition with them, follow the cavalry. He could not see first hand what was happening but by the sounds reaching his ears, he knew that the Austrians appeared to be advancing because the sound of rifle fire and exploding shells seemed to be getting louder with each passing minute. He hastily began to prepare for the retreat when suddenly the noise of gunfire became quieter and he could no longer hear the screaming associated with the battle. Never in his life had he felt less safe. All the drills that had meant to prepare him for any combat experience, did not come near to the reality of the real war.

The field hospital had been erected near to Otto's tent and it did not take long before the first casualties were brought in by the paramedics. A few hours earlier, he had seen a troop of men wearing red crosses on their uniforms and carrying only stretchers leave the encampment and follow the infantry onto the battlefield. Now they were returning. Young men . . . . bleeding, groaning, crying, yelling, cursing, praying and some not uttering a sound were paraded by on stretchers or limped past the tent opening. Constantine was right . . . . he could not imagine a worse scene than what was happening before his eyes. He could not help himself . . . . he stumbled around to the back of the tent . . . . leaned forward and broke into convulsions. He dared not enter the field hospital.

The Pokovnik, on his horse, had led his cavalry into the battle as soon as the first sound of gunfire had erupted. Otto had been instructed to pack a ruck sack with food and water at around noon and walk into the battlefield and find the Pokovnik. He was sure that Constantine was not wounded but would be dead . . . . having already gotten killed. However, Otto did not know, nor was it his place to second guess the situation . . . . his orders were to go onto the battlefield with food.

He packed the ruck sack and began his solitary trip through a hell which was no worse than the one described in the bible. Because the battle field followed the banks of the rivers which were mostly covered by stands of pine and aspen, the battlefield itself was hidden from his view. As he began to make his way to the place where he thought he might find the Pokovnik, he began to realize what had happened. Not a few hundred meters from camp, he came across the first Austrian soldier lying dead on the ground. The sight of a grossly distorted dead face with open pleading eyes along with parts of flesh and bone scattered around, sickened him. How could he go on? How could he deal with the impending sight which would be a thousand times worse than what he first saw. Should he turn back? Should he run away? What were his options? He puked again, sat down, cried and then forced himself to continue. He pushed forward . . . . no one to talk to, no one to give him any assurance, comfort or advice. He prayed. With cannons booming, rifles cracking, horses screaming, men moaning and groaning, Otto sweating and shaking nervously picked his way around corpses, past rocks and trees in his attempt to find his boss.

The human brain is a remarkable instrument, an instrument which is designed to protect the body and mind of the person owning it and Otto soon began to understand that very truth. When faced with horror of extreme proportions, the brain begins to automatically set in motion defense mechanisms. Otto could feel these mechanisms begin to work. He did not understand why it was happening but he knew what was happening. Just when he believed his mind would turn to insanity which would protect him from the sight before him, he began to feel his senses become dull. His ears began to shut out the ear splitting noise. His nose did not send the nauseating odor of excrement, combined with escaping body gases, to his brain for decoding. His eyes that sent horrific pictures to his brain for interpretation, quickly became accustomed to the annihilation and his mind was able to accept the sights before him. Just when he thought that he would go mad, his mind and body were able to compensate, make the necessary adjustments and then give him the courage to continue on robotic like . . . . not feeling, only reacting. It was as if his guardian angel had taken control of him and guided him as he made his way through the ruination left behind by the advancing Russian Army.

It became obvious to him that at first contact, it was the Austrian army which had left their protective foxholes and attacked because as he snaked his way forward, he passed body after body of men in Austrian uniforms lying dead on the ground. He could not tell how far the Russian Army had advanced. He could only keep going until he met up with the Pokovnik's soldiers. What seemed like an eternity of crawling, ducking, running and weaving, he caught sight of a large group of Russian Cossacks. He had found Constantine and he delivered his package to his boss. Following an exchange of a few words, he turned and headed back to camp where he and others would begin the task of packing up, loading wagons and reestablishing their camp. The vacated battlefield would soon be occupied by local souvenir hunters and hungry animals. Most of the fallen soldier's bodies and battle ground would be stripped of anything of value and then and only then, would the bodies be buried in large pits. The prisoners would be taken to Dubno and from there would be sent to work as slave labor across Russia.

The Battle of Gnila-Lipa continued from August 26 to August 30, 1914. All attempts by the Austrians to retake lost ground, were totally unsuccessful and the Austrian Army fell apart in total disarray. Day after day, the Russian Armies would follow the retreating Austrians and day after day, Otto's routine was the same. The advancing armies could not keep up with the retreating Austrians because they had to wait for the supply wagons to catch up. The heavy fighting that occurred between August 26 and August 30, had subsided. What remained was the decision as to how deep they would go into the Carpathian Mountains. By the end of September, it became clear to the generals that the armies would stop just outside of the towns of Tarnow and Gorlitz. They would remain there and await instructions from St. Petersburg.

CHAPTER 13

The winter of 1914-1915 was not pleasant; not only was it dominated by severe cold temperatures and storms, but it also treated the Russian Third Army harshly.

The Russian armies had successfully driven the Austrians out of Galicia and into the mountains and by the fall of 1914 had firmly secured the front. Constantine's regiment had not lost many troops or horses in earlier battles and along with the other regiments, prepared themselves for the coming winter months by stocking up on feed for the horses and supplies for the men. The generals of the third, fourth, fifth and eighth army all had anticipated a quiet waiting period for the winter and then if the war had not ended by spring, would continue their assault against Austria on the Hungarian plain which lay on the South side of the Carpathian Mountains. Their plans for an uneventful winter were soon destroyed by the orders from Russian Army headquarters. The armies along the Carpathian Mountains were ordered to follow the retreating Austrians even throughout the winter months and so a series of forays into the mountains was undertaken.

The Russian armies could not advance on a broad front but would attack along narrow mountain passes. The passes could easily be defended and often the Russians would be caught in an ambush and would be forced to retreat. Often also, the armies would be exposed to the severe blizzards that raged unabated across the steppes, which then slammed into the mountains. Weary, tired and wounded soldiers often found themselves freezing to death and left to rely on their own resources for their survival. The dead could not be buried; the ground was frozen and besides the soldiers had no energy left, so the road sides and many smaller battle sites were strewn with frozen bodies covered by snow drifts left to thaw in the spring time. Often when blizzards prevented the soldiers return to their encampments, they would be forced to fend for themselves. This meant that they would impose themselves on the peasants that lived in the immediate area. The soldiers would scour through the villages in search of food and perhaps shelter as well. Of course the peasants not having nearly enough for their own needs, devised ways to hide their stored food and livestock. They would bury their grain, hide their livestock far in the woods away from their homes, build false walls behind which they would conceal their eggs, flour, pickles, jewelry or anything of value from the soldiers. A large group of armed, desperately hungry and cold men, seeking gratification was not good news for anyone. These men took everything . . . . even the lives of those who would resist handing over their possessions. The cold winter blizzards would leave in their wake, impassable roads, snow bound soldiers, snow bound animals, snow bound peasants. There were no snow ploughs, no heated vehicles, no thermos bottles . . . . nothing that could lessen the impact of the seemingly never ending blizzards.

Following one of the many blizzards while on an unsuccessful foray, Otto and Oleg, along with the rest of the men responsible for the officers field quarters spent the morning digging themselves out from under the snow banks. After digging out and harnessing the horses and after several hours of thawing out frozen buckets of water, then boiling water for the ever present samovar and preparing a pot of gruel for the officers, began the slow trek out of the mountains and back to their winter encampment. Their small group was not the first to retreat from the ill conceived effort to dislodge the Austrians; those that began earlier in the day had created two packed furrows of snow along which men and horses stumbled in their efforts to reach camp. They did not have to travel far to get a clear picture of the damage the blizzard had created. With icicles dangling from nostrils and frost covered faces, they encountered groups of dead soldiers still huddled together on the side of the road. They saw groups of soldiers gathered around fires, attempting to thaw their frozen feet, hands, noses and cheeks. They saw peasant houses and shelters completely covered by hard crusted snow banks. The total death count and disabled would not be know until those who were able, would have returned to the base camp.

As Otto and Oleg slowly made their way on horseback, and as they were passing through a small group of peasant homes, they suddenly became aware of a huge commotion that was taking place in one of the homes. They turned up the ear flaps of their ushanka hats and listened intently.

"Let's look inside and see what is going on, Otto," suggested Oleg.

"Yes, let's," said Otto.

The door leading into the hut had been broken down and as their eyes became accustomed to the dark interior, they quickly became aware of the cause of all the noise. Otto's eyes first focussed on a figure with bound hands and feet. He was tied to a chair and he did not appear to have been in that position for any length of time. He was dressed in a knee length sheepskin coat. His shabby hand knit woolen pants were still tucked into what served as winter boots. Otto noticed that his boots, like those of the majority of peasants, consisted of wool rags or fur wrapped around his feet up to his calf. They were then dipped in water in order to form a thin layer of ice which would prevent the strips of rags from unravelling. His home made ushanka hat lay in the puddle of water forming around his feet as the ice melted from his boots. His nose was bleeding . . . . obviously he had tried to resist the intruding soldiers. What appeared to be the peasant's wife, along with two elderly people, were tied to chairs as well. Their faces were cut, bleeding and bruised. Several children huddled together, sat petrified on top of the oven . . . . eyes glazed and totally silent. No soldiers were to be seen but they could be heard, yelling and arguing. The noise was coming from the cellar.

Apparently, this peasant family had craftily hidden a cistern under the floor and in which had stashed eggs, vegetables, and had hung sausages and hams from the floor joists. They had hoped that the food would remain hidden from the marauding soldiers and that the family would be able to survive the winter. It was hoped that should anyone open the floor hatch and peer into the dark cellar, all that would be seen below would be water. However, on this occasion, these soldiers had not been fooled and had discovered the cache. In their eagerness to satisfy their hunger, all ten of the soldiers had leapt into the cistern to get their share of the spoils. The commotion continued for several minutes. Then, one by one, the soldiers emerged from the cellar. Each one bearing the evidence of the wrestling match that had erupted below. Faces were covered with egg yolk, uniforms soaked with a combination of water, egg and bits of vegetable matter and each was clutching a sausage or a ham or whatever else could be found. They sat down, feasted on their loot, untied the family and disappeared into the freezing cold.

The days, weeks and months passed by drearily. Otto had lost count of the number of expeditions made into the heart of the Carpathian Mountains. He had lost count of the number of letters he had written with no return mail coming through. He had lost count of the number of dead that Constantine recorded in his ledger. One day was just like the previous. The news of the many fights, murders and suicides among the Cossacks and the stories of abuse heaped upon the peasants, no longer made an impact on him . . . . time, for him, was spent attending to the needs and wishes of his boss, Constantine, the Pokovnik. He considered himself to be fortunate to be in his position rather than in the position of a regular soldier.

Winter passed and the spring thaw began to expose the debris accumulated during the winter and with the coming of spring, came the news that the Germans had sent troops to bolster the Austrian/Hungarian forces. News of the German buildup, meant that Galicia would not be spared more fighting and for Otto, it meant that instead of being released upon the completion of his second stint with the Russian Army, he would be forced to remain as long as the war continued. He was stuck. His only hope was that the war would end soon, at which time he could return to Poland.

The events during the winter of 1914-1915 completely demoralized the entire Russian Third Army. It had suffered heavy losses from battle and from the cold. It had suffered from lack of food and ammunition. It had suffered from lack of leadership and sound planning.

Radko-Dmitriev, who had replaced Ruszki as commander of the Third Army, knew of the German buildup but made no special preparations to counter a German offensive or to fortify his position.***** His role was to defend the line in the area of Gorlice—Tarnow. His defense depended on the same type of army that had defeated the Austrians in 1914. The Germans on the other hand brought with them, the latest battle

---

***** *Radko Dmitriew (1859-1918), a Bulgarian, commanded the Russian Third Army in the battles along the Gorlice—Tarnow line in May 1915. His Russian corps was totally unprepared for the strong German attack and in the end it became a senseless slaughter of the Russian Third Army. (Source: Wikipedia)*

equipment and materials. They brought huge canons and heavy artillery . . . . they brought aircraft and they brought with them field mortars. The German plan was to break through in one area of the Russian front and then encircle the rest from two directions. The Germans chose the area defended by Russia's Third Army to be the location of the break through.

It began on May 2, 1915. Hell came to earth before sunrise. Otto was startled awake by the sound of exploding artillery shells and as he stepped outside, the sky before him was lit up like a New Year's Eve fireworks display. His ears were filled with the screams of approaching shells and the subsequent booming explosions. He could not tell exactly what was happening to the thousands of soldiers and horses facing such a barrage of shelling. There was no let up of the bombardment and no retreat possible for the soldiers. They were nakedly exposed to the shelling as they had not dug trenches that could withstand artillery bombing. They could not escape to the rear because any soldier caught running from battle would be shot by their own who had been instructed to do so. The shelling lasted four hours and by later accounts, the Germans had rained over thirty thousand exploding artillery shells on the Third Army. Otto could do nothing but watch and pray. The shells did not reach his location back of the front lines. The shelling was so intense that there were no wounded even being carried from the battle field.

Following the bombardment, the Germans sent in their infantry which was equipped with field mortars. These field mortars were small portable versions of the huge artillery guns.

The cavalry on horseback were totally exposed and the infantry protected only by very shallow foxholes were not much better off.

Constantine had left his protective position immediately as the shelling began and headed into the fire storm. After the major shelling had stopped and since he had not returned to his field headquarters, Otto decided he too would have to enter the killing field. He packed his ruck sack and started forward. He did not go very far, however, before he began to encounter medics carrying the wounded out of the battle field. He met a few, then stopped as he glanced at a victim lying on the passing stretcher. After one glance, he knew exactly who it was that was being hurriedly carried. It was Constantine.

Otto had resigned himself to the inevitable . . . . he was convinced without a doubt that there would be no escape for him this time. He was certain that if he were not killed, he would be taken prisoner by the German Army and judging by the few numbers of men retreating, he knew that there were thousands that had surrendered. In his mind, he felt that being taken prisoner by the Germans might not be a bad thing. He could speak German and he would probably be questioned extensively. With those thoughts, he rushed to the gurney and ran along side the medics as they made their way to the field hospital.

"Is he alive?" he asked.

"Yes, he is but he is bleeding very badly from wounds to his legs and back. We have to get the bleeding stopped quickly or he will die," came the reply.

They reached the make shift operating room within a few minutes. Constantine was stripped of his uniform and placed on the operating table. Doctors equipped with knives, hatchets and saws gathered quickly. They knew that Constantine's leg would have to be amputated and the other wounds cauterized. Ether was quickly applied and the grim task of sawing off the dangling pieces of bone and flesh began. White hot irons were used to sear the flesh and that process began simultaneously with the sawing and cutting. Otto had not witnessed many scenes worse that this and his only concern was the outcome of the efforts to save his boss and friend.

Otto remained by Constantine's cot and waited for Constantine to return to consciousness. The doctors informed Otto that, should Constantine survive, his recovery time would be long considering all the blood that he had lost and the severity of the wounds brought on by the shrapnel.

News came that the German Army had broken through the defenses and, whatever was left of the once proud Third Army, was in full retreat. All wounded would be evacuated immediately and join the remaining retreating troops. Because Constantine held a high rank, he was given preferential treatment and since Otto was his servant, Otto was the beneficiary of the same treatment. Arrangements to transfer the Pokovnik and other wounded officers were made. They would be taken by motorized vehicle to the nearest hospital and from there . . . . God only knew. In the midst of total chaos, with bursting shells all around them and amidst the sounds of the approaching German Army, the rag tag refugees from the battle of Gorlice—Tarnow began their escape to safety.

By the end of the day and with the setting sun, the sounds of exploding shells and gunfire became fainter and fainter; they had put a safe distance between themselves and the advancing German Army.

CHAPTER 14

As the small column bumped and chugged its way along the rutted track, Otto sat silently beside Constantine. He knew that Constantine was still alive but there was no movement from him. Constantine's face was ashen and clammy, his eyes were closed, his hair was encrusted with blood. He was too ill to show any signs of pain or consciousness. Otto had time to think. At the moment, his main thoughts lay with his own safety and the condition that Constantine was in but his mind flashed back to the horror left behind. He could only image the colossal hell that Constantine had come through. Otto rationalized that the entire third army must have been killed . . . . there weren't even many wounded soldiers brought out of the battle field . . . . they must all have been trapped by the barrage of exploding shells around them. When his thoughts returned to the bouncing transport vehicle, he began to realize that he could choose his next course of action. He could easily abandon the Pokovnik, leap off the back of the truck, disappear into the wooded hillsides, wait for the German Army to gain control of the area, give himself up and hope that the Germans would allow him to return to Poland. No one would miss him. Whatever was left of the Russian Third Army was either captured by the Germans or scattered about . . . . each man for himself. He also realized that he would have more time to plan his escape because the German advance would be slowed by difficult terrain and poor roads, making the transport of heavy artillery, very cumbersome. He was not aware of the shape that the flanking armies were in . . . . had they been attacked as well? He reasoned that if they were and if they too were in full retreat, he would not have to wait long for the Germans but if they had not been attacked, they could close the gap left by the obliterated third army and he would still be in the Russian held area. That might mean that he would be given a rifle and for the moment that would be the last thing he wanted. He decided that he would bide his time . . . . he would nurse Constantine . . . . change his bandages, clean his wounds with alcohol, put compresses on his forehead and drip water onto his swollen lips. Otto decided that if his beloved boss should die, he would drop off the back of the truck and head for the hills to freedom and away from all the madness of war.

By sundown, they had been able to put themselves out of reach of the German guns and advancing army. Their little column had come across a company of Russian soldiers. This company had the duty to scout the enemy's position and relay the information to the generals in the front lines. This company was equipped with horses, telephones, carrier pigeons, motorcycles and balloons. Tired and exhausted, still shaking from the horror left behind them, Otto's small contingent stopped at the newly found soldiers encampment. Here they would be given food and petrol for their vehicles. They would stay the night but at daybreak, would hurry on with their wounded in tow.

Otto put three fingers on Constantine's jugular to see if there was a pulse and see how strong the pulse might be. He checked and found a weak, slow pulse . . . .

"At least he is still alive," thought Otto.

Otto then checked the condition of his own body and found that he had survived so far with no injuries whatsoever and as he worked his way off the truck he found that he only was experiencing some stiffness from the cramped and rugged ride.

Otto, the medics and the drivers sat down by the side of the road and rested. In gazing around, Otto noticed that the surveillance company had sent up a balloon that had a basket attached to it and as he watched it, he heard an unfamiliar roar that seemed to originate from the sky. As he peered upwards, three German biplanes were approaching very quickly. Not knowing what to expect, he and the others leapt for cover, from where they watched to see what the aircraft would do. Since the Russians had no planes in the region, the German planes could do as they pleased. The planes roared directly over top of them, then made a U-turn and headed straight back to where they were hiding. This time as the planes flew over them, they heard what sounded like machine guns firing and within seconds, Otto and the others saw the balloon fold up, collapse and come crashing to the ground. Otto became aware of many soldiers from the surveillance operation rushing towards a small wooded area near by. Otto and a few of the medics with whom he had been traveling, also made their way to the fallen balloon, fully expecting to see yet another dead soldier but there was no corpse or wounded person to be seen. The spotter who was supposed to be in the basket had gone AWOL. Such was the commitment of this Russian soldier.

The thought flashed across Otto's mind, "Why should I remain committed to this army if the Russians themselves are not?"

He then wandered over to the small clump of trees and witnessed a terrible sight. In addition to shooting down the balloon, the Germans had dumped boxes of iron spikes out of their planes and on to the soldiers below. He did not stay to watch. He had seen enough. He and the medics quickly hurried back to the trucks, leapt inside and motioned hastily to the drivers to get away from there. Hopefully, they would come to a town soon.

The drivers had gotten directions to the nearest military hospital and by noon the next day, the still unconscious Pokovnik and Otto found themselves in the care of a Russian military hospital.

A day later as Otto was bathing Constantine's wounds with alcohol, Constantine's eyes opened and in barely a whisper said, "Otto, is that you?"

"Yes, sir, it is."

Constantine's eyes closed once again and the slow rhythmic sounds of his shallow breathing resumed. Constantine was going to survive barring some unforeseen trouble which could possibly arise. His wounds were showing signs of healing but there was no guarantee that infection and gangrene would not still occur. Constantine's wounds would have to be kept clean and Otto would have to be the one in charge, as the few attendants were overwhelmed by the huge numbers of wounded entering the facility. Attending to Constantine's needs was a full time job. The severity and number of wounds inflicted required detailed and constant attention. Without x-rays or penicillin, there was no knowing for certain the extent of the initial damage and the subsequent damage resulting from the rough tossing and bumping that occurred during the hasty evacuation. Instinctively, Otto went about his nursing duties, caring for the man who was responsible for saving him from becoming a front line soldier. He owed Constantine his life . . . . now he would try to save Constantine's. Now that Constantine had come out of his coma, all thoughts of deserting Constantine and the Russian Army vanished from Otto's mind. The debt that he felt he owed Constantine and the lure to embrace Anya and the children, outweighed the notion of desertion in order to gain his freedom from the army and return to Poland. Surely the war would end quickly and surely he would convince Anya to leave her husband to go with him to the promised land of Saskatchewan in Canada.

Day after day and little by little Constantine's condition improved and he was able to do many things for himself. He could eat and drink on his own and he was able to assist Otto in changing his bandages but most importantly, he was able to tell Otto the severity and location of his pains. There had not been any communication with Constantine's family so Constantine and Otto were totally unaware of the conditions back home or in the rest of Russia as well. All they knew was that in Galicia, the Russian Army had suffered terrible losses; this news coming from the other wounded soldiers and from the medics that came by occasionally. The medics that came by would always carry a chart with them and would record the progress of the injured and maimed service men. When a patient's chart read that the patient was able to travel, arrangements would be made to bundle up the patient and ship him either back to his unit or further away from the front into a rehabilitation facility. The decision where and when the transfer would take place was left up to the officer in charge.

One afternoon as Otto was attending to Constantine's wounds, a group of officers approached Constantine's bed and sat down.

"Constantine Zaharoh," began the Colonel, "we are here for two reasons; one, to give you the news that you will be returning to St. Petersburg, now called Petrograd, and the other to give you some information regarding the progress of the war. First, you along with your valet, will be leaving by train; you will be given a few hours advance notice and I expect that you will be on your way within two days. Now for the other news. It amazes me that you were able to escape from the German attack on May 2. I know that you have not been given the details so I will give you a short summary of what happened and what the results were. Radko-Dmitriev, your Third Army commander, has written an account of the battle and I was given a copy to read. There is no good news coming from his report. He writes that the Third Army resisted courageously but could not withstand the overwhelming pounding they received. After two days of trying to defend their position, the army was given permission to retreat which, what was left of them, did. They retreated as far as the San River. I am sorry to report that out of the two hundred forty thousand men of the Third Army, only forty thousand reached the San River. The rest were either killed, taken prisoner or had deserted. Your Cossack Division of five thousand men was reduced to fewer that seven hundred. You were only one of the few officers to have escaped with your life. The Third Army suffered the greatest number of casualties. Also, we have been able to send a message to your wife and children that you survived and that you would arrive back home within a week or two."

Following a short conversation, the men left and Otto and Constantine began preparations for the long train journey back home. What were they going back to?

During the last few days before the trip home, Otto and Constantine spent plenty of time together and had the opportunity to talk. Over and over, Constantine thanked Otto for staying by his side and looking after him.

"Without you helping me Otto, I surely would have died. You know that I can never repay you and I don't understand why you stayed by my side. You could easily have left me . . . . you could have easily slipped away into the night and no one would ever have known what had become of you. Also Otto, I am sure a guardian angel is looking after you . . . . look at you . . . . how many battles have we seen? . . . . how many times, when you were attending my needs during the fighting, did you escape injury from shells that exploded right next to you? . . . . how many times were you exposed openly to rifle fire and not one bullet hit you . . . . not one! Otto, it can only be described as a miracle. Just look at you . . . . no broken bones, no bullet wounds . . . . nothing . . . . how could this have happened? Surely you are in God's hands. And now, look, because of my wounds and my injuries, you are going back to safety. I cannot see how I will ever be able to return to the front lines. I have deep wounds that won't heal for many months and I am missing a leg . . . . it's hard to ride a horse with only one leg, you know, Otto," he said with a faint smile.

"Otto, I don't know what to expect when we return to St. Petersburg. I know my family is waiting but I have not heard where Anya is. I suspect that part of the reason for your dedication to my health has something to do with Anya. It will be good to get back home nevertheless, and I give you my word of honor, you will be my valet as long as you are forced to stay in the army and that as soon as your obligation is over, I will send you back to your own family and hopefully you will be able to emigrate to Canada with them."

The troop train carrying the wounded for treatment in Petrograd, chugged slowly through the outskirts of Petrograd and made its way to the Moscow Train Station. Otto had traveled this last leg before and was familiar with the route but as the train slowly made its way along, he became aware of what was going to greet them. The first thing he noticed as he gazed out of the window, was the look on people's faces and their movements. On previous occasions, the people he saw walked briskly, heads held high and they walked with assurance. Now, as he looked upon them, he saw that they walked with heads bent low, their faces showing signs of apathy and fear. They no longer walked with a purpose; they seemed to be just aimlessly wandering. As the train continued, he saw hundreds of men in front of factories carrying placards denouncing the Tsar and the war effort. He saw shop after shop boarded up with slogans posted on the boarded up windows. He saw soldiers everywhere. At a time, when he should have been feeling jubilant, he found himself feeling depressed.

"Obviously," he thought, "there is big trouble in Petrograd."

As the train finally stopped, he caught a glimpse of Tatiana and her children. She stood there midst the soot and grime of a once proud train station, grasping the hands of her children and desperately trying to put on a brave smiling face. She did not stand out from the others who were milling around and awaiting the arrival of a loved one, a friend or a family member. She looked older, tired and worn. It was clear that the war was creating a hardship for everyone and it was taking its toll.

The reunion became a mixture of happiness, sadness and pain. They hugged, they kissed, they laughed and they cried. Constantine had been taken off the train by two soldiers carrying a stretcher and they informed Tatiana that Constantine would be taken to the military hospital near their army home and there he would remain until he was well enough to go home. The soldiers, Tatiana, her children and Otto accompanied Constantine to the hospital, got him settled comfortably in a bed. Then they went home.

Not a word about Anya had been spoken.

CHAPTER 15

H e did not look up . . . . he did not raise his eyes or his head . . . . he did not have to . . . . he could feel it. It was the same electric sensation that he had experienced years before. With each passing second, his heart raced faster. He began to feel the weakness in his knees that accompanies a warm racing heart. The warm glow that consumed him now felt exactly the same as it did when they first met on that bridge years ago. He became breathless with emotion.

He quickly finished tucking the bed covers over Constantine and cautiously raised his head and let his eyes focus on the two approaching figures . . . . only one captured his complete attention. She had not changed. Her face, her hair, her arms, her walk . . . . everything about her urged him to run to her, throw his arms around her, embrace her, kiss her, hold her; he didn't.

He remained frozen, trance like, beside Constantine's bed. His body drew him to her; but, his brain told him not to touch her. They had not been together physically for over two years. He was not certain of her feelings toward him, even though they had been writing to each other until the past year when the war prevented the mail from reaching its intended destinations. How would she react? Would she stiffen up and greet him coldly? He did not know. He did not even know whether she was aware of his return to Petrograd. Would the same fire be rekindled in her or was this damn war which was systematically destroying all of Russia, also destroying the passion she felt for him? He watched as she abruptly came to a complete stop. He watched . . . . the almost vacant look on her face suddenly changed and within the time span of only a few seconds, he saw color drain completely from her cheeks, he saw her eyes grow larger and larger, he saw the initial quizzical expression change to what appeared to him as a combination of surprise, horror, joy, relief and momentary apprehension. Without a word, they reached out to each other. He knew, she knew, Constantine knew. Only Olga, Anya's mother, stood by in total silence and observed the scene before her . . . . she did not know.

They did not care, nor were they aware of anybody else or anything else around them. The rest of the world was shut out and they were aware of only each other. And they embraced in ways that only people who are truly in love would embrace. Anya no longer cared about concealing their secret . . . . she had kept this to herself for much too long. She did not try to hide her feelings. No one interrupted them and after what seemed like hours to Constantine and Olga, Otto and Anya loosened their grip and turned their attention to Constantine.

Olga did not speak to Anya until they returned to their home but within minutes of their arrival back there, Olga sat Anya down and demanded an explanation.

"What were you doing with Constantine's aide?" Olga demanded. "Tell me everything. There is something going on here that I do know about and that I do not approve of . . . . you should be ashamed of yourself."

"No, Mama," came the reply, "I am not ashamed of myself or of what I have done. You sit down and listen. It is time that you know the truth. First of all, you know how fond you are of my children . . . . Mother . . . . Ivan is not their father. Otto is. You know that it was you who arranged my marriage to Ivan and the only reason that I consented was because I knew that no one would accept Otto as my husband. Besides, he was not in any position to marry me and take responsibility for Albert. You thought that it was Ivan with whom I was pregnant and therefore the hastily arranged wedding. I must admit mother, that as the years slipped by and I saw nothing of Otto and only occasionally received a letter from him, I was beginning to forget him and to accept Ivan. But now, that Ivan was killed in battle, I am free to associate with whomever I please. Mother, I accepted Ivan as my husband but I never accepted him as my lover."

"I am sorry but I cannot change how I felt then, and how I feel now," continued Anya. "I don't know how you feel about father and I don't know if you truly are in love with him or not, so you may not understand what I am saying. Mother, this war is destroying everything around us; it's destroying our beloved city, it's destroying our beloved Tsar, it's destroying our country, it's destroying father's business, it's destroying millions of families . . . . but, I will not let it destroy how I feel about Otto. You can chase me and my children from your home because of my attachment to Otto, but I will not give that up. After hearing about the outcome of the Battle at Gorlice, I was convinced that Otto had been killed or taken prisoner and that I would never see or hear of him again. I am still in total shock. Mother, I beg you, give us a chance at happiness. Who knows how much time there is left for us all anyway?"

Olga who sat and listened with tears running out of her eyes and down her cheeks finally spoke, "Do you want me to pass this on to your father? What about Albert and Ivanka? Should they know?"

"Mother," said Anya, "I would like to tell father myself and I will tell my children when I feel they are ready to understand and accept this news. Right now, they are still missing Ivan too much . . . . let it be for now."

The decision was made. As long as Russia was at war and as long as Petrograd continued in it's present state of turmoil, Anya would stay where she was. Other plans would be made after things settled down.

Days passed into weeks and weeks into months and with each passing week, only bad news was circulated. Russia was losing battle after battle; soldiers, by the hundreds of thousands, were either killed or taken prisoner. Russia had conceded Poland to the Germans; Tsar Nicholas II himself, had taken over the position of supreme commander of the armed forces. He left his domestic duties in the hands of his wife, Alexandra.

Nothing was going right for Russia, but life in Constantine's realm settled down into a manageable routine. Constantine's health had improved with each passing day and after a two month recovery period in the military hospital, he was able to return home and take up military duties once again. Because he had lost a leg, he was not able to ride a horse and therefore he would not ever serve on the front lines again. He was assigned to the military academy in Petrograd where he would instruct younger soldiers who were singled out to become higher ranking officers in the military. He had been fitted with a wooden leg and with the help of a cane, he became independently mobile and each day would find him in his classroom. He would be driven to the academy in the morning and then back home again late in the day. Otto would not remain with him during the day but would travel back and forth with him . . . . helping him in and out of the carriage and helping him transport his instructional materials. Constantine and Otto had lots of time to talk as they traveled the 5 kilometers back and forth to the Academy. However, they did not talk a lot and when they did, Otto could sense that Constantine was not the same man he had gotten to know so well before the shrapnel had ripped him to pieces. The physical wounds he had suffered were healed leaving scars on his flesh, but the deeper emotional wounds that he suffered, had not healed. These wounds would never completely heal and the scars left behind would remain even deeper and would affect him much more than those acquired from the physical wounds. He talked about it with Otto.

"War will do this to a man, Otto," he confided.

They talked about other things. They talked about how things were so different without Oleg. They had waited and waited to hear some news of him, but nothing had come. The newly assigned driver was fine but he was not Oleg. They both wished they knew what had happened to Oleg . . . . had he died? . . . . how had he died? It's strange how the living have a deep desire to know the last words of a dying person . . . . their last movements . . . . was there labored breath . . . . was he calm . . . . every last detail. They would never know the details. Otto had last see Oleg feeding and watering Constantine's reserve horses.

Constantine talked about his now grown up sons, Peter, who was now twenty-one years old, and Alexander, who was nineteen. He talked about how proud he was of his sons but also how he feared for their safety.

Both Peter and Alexander had joined the military and both were serving outside of Petrograd. Peter was a junior officer in the cavalry and was stationed in the Crimea, protecting the oil fields from the Turks. Alexander had joined the navy and was somewhere in the Baltic Sea dodging German submarines. Neither Peter nor Alexander had been home for over a year. They had not yet seen Constantine in his present condition. He also talked about Natalie, his fourteen year old daughter, who was still at home and how she was the joy of his life and how her presence had made his recovery easier.

They talked about how Otto had been Constantine's aide for seven years . . . . how quickly those seven years had passed.

Sometimes they reminisced about the experiences they shared together and they laughed as they recalled the light moments. Constantine told Otto how much he wished that there was something he could do to bring Otto and Anya together as a family. He told Otto that he felt guilty that Otto's duties required him to live on the compound and that the military would not permit Anya to move onto the base. He told Otto that he would gladly release him from the military but that by keeping Otto as his aide, he was, in reality, protecting Otto. Life outside of the base was not safe.

The time spent together on the daily trips and the many conversations between them further cemented the relationship between the Pokovnik and Otto. Over the course of seven years, the experiences, the conversations, the time together changed the relationship that became a partnership, more than a master/servant one. Often, when alone, Otto reflected on this relationship. He often wondered if the strong bond that had been created was a good thing or if it was bad thing. He reasoned that it was a good thing because he was accepted and protected but was it a bad thing because this bond had kept him in Petrograd so much longer than he had planned. If he had not connected with the Pokovnik, he would have been long gone and probably would now be living in Saskatchewan with his real family. Here he was . . . . he was stuck and could not see his way out. It had been his choice to enlist for an additional stint with the Russian army and that choice had put him into his present predicament. He had come to realize that there was no future for him in Petrograd and that if the opportunity presented itself, he would take Anya and the children and return to Poland as quickly as possible. But, he would have to bide his time for here he was safe, for now.

The political situation in Petrograd had deteriorated considerably during the fall and winter of 1916. Tsar Nicholas II had taken command of the armed forces and had left the day to day decisions affecting Russia in the hands of his wife Alexandra. The Russian masses did not like the Tsarista, not only because she was German but also because she had enlisted the notorious Rasputin as her chief advisor. Because neither one had any expertise in governing and because of who they were, others who should have cooperated and promoted unity and strength, worked to undermine their decisions. Karl Marx had published "The Communist Manifesto" a few years previous and the ideas of communism appealed to many of the working class. The working class under the guidance of Lenin, Trotsky and others were organized under the Bolshevik party and began an active campaign to overthrow the monarchy and take control of Russia. They systematically organized strikes and demonstrations. Their supporters shut down factories and disrupted commerce and communication. Inflation was rampant and food shortages in Petrograd became critical.

Some members of the royal family decided to take matters into their own hands. Since they too believed the main problem facing the monarchy was Rasputin, on December 16, 1916, a group of princes, among others, lured the lecherous beast, Rasputin, to the Yusopov palace and there poisoned, clubbed and shot Rasputin to death. Unfortunately for the monarchy, his death had little effect on the whole situation.

During the winter of 1916, there were no parties, no gatherings of the officers, their wives and dignitaries. The champagne no longer flowed and the caviar remained in the bellies of the fish that created it. Trips outside of the military compound were undertaken only when necessary. No one could be trusted outside of the compound. The disastrous war had an impact upon everyone and the good life in St. Petersburg became a distant memory.

During this time period, Otto spent his days dutifully serving Constantine and his family. He also spent many hours with Anya and the children. He read to them, bounced them on his knees, hugged them and even played his flute for them. Even though danger lurked all around them and the conditions were grim, Otto and his own little family were together bringing some comfort to him.

Often in the evenings when all were gathered, the Pokovnik would pass on the news of the day. He related how thousands of soldiers were deserting the Tsar's army and joining the Bolshevik Red Guard. He told of how the newly conscripted troops had no interest in their training and how futile it was becoming, to even attempt to rebuild the army. He tried to sound optimistic but everyone who listened detected the angst in his voice. He assured them all that the troops within the compound remained loyal and that they were in no immediate danger. With the coming of spring, things would improve but he also cautioned, that perhaps it was time to make alternative arrangements to escape the ensuing chaos. He made it very clear to all that he would remain loyal to the Tsar and to the Russia that he was so proud of.

Winter passed and spring arrived but unlike all the other spring times that Otto experienced in St. Petersburg, this one did not rejuvenate the city. As usual, the flowers began to bloom, the birds began building their nests and the buds on the birch trees sent out their green leaves but no one seemed to notice. The feeling of doom and gloom blanketing the city not only remained but rather, it intensified.

March 1 came and it began like most other days. Otto accompanied Constantine to his office, returned home, had lunch, completed his afternoon chores and then along with Metro, the new carriage driver, left to pick up Constantine to return to his house. There did not appear to be anything unusual happening as far as Otto and the driver were concerned. They helped Constantine into his seat and proceeded on their short trip back home.

"Otto, Metro," began Constantine, "I want both of you to come into the living room as soon as you put the horses in the stable. I have important news and advice to pass on to you immediately."

"Yes, sir," both replied simultaneously.

When Constantine had his family, Otto and Metro gathered together in the living room, he began to deliver the sad news.

"Russia will never again be the same," Constantine began. "The Tsar has abdicated his throne and he along with the Tsarista and children have been placed under arrest. The new president Kerensky, has sent them, under guard, to Tsarskoe Selo. No one knows what will happen to them."

"Along with this bad news," continued Constantine, "the reality is that what is left of the Tsar's army is in compete chaos.

Our camp commander called us officers together today and told us that he was resigning his post but is giving us a few days to decide what we are going to do. I am not moving unless this base is taken over by the revolutionary forces and, believe me, they are growing in great numbers and are becoming more belligerent with each passing day."

"So," said Constantine, "what does all this mean for you, Otto and Metro? Since there is no one in command to tell me otherwise, I am giving you a release from your service to me and from the army. Now go and do what you must, but Otto, I want to see you in my chambers."

Once Otto and the Pokovnik were alone, Constantine continued, "I have called you up to my quarters because I want to talk to you in private. Otto, I would love to have you stay here with me . . . . your loyalty to me and your care for me are unquestioned. I love you like a son but Otto, you are German, not Russian. This struggle is a Russian struggle and I do not want to see you die because of a Russian problem. Honestly, it does not look good for me and my family. A few moments ago, I said that I am remaining here . . . . that is not true . . . . I am not certain of Metro's loyalty. A group of officers have arranged for ourselves and our families to board a troop train that will take us from Petrograd south and hopefully to the Crimea."

"Otto, I can't force you to leave Anya and the children, but my strongest advice to you, is to get rid of anything and everything that would link you to me. By tomorrow, I will have some false identification for you which I have already arranged. The Red Guards are not to be trusted. They would shoot you on the spot if you were linked to the Tsar's army in any way and having a German name would not help. Go to Anya now, say your goodbyes and get out of Russia any way you can," expressed Constantine sorrowfully.

Even though it was shocking to hear those words, Otto knew what was coming and he had mentally prepared himself for the bad news but did not have a plan for what to do when this news broke. He was surprised though that the Pokovnik had given him release from the army.

Otto rushed to his room and changed his clothing as quickly as possible trying to make himself look as much like a Russian peasant as possible. Taking his army identification with him, he began the two kilometer walk to Anya's mother and father's place. He walked hurriedly but cautiously as he made his way along. Everywhere he looked, he could see the turmoil and confusion that existed in Petrograd. The sound of guns firing could be heard . . . . he saw people cheering and waving . . . . he saw people huddled together crying . . . . he saw people wearing uniforms that he had not see before. Not all of the shabbily clad armed troops were men . . . . women too were carrying rifles fixed with bayonets.

"Those must be members of the Red Guard," he thought to himself. He passed buildings that had their windows broken and some were on fire. He picked his way through the melee and eventually made his way to the locked and barred garden gate of the Oleshenko household. Quickly, he unlocked the gate and ran into the house. Anya and the children were waiting.

"I came as quickly as I could. Have you heard the news?" asked Otto.

"Yes," came the reply.

"I am so scared. I didn't know if I would ever see you again," cried Anya.

"I am frightened also, Anya, but let us try not to show our fear to Albert and Ivanka. I don't want to upset them," replied Otto.

So with brave faces Anya and Otto went into the parlor where Olga and the children were sitting. Anya said that she would make a cup of tea and perhaps that would make them all feel a little better. She went off into the kitchen leaving Otto with Olga.

Olga began to talk. "Otto, this is not the outcome I had planned for us. Everything before the war was good. We had money, we had comforts, my husband was a very successful business man, we travelled to nearly all parts of Europe and vacationed in many luxurious resorts. Then this damn war came. Now we have lost almost everything and if the Bolsheviks get into power, they will seize whatever we have left. My husband is at our dacha preparing it for when we will have to leave here. Our only hope of surviving is if we cooperate with the Bolsheviks. They too will have to run the economy and businesses. My husband is able to do that very well. I know that we will lose the title to our property but perhaps they will let us live there. We will be taking Anya and the children with us." Anya came with the tea cups, ending the conversation.

That night, alone on the sofa, Anya and Otto, huddled together, arms around each other and pillows soaked with their tears, they talked. They talked about everything that had happened to them; how years before they had met on the Liteiny Bridge, and how they had to keep their lives together a secret from everybody else. They talked about the children and what a joy they had brought. They talked about Ivan and how he was killed in the war. They talked about the plans they had made for themselves once the war had ended. Eventually, they had to talk about what was going to happen to them over the next few days.

"What are you going to do Otto? What is going to happen to you?" Cried Anya. "You know how much I want you to stay with me and the children. You know that I have loved you and still do, more than anyone else in my life. I don't want to lose you . . . . oh I don't want to lose you."

Otto held her close and said, "Anya, I am going to stay here with you."

"No, you can't stay Otto, you will be shot for sure. You would not survive if you stay. The only hope for us Otto, is if you can make your way safely back to Poland and if I remain safe at the dacha, we might have a chance to reunite once everything settles down. But for now, you have to leave. I am not even sure that my mother would not hand you over to the Bolsheviks. She really does not like you. You must get out while you can . . . . if you still can. The rabble are everywhere and they will show no mercy."

No sooner had those words left her lips, when the sounds of people approaching filtered into the room. Anya pushed the curtains aside and gazed into the darkness.

"Otto," she whispered, "there are many men carrying torches and carrying guns at our gate. They are rattling the gate and demanding to come in. They seem to be drunk. Otto, you have got to get out of here. Quick . . . . out the back door and into the alley. I will stall them as long as I can, but I have to let them in . . . . now, go!"

After a very brief farewell, Otto, with tears running down his face, heart racing and thoughts totally confused, he slipped out of the house and as he made his way back onto the street and into anonymity, he realized that he would never see Anya and the children again. He sat down and cried and could only imagine what Anya, her mother Olga, and their children were going through back at Olga's house. He dared not go back. It was over.

All night long, he wandered the streets . . . . he was not the only one. He even went back to Olga's house to catch a glimpse of it and try to find out what had happened. From a distance, all seemed quiet. His heart urged him to run back to Anya but his head told him that it was indeed over and for his own survival, he would have to plan his exit from Petrograd. Where would his road end? He sat under a tree to assess the situation and to plan his escape. The distance from Petrograd to Piotrkow, Poland was one thousand, five hundred kilometers by train. He could possible leave on a ship or he could make his way back on foot. The only logical option was by train and even the train option left many unknowns. There was no way of knowing where the trains would end their trips or whether the trains would be occupied by revolutionary soldiers. Where and how would he be able to cross the border into Poland? How many belongings would he be able to take with him? Would he have to walk great distances to get to his destination? There were no clear or obvious answers to his questions.

CHAPTER 16

After the sun had risen and when he felt it was safe, Otto made his way back to the military compound, knowing for certain that this would be the last time he would see the place where he had spent many years and where a million memories had been created.

With a sad and heavy heart, he presented his pass to the compound guard and entered the facility for the last time. He knocked gently on the Pokovnik's door; the door opened slowly and he was met by a teary eyed Tatiana. She welcomed him with a hug and a kiss on each cheek and led him into the kitchen where she had a pot of tea ready for drinking. Constantine and Natalie joined them and they sat around the table, for what they all knew, was for the very last time. There was no reminiscing: there was no time for that. Quickly, they confirmed where they each would be going and how they would perhaps be able to contact one another. All information would have to be stowed in their memory banks and not on paper.

Following their short lived reunion, Otto hurried up to his room to sort out those things that he would be taking with him. He packed sparingly, discarding anything that would connect him with the Russian army or with the Pokovnik. He gathered some civilian clothing, sorted his money, concealing as much as he possibly could on his person and in some secret pockets that he had sewn into his ruck sack. He put on his cap, stuck his flute into one of his tunic pockets and then went down the stairs to pack some cheese, sausage and bread. There waiting in the kitchen, with his train ticket and new identification papers, was Constantine. Tatiana and Natalie were there also, ready to say their last goodbyes.

Finally it was time to leave. Natalie was the last to give Otto a goodbye hug. She gripped him hard for several minutes and did not want to let go. Spontaneously, Otto reached into his tunic pocket, withdrew his flute, bent down, handed it to Natalie and said,

"Natalie, take this, make it a memory of me. I no longer have any use for it. I will never play it or any flute ever again."

As he handed it to Natalie, he understood what that flute symbolized and now, everything . . . . all the joys it had brought to him and all the happy hours of playing in the band, practicing on the canal banks, playing it for the Pokovnik family and serenading Anya, was lost. From that moment on, the flute would only reopen memories . . . . memories which he felt would be best suppressed and forgotten. He was leaving . . . . leaving everything behind . . . . memories and all. He would have to start all over again at age twenty-seven.

He pulled his cap low over his eyebrows, slung the ruck sack over his shoulder and headed to the nearest train station that had not yet been seized by Trotski's Red Guards. The train station was clamoring with others who were hastily leaving Petrograd. Many of the individuals milling around and boarding the trains did not even have tickets. He scurried about the station until he finally found a train that was heading south and he boarded it with no trouble.

The train he boarded was jammed full with other people, many in the same position as himself . . . . people escaping from a dangerous situation. No one spoke. No one could be trusted. Who was a Bolshevik supporter? Who was loyal to the Tsar? Who was a thief? What were they running from? The answers lay hidden in the minds of the individuals not to be shared with anyone else.

Fortunately, the trip out of Petrograd began uneventfully. The trip he decided would be uncomfortable but bearable . . . . hopefully his good luck would continue. He had a bit of food and he was able to secure a window seat at the back of one of the four passenger cars pulled by a small steam engine.

The planned route as outlined by Constantine, would take him from Petrograd to Riga, Latvia . . . . then on to Vilnus, Lithuania . . . . further along to Minsk, Belarus . . . . and from there on to Lodz, Poland. He had no idea where the German occupied area began or where it ended. He knew that Lodz was in German hands so somewhere along the way he would have to change from being a Russian peasant into a German sympathizer.

Otto sat down, placing his ruck sack on the floor by his feet. Then he surveyed the passengers, making a quick assessment of each one, including the elderly woman sitting next to him. The car held thirty-six passengers and to Otto's relief, no one appeared to be a bandit or a thug. Most of the passengers were elderly or were families with small children. Several appeared to be leaving in haste but he could not see anyone who would create a problem.

He was not familiar with domestic travel in Russia because most of his travels had been on troop trains. However, he had travelled back to Poland once, so he knew that the train would stop frequently and the trip would be slow. He also knew that he would have to get off the train for a bathroom break and to get some water. He did not know if that would present a problem.

The first day's journey would be critical for a successful escape. Petrograd was a very large city and it would take some time for the train to get from central Petrograd to the relative safety of the outskirts and open countryside. As the train pulled out of the station, Otto could see evidence of unrest and uncertainty that gripped the city. Soldiers were everywhere and mingling among them were people lugging their precious possessions to perceived safety. However, the train did not pass through areas where open hostilities were in progress. He was in luck.

By night fall, the train was safely out of Petrograd and on its way to Riga. The sun had already set as the tired old steam engine pulled off the main track and onto a siding where it would rest until daybreak, at which time it would resume its journey towards Riga. The locomotive would be unhitched from the lead car and taken away for refueling. The four passenger cars, with their passengers inside, would be left on the siding for a few hours, but the passenger cars would not be cleaned until the turn around point in Lithuania.

Otto deliberated whether he should risk vacating his seat for a few hours and try to get some sleep outside or whether he should stay inside the car and put up with the stench, accumulating debris, groaning, crying and snoring of fellow passengers. He weighed the alternatives and decided it would probably be safer to remain in the car. At least he would still have a seat.

After the train had stopped and after the soot from the train smoke stack had settled and after the passengers had seemingly settled down for a few hours nap, the end doors of the car opened and six men brandishing pistols and swords burst in. The passengers immediately sat bolt upright and let out a collective gasp and began clutching their belongings and hiding them as best they could. Everyone, including Otto, realized that they were not police or the Tsar's soldiers. They were either some of Trotski's henchmen or just plain outright thugs. Otto pulled his cap lower over his eyes and pretended to be asleep. There was nothing he could do.

The thugs systematically began taking everything of value away from the passengers. Anyone who showed the slightest sign of resistance was jabbed harshly with the point of a sword or the barrel of a pistol. Otto glanced out of the window and saw that these men were not alone . . . . the whole train was surrounded by men on horseback. There was no escaping. He could do nothing but give up his possessions and hope to escape being killed or cut up and left to bleed to death. Earlier in the day, Otto had anticipated that something like this could happen so he had carefully taken as much money as he could and had folded it carefully into his clothing . . . . some in his boots, some in his underwear and some folded cleverly into the creases of his tunic and baggy pants.

"What have we here?" Grinned the brute displaying his stained rotting teeth.

"Looks like someone who does no hard work," replied a younger, more pleasant looking man.

With those words, the brute cocked his pistol and jammed it against Otto's temple. Otto trembled but said nothing.

"Hell," he thought, "I spent a year on the front lines fighting the Austrians and the Germans. I survived bitterly cold winters on the steppes. I survived the horrific German assault at Gorlice. I even escaped the nails dropped from the German biplanes. Nine years away from Poland and I have no scars, no broken bones and I have lived in comfort most of the time. Now look, am I really going to get my head blown off by a group of smelly, illiterate outlaws? God, if it is your will, let me survive!"

Otto did not move a muscle but merely stared straight ahead. There was no use resisting. The robbers collected whatever they thought that would be of use to them and began putting their loot into potato sacks. Otto's belongings were ripped from him and thrown wholesale into the robber's sack.

Just as quickly as the robbers had come, they suddenly left the train, jumped onto their horses and rode off into the darkness.

"Thank God," thought Otto, "I had enough sense to hide a few rubles on my person."

Glancing through the window Otto began to understand why the robbers left as quickly as they did. The railroad guards had been alerted and could be seen hurrying to find out what was happening.

The rest of the journey through Latvia and Lithuania was uneventful. He was able to make the connection necessary that would lead him to the front between the Russian and German forces. He had no plans for how he would manage to get through to German held territory. Those plans would have to wait until he would be confronted with the problem.

The train slowed and the conductor entered the passenger car. The announcement made was that it was no longer safe for the train to continue towards Poland and all passengers would have to get off because the train would be turning around at the nearest round house. It would then head back to Russia. During the time that Otto was traveling on the train, he had become acquainted with several other passengers who were in a situation similar to his. Following their departure from the train, the small group began their quest to reach the Polish border on foot. They had some knowledge as to the distance to Lodz but no one knew where they would encounter the German held border.

As they made their way along, they soon met up with other escapees and together, they slowly made their way along. After two days of travel, they came across some Russian soldiers on patrol and were told that the front was silent for the moment and that it was only a few kilometers away. Otto had previously decided that when the time came for him to cross into German held territory, he would leave the group and sneak across the front line at night. He believed that he would avoid much trouble if he would not have to try to identify himself to the German soldiers.

He set out. He found a small dirt road that headed southward and he followed it. After five fours of walking and as the sun began to rise, he spotted an army patrol heading towards him. Quickly he stepped into the tall grass that lined the road and there he waited patiently for the patrol to pass. He would soon know if the soldiers were Russian or German . . . . it really didn't matter . . . . he just needed to know with whom he would be dealing. The small patrol passed and Otto recognized them as German. He had actually made it into German held territory sometime during the night! Now if someone apprehended him, he would not be sent back to Russia. Now he could relax and get some rest. The rest of the journey home, would take a while.

Even though he had been abroad for several years, Otto recognized the landmarks and buildings on his walk back to his boyhood home. The road on which he walked passed through several towns, villages and open countryside. The evidence of armies having passed through, was all around. Burned out homes, barns, mills, storage buildings and hay stacks could be seen as he made his way ever nearer to his waiting mother, brother Hugo and little sister, Olga. He wondered what he would see when he would finally walk into Moszczenica and into his mother's home. There had been no news coming to him from Poland for nearly two years. Perhaps there was not even a home to go to. Perhaps his family had been killed or displaced during the battles that raged in this region. The armies had passed through this region three times and the news that he had gotten while on his journey persuaded him to avoid going through Lodz. So rather than going through Lodz, he skirted it and in doing so, his return journey would take him through several villages and towns that he came to know in his youth. He would first pass through the town of Alexandrow. It was here that he was born and where he had spent the first few years of his life. As he passed through, he wondered if any of his relatives still lived there or if they had permanently left their homes and gone abroad. He was anxious to reach Moszczenica so he kept going. Next he passed through Pabianice where several more of his relatives either had lived or were still living. He promised himself that he would return to Pabianice as well, once he was settled back in Moszczenica. He had been walking all day and he knew that the distance from Alexandrow to Moszczenica was over fifty kilometers. He had no money left on his person; the money that he had hidden from the robbers had now been spent and he would have to rely on hand outs from the villagers. He walked until it became dark. He then noticed a bombed out vacant house which he entered. Inside, he found a space that was still intact and here he would spend the night and complete his journey home come morning.

It had rained during the night making the narrow dirt road, leading to Jarosty, through Gajkowice and finally to Moszczenica, quite muddy. It would be in Moszczenica where he hoped his journey would end. He had completely lost track of the days and of the weeks. As he trudged along nearing Jarosty, he figured it must be one day other than a Sunday because he saw people outside of their homes working in their yards. They were cleaning up debris left over from the winter and from the damage caused by the armies. As he walked through Jarosty, he paused in front of the Lutheran church. Numerous memories of his boyhood flashed before him. He recalled the bible lessons he had heard, the hymns he had sung, the confirmation lessons he had attended, the many weddings and funerals that he had witnessed. The church stood there as before he had left. The church had indeed escaped the battle scars evident on many other buildings.

As he stood there realizing that his life had come full circle, his eyes filled with tears which slowly spilled over and inched their way down his cheeks. Were they tears of relief that he had finally made it back safely to home territory? Were they tears of sadness as he looked upon the ruination of the buildings and countryside? Were they tears of despair knowing what he had left behind in Russia? Were they tears of fear anticipating what he would find following the last few kilometers to where he hoped his family would be? If he was to find his family, he would find them in the house that his father, Martin, had secured for his family several years ago.

He did not see any activity in the yard when he finally stopped in front of the house that he, as a youth knew so well; however, signs of people inhabiting the home were everywhere. The garden had been dug and planted as signs of newly emerging vegetables were evident. The few flower beds had been weeded and healthy looking shrubs and flowers were beginning to leaf out. Otto took a deep breath and knocked on the door. The door opened slightly and two eyes peered through the small opening. The eyes blinked . . . . then squinted . . . . then got wider and wider. Suddenly the door flew wide open and Paulina rushed forward and grabbed Otto . . . . hugging him . . . . kissing him. The commotion that Paulina and Otto created, brought the rest of the family to the door.

After gaining her composure, Paulina was finally able to talk, "Otto, look at you. You are alive. I thought you were a beggar when I first laid eyes on you. Come, sit. I will make a pot of tea and bring you some freshly baked bread."

Otto managed a broad smile as he wearily walked into the house. Both Hugo and Olga were hugging and touching Otto to make sure that he was real, as he made his way to a chair by the table.

"We thought that you would never return from Russia," said Hugo as Paulina rushed about preparing the tea. "We know that countless soldiers have died so far and since we had not heard from you, we had given up any hope of your safe return . . . . but, look at you . . . . you are in one piece!"

"Yes," replied Otto, "I am in one piece. I have not had a decent rest or a decent meal for days. I have to lie down and get some sleep. We will talk later. Thank God! I am home!"

CHAPTER 17

POLAND

Gustav Jung was not a tall man and as a matter of fact, he was rather short compared to most other men, but what he lacked in height, he made up in bulk. His five foot eight inch frame carried nearly one hundred and eighty pounds of muscle and bone. His thick calved legs were connected to sturdy heavily muscled thighs. His waist measured forty inches and his chest, fifty-two inches. No sign of his seventeen inch circumference neck could be seen when he was wearing a collar and set on top of his thick neck was a somewhat rounded head. When engaged in close conversation with him, one could not help but notice his kindly round grey-blue eyes and the slight smile that appeared as he spoke. Very noticeable was his greying beard and light streaks of grey in his otherwise dark brown hair. Also, those whose hand he shook, experienced a thick fingered meaty hand that held a powerful grip. It was obvious that Gustav was a product of many years of hard work. The many years of building, digging, pounding, lifting and shoveling had left its imprint on not only Gustav's body but also on his personality.

The statistics on Gustav's birth are not exactly certain, but it is known that the year was 1856 and the place was possibly in Pfalz, Bayern, Germany. As a young man, probably in the early 1870's, he had come along with many others to find work in the many thriving textile mills which had sprung up in Piotrkow. His family, which for centuries had made their living in the Black Forest area and even though the times were hard and they were suffering financially, was not prepared to pick up and leave to a place unknown some 500 miles away. Gustav, on the other hand, felt he had nothing to lose. He owned no land, had no job, was single with responsibility only for himself and was somewhat of an adventurer. He was a man who possessed a good work ethic, an ambitious nature, a sound healthy body and enough intelligence to make sound business decisions. It was not long after his arrival in Piotrkow that he could see the opportunities that presented themselves and he quickly seized upon them.

He saved his money and lived frugally and by doing so, was able to buy a plot of land. He secured some carpenter's tools and set out to build himself a house. The plot of land that he had purchased fronted on to a narrow muddy rural road just on the edge of Moszczenica. There were no services to the property nor was there a well. He surveyed his property and decided where the house, the barn, the storage sheds, the garden and the well were to be located. He knew that it would take a long time to complete the project but that did not deter him. Once he decided where to place the house, he gathered all the building materials needed to start with and went to work. Stone by stone and piece by piece the structure took shape and within a short time, he was ready to move into his house. The completed house boasted two rooms, one entrance door and two windows. The house sat on a stone foundation. The rest of the house, except for the chimney, was made from slabs of lumber. The trap door located in the kitchen part of the house led to a cellar where he would store his vegetables and other things not required on a daily basis. Before winter arrived he had dug his own well. He had surprised himself that building a house was relatively easy and upon completing his house, he decided that given another opportunity he would build another but first, he had more pressing issues with which he had to deal.

After taking stock of his situation, he was truly amazed that the years had slipped by so very quickly. Gustav realized that he was thirty-three years old and still single. He had been so busy working and saving that he had found little time to court and find himself a fitting bride. Here he was . . . . thirty-three years old . . . . a proud owner of property on which he had a house . . . . a man with a good paying job in the textile mill . . . . and no wife. He would have to rectify that situation before it was too late. He did not want to remain a bachelor for life.

Beginning in the early 1800's, Lodz and surrounding area had attracted thousands upon thousands of evangelical Lutheran Germans. In addition to attracting Germans, Jews flocked to the region as well. The reason being that somehow Lodz had become a main center for the textile industry. Huge factories had been built in Lodz and skilled weavers and entrepreneurs established themselves in the city and many of them spilled over into the surrounding areas even as far as Piotrkow, which lay eighty miles south of Lodz and also boasted large textile mills. Surrounding Piotrkow, the established neighboring towns and villages such as Pabianice, Alexandrow, Moszczenica and Jarosty, supported smaller operations and farmers which supplied the cities and larger towns with meat, dairy products and vegetables. Lutheran churches and German schools were built in order to maintain the German heritage. Any person of German heritage living in Lodz or any of the surrounding areas need not feel that they were living in a foreign land.

There were many German girls of marrying age available. The only problem that Gustav would be confronted with, was that most of the girls his age had long since been married. He would just have to find a younger one. Gustav's search for a bride led him to various churches in the area. Since he himself was a devote God-fearing Lutheran, he thought that the churches would be the first and probably his best place to meet his future wife. Finding a suitable partner from his perspective was not that difficult, but in the late 1800's, most potential husbands would have to have the prospective bride's family approval. He soon realized that he was at a slight disadvantage when in competition with other suitors. Most mothers and fathers preferred men near to their daughter's own age; but, on the other hand, he was a man of means and he possessed a certain charm. His obvious strength and energy would be a bonus and he was not easily discouraged. Besides having spent the fall and winter alone in his new house, convinced him that the bachelor lifestyle was not for him. Cooking, cleaning and washing clothes was not his forte: building, farming, making money and socializing suited him much better. He was not a loner.

It was early spring of 1890 when Gustav determinedly set out to find a bride. The winter had been long and cold; he had spent too many evenings by himself. After working all day at the mill, he was coming home only to find an empty cold house where he would have to begin the many chores and household duties by starting up a fire in the kitchen stove to warm the place. Each evening would see him tending to his small brood of chickens, his two pigs and a cow that he had acquired the previous summer. Following his daily outside tasks, he would then prepare his evening meal, wash up his dishes, sit down and read a few passages from the Bible, extinguish his coal oil lamp light and crawl into bed. This routine was not for him and he convinced himself that if he could not find a suitable partner by fall, he would sell the property and become a boarder once again.

It was not as though he didn't have previous opportunities for marriage but each time a suitable partner would appear, something interfered and the partnership never was realized. There was Marie, a very pretty, fun-loving girl, but she happened to be Catholic. There was Hilda, a nice responsible Lutheran girl but Gustav had been so busy establishing himself that he hardly had any time to court her; she became tired of waiting for Gustav and accepted another man's proposal. There was Stella but that relationship did not work out either. Several more names could be added to the list but he soon discovered that in being thirty some years old, the number and choice of eligible brides dwindled. Now that he was really serious, he had some searching to do. Gustav had been attending various churches within a couple of hours walking distance of his home but still after several months of dedicated attendance, he had not yet met anyone that he believed would be a good match for him.

Sunday, June 15, 1890, began like most previous Sundays had. Gustav rose early in the morning and before having his own breakfast, he attended to his chores in the barnyard. Following the completion of his outside chores, he went back into the house, where he made a pot of tea, scrambled a few eggs, sliced a large piece of bread from the fresh loaf that he had purchased on Saturday, sat down and enjoyed his breakfast. Following breakfast, he washed, shaved, changed into his best three piece suit, gave his dress shoes a quick wipe and set off for the church in Jarosty. The Lutheran Church in Jarosty was only a little over an hour's walking distance from his own place so there was no need to hitch up his horse and ride to church. He could walk.

He engaged in casual conversation with other parishioners as they made their way to the morning's church service and after the hour walk, he entered the church and took his usual seat on the left side of the nave near the back. On this particular Sunday he had arrived a little earlier than usual so he was able to observe the families as they entered, with the men separating themselves from the women and children. He recognized the faces of most of the people that came, but just as the service was about to begin, an unfamiliar family entered. There were three people; a man, probably the father, a woman, probably the mother, and a young woman, probably their daughter. This family was unfamiliar to him but it appeared, by the way others nodded and smiled as they sat down, that this family was not entirely new to the area and that they were acquainted with some other members of the congregation.

Mother and daughter took their seats on the right side of the nave and near the back of the church and the man sat with the other men on the left side benches. Gustav had a clear view of the young woman that had just sat down and immediately all of his attention was focussed on her. He had no knowledge of who she was or from where she had come but she definitely got his attention. He guessed that she was younger than he was by several years but she certainly was no longer teen aged. She was definitely older. Since he was viewing from the side, he could not discern many of her physical attributes but he guessed that she stood about five feet three inches tall, had brown hair and probably weighed about one hundred and ten pounds. He noticed that she participated in all aspects of the service; bowing her head when she prayed, responding appropriately to the liturgy and joining actively in the hymn singing. She was definitely of the Lutheran faith . . . . one step in the right direction! It soon became apparent to Gustav that he would like to meet this woman and make her acquaintance, so he decided that he would take the bold step, following the service, and introduce himself to her and her parents. Before the service was over, he was scheming as to how he would accomplish the introduction without appearing to be too forward.

When the service ended, Gustav quickly left his pew. He walked briskly out of the church and waited outside as the rest of the congregation made their way out and for the young woman to make her appearance. He thought that he would be forced to boldly walk up to her and begin talking to her but the introduction happened quite naturally. As he was waiting, he noticed that her mother and father were in conversation with the Schmidt family. He knew the Schmidt family very well as they were neighbors to his property. Mr. Schmidt noticed Gustav standing around and sensing that Gustav might be waiting to meet Ida, he called out to Gustav to come and meet his company. Following the formal introductions, Mrs. Schmidt said,

"Gustav, would you like to come with us to our place and share lunch with us and the Laengers?"

Together, the Schmidts, the Laengers and Gustav made their way back to the Schmidt house where they would visit and partake in a leisurely lunch. The walk would take over an hour and as they strolled along Gustav and Ida had a considerable amount of time to get acquainted.

Gustav was first to tell Ida where he was born, how old he was, a little about his childhood, how he had come to Poland and where and how he had found work. He told her about his ambitions and his hopes for greater and better things. Ida then told Gustav about her family. She told him that she was born in Lodz in 1871 and that she had one older brother named Robert. She told Gustav that she was living with her parents in Lodz and that she worked as a seamstress in a garment factory. She said that her job was to sew cotton dresses and blouses and that the garments from her factory were shipped to other parts of Europe but she did not know exactly where. Ida told Gustav that she loved to sing and dance and loved to have people around her. She told him that she often would go to the ballet in Lodz and that she would attend as many concerts as she could afford. Gustav then admitted that he too would like to attend some cultural events but so far most of his time had been taken up with work and trying to establish himself as an independent person who did not have to rely on wages received while working for someone else. His goal was to become his own boss.

The group eventually reached the Schmidt house where they partook in a light lunch consisting of slices of homemade bread, cheese and sausage, tea and some home baking. As they ate and drank, the conversation centered on the local events and some exchange of information relating to mutual acquaintances. The time slipped by quickly and all too soon, it was time for Gustav to return to his own place to attend to the chores that awaited him. Ida accompanied him to the gate where they said their goodbyes. Gustav had made up his mind that this visit with Ida would not be his last.

"Ida," he asked, "are you returning to Lodz tomorrow?"

"No," came the reply, "we will be staying in Moszczenica for three more days. We have other acquaintances that we are going to visit before we return home."

"Good," said Gustav, "yesterday when I was at the market in Moszczenica, I saw that there was a circus set up. I noticed that there was a carousel, some tents and some other displays. Would you like to come with me tomorrow? I will ask your father for permission. I think we would enjoy it."

Ida did not hesitate for a single moment before accepting the invitation.

The next day, they met shortly after the noon meal and walked excitedly to the market square. No sooner had they entered the square when they were accosted by several gypsy children begging for coins and tugging at their sleeves and directing Gustav and Ida to a stand or tent where the taro card readers, the palm readers, and the tea leaf readers and other fortune tellers were ready to relieve Gustav of his money. There was gypsy music all around and games of chance and gambling were in full progress. Gustav was too shrewd to participate in any games of chance. His interest in coming was the music, the carousel, the freak shows but most of all he knew that there would be people displaying their animals, agricultural equipment and new products and inventions.

They rode the carousel, bought ice cream cones and sat on a bench and enjoyed the entertainment provided by the gypsy dancers. They strolled around some more and in passing a fortune teller's tent, Ida said,

"I would like to have my tea leaves read. Wouldn't you Gustav?"

Gustav, not being romantic by nature, declined the invitation but promised Ida that he would wait for her if she wanted to have her fortune read. Ida paid the reader a few kopeks for the service, sat down and began to sip on her tea as she was instructed to do by the reader. While Ida sipped her tea, the gypsy woman's deeply creased face highlighted by painted bright red lips and deeply set black eyes, shrewdly absorbed every movement, every glance, every gesture that Ida displayed while sipping her tea. The fortune teller asked her a few questions and then settled back in her sheepskin lined chair, closed her eyes and appeared to meditate eventually falling into a trance like state. The gypsy woman then opened her eyes reached across the narrow table and took Ida's hand in hers. After telling Ida that all the tea had to be drunk and when only the leaves remained, she took the tea cup from Ida and began her analysis of Ida's future. Ida, not sure of what to expect, sat aghast at what she was hearing, and was totally convinced that the gypsy woman had a direct link to the Almighty. The old fortune teller's voice cracked and crackled and her eyes squinted and then enlarged with each discovery of the messages hidden in the tea leaves deposit. She analyzed the grouping of the leaves, their proximity to the rim of the cup, the flatness of the deposit and the coloring of each leaf. Everything about the leaves held secrets that only she could unlock. The whole procedure took nearly an hour by which time Gustav was getting anxious to move along.

"Well, what did you learn from the fortune teller?' asked Gustav.

Ida looked at him coquettishly and replied, "It is my fortune and to reveal its contents to another person destroys the fortune immediately. You will just have to wait and find out for yourself."

Gustav merely shrugged his shoulders . . . . then moved on to the display area.

They looked at different breeds of cows, horses, sheep and pigs. They looked at chickens, geese and ducks and finally they came upon the beekeeper. Gustav took one glance at the hive frame that was crawling with what looked like a thousand bees and immediately began asking the keeper several questions. He was hooked! Gustav was so intrigued by the bees that he nearly forgot about Ida but Ida didn't mind because she too became interested in what the bee keeper had to say. Gustav decided that he would purchase a working hive and arrange to pick up his purchase the following day.

Gustav and Ida left the market square fully satisfied with the time that they spent there together and they promised each other that they would see each other again. Gustav went home and Ida returned to the Schmidt house.

The rest of the summer of 1890 went by with no major happenings for either Ida or Gustav. In addition to building fences around his property and preparing more land for crops, Gustav was kept even busier now that he had bees to tend to. He did however, find time on two occasions to venture on to Lodz to court Ida. On both occasions their time spent together was enjoyable and reinforced their desire to become husband and wife. They had talked about the possibility of marriage and both indicated that they were ready to take the plunge. Gustav had however not proposed to Ida during the summer; the proposal had to wait as he was much too busy to have his work interrupted by a wedding. He decided that he would wait until the harvest had been completed and after all his winter preparations were completed as well.

The wedding finally took place on February 10, 1891. It was a joyous affair attended by many of the Laenger clan but none of the Jung family—only several of Gustav's friends. The marriage ceremony was held at the Laenger's home church in Lodz and the reception was in a room rented from the owner of the cotton factory where Ida worked. Ida's father had hired an orchestra to play at the reception and he also had arranged for a good supply of schnapps and beer. February, in Lodz, was not the best time to have a wedding as the temperatures usually remained below freezing day and night but even though it was cold, the volume of alcohol consumed more than made up for the lack of heat. The guests danced and partied until the early morning hours, went to sleep for a few hours, and then returned the next morning to complete the celebrations and send the married couple on their way.

February 12, 1891, saw Gustav and Ida coupled in the house that Gustav had built. Gustav had prepared the house very carefully to ensure that Ida would have no trouble settling in. He had plenty of wood piled up for the fires. He had vegetables stored in the cellar. He had chickens that were still laying eggs. He had a cow that was still milking and he had lots of coal oil for the lamp. Life as a couple started out smoothly and happily.

Ida by nature, was very outgoing and even during the cold winter days she made it a point to visit with neighbors, walk to the market when needed and prodded Gustav to go to church even if it was snowing. Ida made friends easily and soon she had people coming to visit and play cards during the evenings. She talked to everyone she met and those who met her, liked her. The first winter together as husband and wife went by quickly.

Guatav had set out his bee hive a few meters outside the barn yard. He had chosen a good location for the hive because the bees outgrew the one hive very quickly so that by July, he had four queens and hordes of worker bees gathering nectar on their behalf. Gustav had taken a keen interest in raising bees and had become very knowledgeable. He learned how to identify the drones, the queens and the workers. He learned how to control the bees' tendency to swarm by limiting the numbers of queens available and by supplying the bees with an ample supply of frames on which they could build their combs to fill with honey. He diligently attended to the hives every week. Ida generally did not go with him when he worked on the hives but after returning from church on this sunny day in July of 1891, she trotted along side of Gustav. Ida watched intently as Gustav went through his routine of first smoking the bee frames, then carefully lifting the top from the hives and temporarily removing the frames to examine them for their contents. He would destroy the newly laid queen eggs, and then replace the frames. They did not talk during the whole procedure but after Gustav was satisfied with his work, they sat down on a fallen tree trunk and began to talk.

Gustav told Ida how happy he was that he had bought the farm and how happy and content he was having Ida by his side. Then he began to verbally reflect on the events that had occurred in the area during the past year.

"You know Ida, there have been lots of Germans from Moszczenica and other areas near Lodz that have left this area and emigrated to the United States and to Canada. They believe that they will become much better off living in the New World than if they stayed here in Poland to work. Many people say that a man can get eighty hectares of land for just a few kopeks; they also say that there is more than enough work for anyone who has a trade. Even the pamphlet that I picked up in church today was advertising the opportunities in New York, Chicago, ... that is where the world's fair is this year."

"What is the world's fair?" Interjected Ida.

"I think that the countries that put on these fairs, like the one in Paris a few years ago when they built the Eiffel Tower, want people from other parts of the world to come and see what these countries have to offer. I know that some people from around here are going to Chicago," replied Gustav.

"Why are you talking about this? Are you thinking of selling this place and going too?" Quizzed Ida.

"Well, Ida, I must confess that when you hear people talk about America, it does make one feel a little excited and curious. But no, I do not want to sell our place. Mr Becker, was talking with some of us after church today and he said that he wants to sell all his property and land here in Gajkowice and move all his family to the United States. He said that he had talked to the emigration people in Lodz and agents from

America about moving and he is very excited about the prospect. Now I was thinking that we should buy his properties. We have money saved up and I think that I could borrow some from the bank as well. I don't know for sure how much land he has or how much he wants for it but I do know that he has many houses on his land that he lets out to the mill workers. Since several other people are trying to sell theirs and move, I think that we could make a fairly good deal. What do you think, Ida?"

Ida stood up, looked Gustav straight in the eyes and said, "I don't know whether or not it is a good idea to buy Becker's property but I have some news for you. Gustav, I am going to have a baby!"

"Ida, that is wonderful news. Now, for sure, we will have to get a bigger place in which to live. With one child coming, there probably will be several more. Tomorrow I am going to talk to Mr. Becker." And so he did.

Mr. Becker showed Gustav each of his properties and Gustav, with note pad in hand, made notes of every piece of land and every building that was situated on the land. Mr. Becker told Gustav which houses were rented by Jews, which by Germans and which by Poles. Gustav recorded how much rent each paid and where the tenant worked. He noted those tenants that also rented the land and those that only rented the house. Following the tour, Mr. Becker showed Gustav through the large two story house in which he and his family lived. Gustav had been to the Becker's home on several other occasions and was already familiar with some of the rooms but he was also taken down into the cellars, through the barns and the flour mill that he had built. Mr. Becker then asked for some tea to be served, at which time he brought out a map and some pamphlets and showed Gustav where it was that he was planning to go. Mr. Becker pointed to a spot on the map and said,

"Wisconsin. United States of America."

He went on to explain that he was planning to start a dairy farm and if not a dairy farm, he was going to raise beef cattle and hogs.

"The people in the cities need food," he said.

Later Gustav went back to his little house more determined than ever to buy the Becker place. And so he did.

February 16, 1892, came along and so did the first child for Ida and Gustav. They named him Oswald. Four years later in 1896, another arrived and they named him Max. On July 14, 1899, their first of four daughters arrived. They named her Clara. Then came Olga in 1901 and followed by Ludwig in 1903 who was named Ludwig but called Louie. Bertha was not far behind, born in 1905 and finally came Wanda in 1908.

The intervening years had been kind to the Jungs. Both Gustav and Ida worked hard and Gustav was a good manager so he was able to expand his holdings over the years. By the time Wanda was born, he owned over seventy acres of land upon which sixty houses were built and rented out. He had also expanded his flour mill which now had a full time operator. The land that he cultivated came to a sizable portion of the total and he had hired hands to do most of the work. Gustav though, personally looked after the bees.

There had been conflict in Lodz and other major towns because many of the factory workers were becoming increasingly dissatisfied with their wages and working conditions. Karl Marx had published his Communist Manifesto and there were those who travelled to the major industrial cities, Lodz being one, spreading the Marxist gospel. A riot had occurred in Lodz and some factories had been burned but nothing of the sort affected the town of Moszczenica, so Gustav was not excessively concerned. He also did not seem to be too concerned with the large number of German people packing up and leaving the area for the New World. There was constant talk among the German population that those whose relatives had gone to the United States and Canada were doing well. Reports came back that the new immigrants to North America were venturing even further inland so that by the turn of the century, most of the farmers were looking to go to Canada even to a place in the North West Territories called Saskatchewan.

The number of German friends and relatives was slowly decreasing and this was recognized by Gustav and Ida. They discussed this issue often and wondered if they should try to sell their holdings and venture overseas as well. However, each time the topic was discussed the same arguments for remaining, prevailed . . . . their family was intact . . . . they were financially secure . . . . with others emigrating, they were able to expand their holdings. Why should they risk everything by leaving?

CHAPTER 18

1914

"Clara, Olga, come in here. I need to measure you up for new dresses that I am going to sew for you." The call came from Ida to her daughters Clara, now fourteen, and Olga, now twelve.

It was spring time and there was indeed a need for the new dresses. First of all, the girls had grown and needed something nice to wear to church. Clara was going to be confirmed in August and in addition, there were some up-coming farewell parties that the Jung family was either hosting or attending.

During the past few years there existed increased rumblings of war throughout Europe. Russia, which was in control of the Lodz province, had been engaged in a war with Japan and there were new rumors abounding that Germany and Austria were planning to expand their borders at the expense of countries which they bordered. Several young men from the Moszczenica area had been conscripted and were presently serving in the Tsar's armies.

A new wide gauge railroad linking Piotrkow to Lodz had been completed in 1910. The railroad was built to transport raw materials and finished textiles between Lodz and Piotrkow, but in the spring of 1914, the railroad carried more troops, their horses and weaponry, than it did consumer goods and passengers who often travelled to Lodz. Many of the people living in the area became fearful should war break out. They feared for their sons lives, they feared for their wives and daughters and they feared for their property. The Germans, as well as the Jews, had more reason to be fearful than the Poles. If the Germans attacked Poland, then the Germans would be seen as the enemy and would become the objects of vengeful seeking citizens. Because of this build up of arms and the increasing talk of war, the exodus of Germans from this region increased.

One of the families that had made arrangements to leave was the Martin Flath family. The Martin Flath family had come to Moszczenica a few years earlier from the Alexandrow area and had purchased a small plot of land in Moszczenica. Martin's family and Gustav's family attended the same church and their children attended the same school. Martin, who operated a flour mill, would often visit with Gustav who also was interested in milling flour. Martin's oldest son, Otto, was one of the young men in the area who had been conscripted and was presently serving the Tsar's army in Dubno, Galicia.

Martin, in conversation with Gustav informed Gustav that he and his two younger sons, Adolph and Teofil, would be emigrating in April of 1914, but would be leaving behind his wife Paulina, his son Hugo and his young daughter Olga. Hugo would be responsible for looking after and providing for himself, Paulina and Olga. Martin told Gustav that he would have liked to have taken the whole family, but Paulina, even after the pleading and begging, insisted on waiting for Otto to come home from the army.

"I will come back for them!" Martin had stated.

"You girls know that your school friends, Adolph and Teofil, are leaving for America soon and you need to have new dresses for their farewell gathering that is being held in the church. Clara, I will take your measurements first, then yours Olga. Then we can choose the fabric and pattern that you would like to have. We'll cut out the pieces and then we'll sew."

Ida had always sewn all the clothing for the children. She had a sewing machine and the room which she used for sewing, contained some shelves, a cupboard and a full length mirror. Ida positioned Clara in front of the mirror and began.

Clara stood in front of the full length mirror dressed only in a petticoat and as her mother began to take her measurements, Clara too began an analysis of the figure reflected in the mirror. What stared back at her was a five foot tall girl.

"Maybe five feet one inch if I stretch my neck and put more weight on my toes," thought Clara.

She weighed about one hundred pounds and liked what she saw. Her eyes that stared back were large and round . . . . the black pupils were surrounded by dancing grey blue eyes . . . . her eyebrows were thin and light brown in color. When first seeing her face, it was the eyes that captured one's attention. Her face was nearly as round as her eyes. Her cheeks were full, firm and rosy and when she smiled at the mirror small dimples revealed themselves. Her nose, she decided, was not the prettiest feature, being just a little wide and she thought, a little too flat. Her mouth was full with rosy full lips. She thought that her neck was too short. Then from reviewing her face, she continued downward to her waist and her legs and ankles. After examining fully the image in the mirror, she concluded that if only she could grow another inch or two, she possessed the necessary means to marry a handsome man. Then when it was Olga's turn to be measured up, Clara sat on a chair and began peppering Ida with the many questions that had been troubling her for a while now.

"Mama," she said, "many of my friends here in Gajkowice and at church are afraid of what is happening. Should I be scared?"

Even before Ida could answer, came another question.

"Could we also leave like the Flaths? I do not want to get killed in a war. The soldiers frighten me and when my friends talk, they frighten me even more. I have bad dreams at night and I worry about what could happen to us."

"Clara, Clara," soothed Ida, "don't worry. Everything will be all right. We live far away from any big city and far from any border where, if there should be a war, the fighting would take place. The soldiers that you see are just passing through and going much farther towards Germany. Don't worry. We will be safe."

Feeling somewhat relieved, Clara then asked if she could be excused because she wanted to attend to the needs of her two younger sisters, Bertha and Wanda.

Evening came and the whole family gathered around the large kitchen table to partake of the usual evening meal. Since it was early spring, the cows had calved so there was fresh milk and cream for the table. The chickens had also resumed laying eggs after having a rest from their expected daily offerings so there were fresh eggs available as well. This evening the supper consisted of boiled eggs, a slice of homemade bread and a cup of hot milk or tea depending on the age of the person who drank it. Clara, now nearly fifteen years of age, could have tea if she wanted but Olga who was twelve would not be offered tea to drink. The family was large and there existed a wide range of age between the youngest and the eldest, so it would be expected that there would be much chatter and commotion at the table. Usually there was, but on this evening very little was said except for the chatter of the two youngest. Gustav attempted to lighten up the mood but failed. The uncertainties and general anxiety that permeated the whole community left its imprint on all but the youngest members of the Jung family. Following the meal, Ida, as usual, brought out the family bible, read some passages from it, then all bowed their heads, folded their hands and in unison repeated the evening prayers that all had learned from previous generations, the last prayer being Das Vaterunser (The Lord's Prayer). Following the supper clean up, Clara and Olga solemnly went to their room and prepared to go to sleep. It was a day that had been filled with mixed emotions for Clara. She was excited that she would be sewing a new dress and that she would be confirmed but at the same time fearful of the unknowns that lay ahead.

Two weeks later, the dresses had been completed and all the preparations for the farewell gathering for, not only Martin Flath's family but also for two other families as well, had been completed. The church service on this day took on a serious and sad tone. The pastor delivered a comforting emotional sermon which kept the men of the congregation in deep serious thought and brought out waves of tears from the women but most of the children couldn't understand what the crying was all about. Clara and Olga sat next to their mother with Bertha and Wanda between them and from their pew they could survey most of the congregation. Clara sat upright throughout the service and kept a constant eye on Adolph and the rest of the Flath family. She also kept watch of Paulina and young Olga. Throughout the sermon, Paulina sat stoically erect trying her hardest not to show any exaggerated emotion to the knowledge that her husband and two of her precious sons in a few days would be leaving for good. Her heart was being ripped apart by the thought. Martin, too, sat quietly, immersed deeply in his own fears and uncertainties, wondering if he was making a wise move. As Clara watched, she was not totally overcome with emotion because, although she was acquainted with the families that were leaving, she was not really close friends with any of them. Her roll in the day's proceedings was that she and other girls from the Sunday school classes would sing two songs for the families that were leaving.

When it became apparent that the threat of war would soon become a reality, the exodus of Germans changed from a trickle into a flow. As many as could, arranged for passage elsewhere. Each Sunday the congregation at Jarosty saw their numbers dwindle. Clara had several more opportunities to wear her new dress and sing some farewell hymns for those who were leaving in haste.

Clara celebrated her fifteenth birthday on July 14, 1914, and the following Sunday she was confirmed into the Evangelical Church of Poland and come what may, the Jung family was not moving and refused to be caught up by the hysteria that consumed most of their neighbors. Life for the Jungs went on as usual. Each member of the family had his or her role and by keeping very busy, was able to forget momentarily, the possible effects a war would have on them. Life went on, but throughout the summer of 1914, there was troop movement everywhere and the Tsar's armies were kept busy fortifying the areas fronted by the German troops. Several more families from the Moszczenica area were able to secure passage elsewhere but by the middle of July, Poland became closed to emigration and even if one had the means by which to leave, could no longer do so.

The news that war had broken out between Russia and Germany reached Gustav Jung on August 28, 1914. He learned that there had been battles fought in East Prussia and that the Russians had attacked the Austrians in Galicia. Gustav was fully aware of the fact that Paulina Flath's son, Otto, was stationed in Dubno, Galicia, and upon hearing the news passed it on to Paulina. There had been no news of any fighting near to the city of Lodz but surely if there was fighting to the northeast and to the southwest of them, there would also be battles fought in between. The only hope that Moszczenica would not be affected, would be if Russia defeated Germany very quickly and that the German armies would not have an opportunity to pass through the area should the Russian army be in retreat. Gustav reasoned that as a family, they would have to make plans as to how they could protect themselves.

Quickly, Gustav summoned his family to the kitchen and hastily began making plans for their safety and for the protection of their livestock and crops. After a quick consultation with Ida and their two oldest sons Oswald and Max, Gustav said,

"We will put as much food and supplies as we can into the grain cellar. We can make a solid trap door to replace the iron grate through which the threshed grain is shoved and then we can pile some hay or straw on top. It is large enough to hide all of us if need be. If the soldiers come, we will quickly go there. One never knows what kind of demands soldiers in battle will make on us civilians. We definitely will have to hide mother and our girls. As far as the livestock goes, there is not much we can do but we will take some of the pigs, some of our milk cows and two of our horses and try to hide them in the forest. We will build a shelter for them and store some grain and water there. Hopefully, the soldiers won't wander into the forest. We cannot protect our house but we can partition off parts of the cellar and put things behind false walls. Perhaps we could dig deeper into the ground and make some secret compartments there as well."

And so the preparations commenced.

News on the progress of the war came sporadically to Gajkowice and as usually is the case, the various accounts given were often in contradiction to each other, but the general consensus was that Russia had defeated the Austrians in Galicia but the Germans inflicted heavy losses on the Russians in East Prussia. Since East Prussia was closer to Gajkowice, most believed that the Germans would invade their region and capture Lodz. They heard that there were staggering losses on both sides and because of that, the war would not last very long.

The German offensive in Poland began on September 28, 1914, and by November, the German army had driven the Russian forces ever closer to Lodz. The Russian forces in their plan to protect Lodz had entrenched themselves in defense only a few miles outside of Gajkowice in a line which started far to the south and then to the north past Aleksandrow and up to Lithuania. Word had come to the villages that, should the Germans advance, the deciding stage for victory or loss was being set up just a few miles away.

There had been a definite increase in military traffic along the roads throughout the countryside and no one ventured far away from their homes. All the civilians, Poles, Germans and Jews alike were apprehensive of what all the troop movement might mean. It did not take long for the residents of Gajkowice and Moszczenica to experience war, first hand. On November 11, 1914, the advancing German ninth army met the entrenched Russian second army under General Scheiderman. Within hours of making contact, the battle began to rage.

Gustav, Oswald, Max and Louie, all had gotten out of bed that morning a little earlier than usual because the temperature had dropped steadily during the night and by morning, the thermometer had reached minus fifteen degrees. This meant that the milk cows would stay in the barn and they would be milked and watered there. Also, the animals hidden in the bushes needed attending. Louie was the first to detect the sound of cannon fire. His eyes widened as he spoke.

"Papa, what is that noise?"

Gustav put the pail of water down on the ground, lifted the ear flap up on his winter cap and listened.

"I don't like to say this Louie, but I believe it is the sound of war at our door step. Go quickly and tell your mother and sisters to be ready to go into hiding. We don't know which way the armies will go. Tell them that the bursting shells will not reach us yet and as long as the sounds don't get louder, we will be fine. Don't be frightened. Everything will be okay. Oswald, Max and I will finish the chores. Then we will come to the house and help carry supplies to our hiding places."

Louie, being only eleven years old and not fully appreciative of the gravity of the situation, scurried off to relay the message.

The whole family spent the rest of the morning preparing their hiding places. By noon, they all went back into their house, said a few prayers, ate a good dinner and then sat and waited. The pounding sounds of exploding cannon fire continued constantly but the volume didn't change. Neither side was giving way and as evening approached, Gustav and his sons ventured out again to tend to the livestock. They took their milk pails and watering pails and began their chores. Gustav had the foresight to move his beehives deep into the woods and had covered them with branches. He knew they would winter there. Ida and the girls remained in the house and were expected to remain there. Clara, though, being naturally curious, soon became bored.

"Olga, let's sneak outside and listen to the cannons," whispered Clara to her sister.

"Okay, let's go," replied Olga.

Once outside and out of sight of their parents, Clara said, "I wonder if we could see anything if we climbed to the top of the flour mill. If we look out of the top opening, we might be able to see something."

Olga, being adventurous herself, soon agree and off they skittered to the mill.

The terrain around Gajkowice was mostly flat especially in the direction from which the battle was raging. The mill had been built to a height of more than thirty feet to accommodate the fifteen foot long blades that turned the grinding stones. The girls climbed to the top of the mill and peered through the opening.

"Look! Clara, look! I see dust and I see fires. Can you?"

"Yes, Olga, of course I can."

Silently, they continued to watch but it wasn't long before a loud booming voice commanded, "Clara! Olga! Get down from there, right now! What do you think you are doing? Are you crazy? You could get yourselves killed up there. What if an airplane would come by . . . . if they saw anyone in the tower, they would shoot. Get down now!" Gustav was furious.

"Papa, we just wanted to see what we could see . . . . sorry . . . . sorry . . . . so sorry, Papa," whispered the girls.

The same level of noise continued for three days. The explosions would stop during the night only to start up again in the morning. The residents of the villages and towns bordering the battle field were not fully aware of the carnage that was being created only a few miles away. They could only imagine the horror, pain and suffering being inflicted on the soldiers on both sides. The peasants living within a mile or so had vacated their homes and had gone to relatives living elsewhere. The people in the villages remained in their homes helplessly awaiting the outcome.

Clara and Olga did not venture outside again, but the men went out twice daily to attend to their chores. Following the completion of the outside chores, the men would return to the house and recount what they had observed. On the evening of the third day, Gustav announced that the sounds of exploding shells was increasing in volume and that many columns of wounded men and horses were passing by on the main road.

"We will spend tonight in our hiding place. I think that the German army has broken through and the Russian army is in retreat."

Gustav and his sons had brought in a large mound of hay and placed it over top of the trap door, leaving a tunnel through which they could crawl to enter their shelter. They each took a personal item with them but Gustav would not allow anyone to bring a candle or a match. One by one they crawled through the tunnel with Ida leading the way and urging little Wanda to follow close behind. Gustav was last to enter and as he made his way along, he pulled the hay over the tunnel opening hoping that he would not leave any signs of its existence.

The pounding and clattering of horses' hooves, the yelling and shouting of panic stricken soldiers combined with the roar and rumbling of assorted motorized military vehicles echoed in the cold night air. It was those sounds that filled the ears of the Jung family and along with the tremors felt, which caused all of the Jungs, from youngest to oldest, to huddle together and silently wait for the commotion to abate.

By the time the sun rose, all was quiet but no one was yet brave enough to venture out into the open and their decision to sit tight and wait proved to be a wise one. Some light came filtering through the narrow cracks which had been left for air to enter the cellar. The narrow streaks of light made it possible for the family to see as they broke off pieces of bread, shelled some cold boiled eggs and poured themselves cups of milk. Following their breakfast and talking in whispers, the various members of the Jung family offered their feelings and reactions to the event that had occurred during the night and what could possibly befall them in the near future. They all agreed that it was quite probable that their village was now under the control of the German army but they could not agree on what that could possibly mean for them. As they continued to quietly and patiently remain in hiding, a different kind of sound came from the ground above them. This sound signaled the presence of several horses and the voices clearly heard, told everyone below that there were a number of troops right in the threshing shelter. Quickly assessing the voices heard, Gustav was convinced that a squad of mounted soldiers had entered their yard and within a few moments realized that the voices above came from German soldiers. The sergeant in charge of the squad began to give his orders.

"Dismount," he ordered, "and quickly go from building to building. Check every single one. There may be some enemy troops hiding out here. I don't see any smoke coming from the chimney nor do I see anyone around here. Check thoroughly and return here within ten minutes."

With those orders, the other members of the squad went in separate directions to check all the various buildings. The sergeant dismounted, tied the horses' reins together and allowed the horses to eat freely of the hay that was covering the grain cellar. Within minutes, the troop members returned giving the sergeant their reports.

One said, "I have checked the house thoroughly. The people living here must be German as there is all kinds of German literature in the house. I could not find anyone inside."

Another spoke up, "I have checked the barns. The animals are tied up in their stalls which have straw, and there is hay to eat."

"Likewise with the pig pen and the chicken and goose sheds," said a third.

"I checked the mill and there was no one there either," reported another soldier.

"They must have gone into hiding in the forest last night when they heard the enemy retreating along the main road," concluded the sergeant. "We will stay here for an hour or two. Our horses are tired, hungry and thirsty as are we. Find some water buckets and bring the horses some water. Private Willie, you go into the house and light a fire and try to find something to eat. Do not destroy anything. Let us just see what this family has here."

Gustav and his family heard exactly what the sergeant had said. In whispers, Ida and Gustav discussed whether or not to reveal themselves to the soldiers, but after a short debate, decided to leave everything as it was. True to the sergeant's word, the squad returned to the shed, some of them carrying a few rolls of newly made garlic sausage and some unidentified objects which they carried in sacks. The last words from the sergeant were,

"We are some of the last troops to leave the battlefield. There will not be many soldiers behind us and we need to hurry to catch up to the rest of our regiment."

The danger had passed. It was now safe to come out of hiding. The Jungs were very fortunate to come out of this ordeal with only very minor consequences. The Russians as they retreated did not fight any rear guard battles with the advancing Germans. The cold weather had prompted the advancing German army to advance slowly because the other German armies at their flanks had not yet broken through the Russian lines. The German army would take some time to bury as many of the dead that they could before having to move on. Thousands of Russian and German soldiers that lay dead were left where they fell. The battle field would now become a mecca for local souvenir hunters and for peasants who would strip the dead soldiers of their weapons, their boots, their coats and belts, their rings and even their gold teeth. The spoils of war!

The Jung family emerged from their hide out and quickly began to normalize their day to day life. Gustav, Oswald, Max and Louie ventured out to the main road leading out of Gajkowice and there they witnessed hundreds of men, boys and even some women heading toward the deserted battle field. Gustav was fully aware of their intentions and quickly informed his sons that they were not to go anywhere near there. Gustav had not ever seen first hand how a recently deserted battlefield would appear to an observer, but he easily painted a mental picture of what awaited those who were heading in that direction. The thousands of partially frozen corpses of men and hundreds of horse carcasses did not create a very pleasant image in his brain. He visualized men with decapitated bodies; their heads severed by the bayonets of enemy soldiers. He visualized grotesquely shaped humans piled one atop the other, eyes still wide open, glazed with terror as the bullet, bayonet or shrapnel pierced their bodies. He visualized the hundreds of gallons of blood lying in pools waiting to be devoured by animals that lived in the forest. He visualized the ghouls who went from body to body, stripping each bare of artifacts and clothing, showing no respect for the individual who, only a few hours earlier was a living father, a son, a brother, an uncle. No, he would not allow any of his sons to witness anything like that. He offered a quick silent prayer that this battle would be the end and that there would never ever be another one like it.

God did not answer his prayer in the way that he had hoped. Two weeks later the whole scene was replayed. The Germans that broke through the Russian defenses had continued on past Lodz and decided to attack Lodz from the rear flank. They believed that the German armies attacking from the west would drive the Russians back and if they also attacked from the east, the enemy would be surrounded and would be forced to surrender. But, that did not happen. The Russian forces were able to hold those German forces that attacked from the west at bay, while at the same time, allowing the Germans to enter Lodz from the east. When the Germans had entered Lodz, the Russians quickly closed ranks behind the Germans and had apparently trapped them inside Lodz.

The news of this was not known in Gajkowice but Gajkowice would feel the effects of these events very quickly. Rather that seeing the German army advance farther into Poland, the German army had to scramble to get out of Lodz and retreat back to the west. Part of the retreat route went by Gajkowice once again and so near the end of November, the Jung family found themselves hiding in their grain cellar. Unlike a few weeks before when the German troops entered their yard, this time it was a troop of Russian Cossacks. This time also, the Cossacks caught them by surprise and the family had no time to run and hide in their shelter. The girls, rather than head for the grain cellar, ran up to their rooms and peered out of the windows to witness the event happening in the back yard. When the Cossacks came trotting into the yard, Gustav and Oswald quickly left the house and went into the yard to meet them. It was obvious that they were in a hurry and did not have much time to spend before they would leave. The Cossacks' horses milled around and the Cossacks, with their fur hats, their sheepskin coats and long sabers dangling by their sides, created a frightening picture to the little eyes that peered through the windows. After a brief exchange of words, the Cossack leader spied the poultry pens and since the temperature had risen somewhat, the flock of geese was outside strutting around with their heads held high, busily cackling to each other. Without a word, two of the Cossacks stormed the gate to the pen, broke it down, leapt off of their horses, withdrew their sabers and systematically began popping off the heads of the unsuspecting frightened geese. Within minutes and covered by the splattered blood of the crudely butchered geese, the Cossacks picked up the fallen blood dripping carcasses, and threw them into the waiting arms of the rest of the still mounted Cossacks. Nothing more was said. The Cossacks, with geese in tow, turned and galloped out of the yard. Gustav, Oswald and those who were watching from the house just stood there, bewildered by the actions of the Cossacks but totally relieved that the Cossacks only wanted a good meal and nothing else. Even in the midst of tragedy, it was a humorous moment bringing smiles to the faces of those who observed.

The battle for Lodz became pivotal in the struggle for dominance in Poland and by December 6, 1914, the German forces prevailed and the Russian forces fell thirty kilometers back, with the result that the Jung family holdings were now located in German held territory. Most importantly, the fighting, the killing and the suffering had come to a halt in that area and the Jungs and others like them, were able to once again pursue their daily activities in peace.

The two women were in the kitchen by themselves. They were in the process of finishing up the washing and cleaning up of the dishes and area following the dinner enjoyed by their respective families. Their daughters, after having helped in the preparation, the serving and then following clean up, had been dismissed. The men and boys remained in the dining room and living room where the older men and sons smoked their cigarettes and played cards and at the same time enjoying a glass of schnapps. The visit of Paulina Flath, her son Hugo and her daughter Olga had been arranged by Ida. Not having had an opportunity to have a meaningful visit with some of their friends from the church or even to see some of their acquaintances due to the turmoil in all of their lives in the past few months, Ida had decided that it was time that they renewed some friendships.

Ida had always held a certain admiration for Paulina and there, talking with her and watching her, certainly did not diminish her previous respect for Paulina. Paulina was a tall, physically strong woman. Not only was she physically strong, but she was also mentally and emotionally strong. Everyone who found themselves in her presence immediately felt her strength. She always stood erect and she always projected a look of confidence, assurance and determination. She had not been concerned in the least that she would not be able to manage by herself, along with Hugo and Olga, when Martin had announced that he was emigrating to Canada. In fact, she was more concerned that Martin would not be able to manage without her. She had been most reluctant to permit Martin to take two of her sons with him, especially young Teofil. Adolph, she thought would be fine, he was older, but Teofil was just a youngster and still required adult guidance. But after much pleading by Teofil and continued assurance from Martin, the practical minded Paulina had agreed to the arrangement. To many of her acquaintances her explanation that she would remain in Poland until her oldest son Otto returned from the army, was more of an excuse that a reason. Many felt that Paulina was not completely convinced that Martin would be able to support the whole family in Canada and because she was more of a realist than a dreamer, had refused to subject herself and little Olga to the uncertainties of emigrating and Martin's ability to support all of them.

"Paulina," Ida began, "I am sorry that it has been so long since we have been able to get together. It has been a long terrible year for all of us, hasn't it? How are you managing and how did you manage to get through all the turbulence that was all around us last fall and winter? Have you had any word from Martin or from Otto? You must be worried about what has happened or what is happening to them."

"Oh yes, Ida, I have spent many sleepless nights thinking and worrying about my dear Martin and my sons," confided Paulina. "It has been most difficult and at times, especially during the fighting around here, I have almost given up hope. I have not heard anything from Otto and I do not hold out much hope for us ever seeing him again. All I know is that his regiment was in the battles that took place just a few weeks ago in Galicia and that the Russians had suffered huge losses. I don't think that Otto could possibly escape all of that . . . . I can only hope and pray that he did. As for Martin, I have sent letters to Canada but I don't think they will reach him either. The Germans will not be allowing letters to go through to Canada and so, in answer to your question, no I have not heard a word from Martin, other than his last letter that I received almost a year ago. He, Adolph and Teofil had reached Radisson, Saskatchewan safely and they were living with his cousin, Louis Flath. That is all I know. Hugo, Olga and I are managing fine now. Hugo is back working in the mills and I am able to look after our home and property. So things for us are fine but I do worry about the rest of my family. And you, Ida, how are you doing? How is your family in Lodz? I hear that many buildings and factories in Lodz were heavily damaged," inquired Paulina.

"I guess that God was looking after us, Paulina," stated Ida. "We are all well and I thank God that the people here are able to return to a more normal life. It has been a struggle. We now just have to wait for the war to end for good and after that, we all will know what to do with our lives."

CHAPTER 19

1918

The combination of ample summer rains combined with hot humid days and nights had resulted in a bountiful harvest. The two young men had used sickles and scythes to cut the small plots of wheat and oats. The stalks of grain had been gathered by hand and tied into bundles; strands of grain had been used to keep the bundles together. The bundles were then stooked in the fields and left for the warm sun's rays to do their job of drying and hardening the kernels. When it was deemed that the grain was sufficiently dry, the bundles were then hauled to the threshing shed where the young men would use a flail to beat the grain heads to separate the kernels from the chaff. The men would then wait for a light breeze to occur, at which time they would place the kernels and chaff on a blanket and throw the grain into the air and hope that the lighter chaff would be carried away by the breeze and the heavier kernels would fall back on to the blanket. It was very time consuming and tedious work and because of that, only enough grain would be threshed for what would be needed to feed the poultry and supply enough grain for flour, which would be needed to make bread, pancakes, noodles, cakes and pastry. The rest would be left for feed for the cows, the horse and the pigs. It was well into the latter part of September and the grain had successfully been harvested. All that was left to harvest now and to be stored in the root cellar were the remaining root crops and cabbage that had been planted in the garden.

The back door of the house opened and the two young men that stepped out, walked leisurely to the shed that housed the tools they required to do the work that lay ahead for them. They were in no hurry; the morning sun had taken the chill off the air and removed the dew that had accumulated on the potato plants during the night. They knew that there was no advantage to dig potatoes early in the morning; potatoes needed to be exposed to the warm sun for a few hours before they could be stored successfully in the root cellar. Hugo pulled at the home hewn handle and the heavy slab door to the shed swung open and revealed the forks and buckets that would be used to extricate the potatoes. Hugo reached in and removed a fork and a bucket and then handed them to Otto. Then reaching in again, he removed another fork and bucket that he would use.

Silently, they meandered over to the potato patch and began the day's work. Digging potatoes does not require a great deal of thought; there is not much that can go wrong, so Otto, after settling into the routine of first removing the dried up potato tops, driving the fork into the ground, lifting the fork's contents to the surface, and then lastly shaking as much soil as possible from the freed potatoes, had ample time to reflect on the events which had transpired since his return a few short months ago. After they had dug potatoes for about two hours, Hugo suggested that they sit down in the shade for a rest and a drink of water.

"Otto, you have not said a word to me all morning. Is something bothering you? Are you not feeling well? I know there is something wrong because I have dug twice as many potatoes as you have," stated Hugo.

"No Hugo, I am not ill and if you must know, I have been thinking about my whole situation," replied Otto.

"I am sorry that I have not been keeping up to you," continued Otto, "but I was just thinking. I have just realized that it has been nine years since I have been doing this chore . . . . nine years. I left nine years ago with nothing and here I am back again, with nothing. I have no money, no property, I don't even have a record of what I have been doing for the past nine years. Honestly, Hugo, I feel almost like a stranger here. Besides our family, I hardly know anyone. None of my friends are here anymore. Most of them, I guess, had been conscripted into the army and are dead. I feel guilty about stepping back into this family the way that I have. You have been here all along . . . . working and taking care of our mother and sister. Where was I?

I was serving in an army that is at war with people of our own heritage! Really, I feel like an intruder. I am saddened and at the same time, I'm angry. If it wasn't for me, you, mother and Olga would all be safe in Canada now. Hugo, just think about it . . . . here we are living in a place that is not even a country. There is no Poland, is this Germany now? Is it Russia? What is it? There isn't even any common currency. Whose money do we get paid with for our work in the factories? Sometimes it's in rubles, sometimes it's in marks and sometimes it's nothing. Why are we digging these potatoes anyway? These damn potatoes are now your money. It's almost funny . . . . we are digging up money!"

"Hugo, I get sick to my stomach when I think about it. If only I hadn't signed up for a second stint, we could all have been far away from here . . . . Hugo, the army, this damn war and the robbers have taken not only nine years away from me, they have taken my life. I am left with nothing!"

Hugo sat silently and listened.

Finally, Otto said, "Well, I guess I have to restart somewhere. Let's go dig some more damn potatoes."

It had not taken long for Otto's body to physically recover from the beating it had taken during his escape from Russia, but the emotional wounds that had been inflicted upon him during the past few years refused to heal. Now that his body had recovered, his mind would now focus on the emotions, but rather than heal, old wounds that had partially healed were reopened and bled harder than ever. There was no doctor, no nurse, no therapist, not even a friend that could apply the salve that would begin to close those wounds and hide the scars left deep inside. Time was the only healer available and Otto learned that along with time, hard physical labor helped. He found that if his muscles ached and if his body felt weak from hard physical work, his mind could rest and he could sleep through the night and not be tormented by recurring nightmares that had been haunting him since his return to Poland. Otto was not the only one who felt the emotional strains that this war had produced. There was not one family, one village, one city, one country in all of Europe, that had escaped its effect. Individuals were affected, families were in turmoil, institutions suffered and governments struggled and in their emotionally weakened condition were left vulnerable to be attacked economically, socially, politically and physically. Because of the war, Otto's family would never be the same, Moszczenica would never be the same, Poland and Russia would never be the same; the war that was supposed to last for a few months was taking its toll.

It was after coming home from their usual day's work in the textile mill when Otto and Hugo came into the house to find Olga crying. She was sitting in a chair beside their mother's bed. There was no warning that something was amiss when they had left for work that morning. The virus struck fast and it struck hard! Within a few hours of the virus attacking Paulina, she fell into a fever induced coma and within twenty-four hours she was dead. In what seemed like a blink of an eye, the stalwart of the family, the strong one, the one whom all looked to for stability and reason was gone, leaving behind two grieving sons and a now motherless, vulnerable young daughter.

Tears, grief and uncertainty consumed the three helpless onlookers as they watched neighbors and other family members prepare Paulina's body for burial. What would they do without her? Who would look after Olga? Who would look after the house? Who would keep the family together? There had been no warning; there had been no time to prepare, there was not even any time to cry. It was all so sudden, so devastating that it was days before the shock of her sudden death would subside and they were able to come to grips with reality and make plans for their future. Any permanent plans though would have to wait because, not only did the Spanish Flu pandemic virus strike the Flath family, it attacked nearly the whole population of Moszczenica. Within days, hundreds of people had died or were sick with the virus. Some families were completely wiped out by the virus and others escaped it completely. It struck quickly and it subsided nearly as quickly. Within a month of the first casualty, it had left to move on to other parts of the country and the world where it would continue its mayhem. Moszczenica, which escaped serious damage from invading armies did not escape the Spanish Flu. The Jung family escaped but the Flath family was not so fortunate.

The year of 1918 was a pivotal year in the annals of human history. It was one of those years during which the events that occurred would permanently change the direction for many. The year, 1918, saw the Bolsheviks firmly take control of Russia and begin introducing communism to the nation. As a consequence, Tsar Nicholas II Romanov and his entire family was murdered which ended hundreds of years of Tsarist rule over Russia. November 11, 1918, witnessed the surrender of the German army in World War I. The signing changed the map of Europe forever. It also meant that communication between many parts of Europe and the Americas would resume. The loss of 50,000,000 to 100,000,000 peoples' lives due to the Spanish Flu pandemic had effectively reduced the total world's population by an estimated five percent. For Otto and others in Moszczenica, 1918 meant that they were now living in a country called Poland and they were now free to correspond with friends and relatives abroad. For Otto, it meant that he could never return to Russia; he would never be able to find out what happened to his beloved boss and mentor, Pokovnik Constantine Vasiletvich Zaharoh and his family. It also meant that there would never be any hope of his returning to Anya's arms. The loss of Paulina meant that someone else would have to take care of and raise eleven year old Olga. It also meant that the urgency to reunite the whole family in Canada was gone and remaining in Poland to live and work appeared more realistic. If ever there had been any doubt as to where Otto would be for the next few years, that doubt had been removed in 1918.

As in the case whenever any war ends, there are celebrations held to mark the end and to start anew. Gustav and Ida who were fond of inviting guests to their home, found that the end of the war to be a very good reason for celebrating. In fact, they had another reason for celebrating; their oldest son, Oswald was going to be married. So in honor of

Oswald's engagement and to celebrate the end to the war, Ida and Gustav invited many of their friends and acquaintances to join with them in an afternoon and evening of eating, drinking and dancing. The guest list included Otto and Hugo Flath.

Clara had turned eighteen and Olga had turned sixteen, so it was only natural that after several years of cloistering, they were more than ready to celebrate. In preparation for the event, new dresses were sewn, the inside of the house had received a fresh coat of paint, the yard was carefully manicured, a pig had been slaughtered and by 1918, the goose flock had been regenerated so there would even be roast goose. Several of the musicians had gotten together and were prepared to entertain for the entire evening. The furniture that usually sat in the living room had been moved out to make room for the musicians and the dancing. Extra chairs from neighbors had been brought in, as well as extra dishes and cutlery. The party was to be held on the last weekend in November.

The guests began arriving by three o'clock in the afternoon and by five o'clock, the last guests, Otto and Hugo, appeared. It had taken much prompting and persuading on Hugo's part to get Otto to agree to go. Hugo reminded Otto, that Otto and Oswald were close in age and had been well acquainted years before. Hugo told Otto that it was time that both of them should remove the black arm bands from their sleeves and participate in social events. Max met them at the gate and escorted them into the yard where several people had gathered and were busily engaged in conversation. Otto had not seen many of these people for over ten years. He recognized many of them and many recognized him. One by one, they came over to him and Hugo, offered their condolences on the death of their mother and wished them well. Within a few minutes, Otto and Hugo felt right at home, chatting with old acquaintances. Some of the women at the gathering remained outside with the men but most of them, had gone into the house to help with the preparation of the food. Every few minutes someone from the kitchen would appear with some homemade whisky, trays of sliced sausage and cheese. Otto and Oswald were busily engaged in conversation when a young woman with a ready smile and a very pleasant voice approached, carrying a plate of sliced kielbasa, asked them if they would like to have a few pieces of sausage. Otto's eye quickly scanned the young woman, then turned toward Oswald with a quizzical look on his face. Oswald quickly realizing that Otto did not recognize his sister, said,

"Otto, surely you remember Clara, my sister."

"Yes, Oswald, I remember your sister Clara, but this is not how I remember her."

Turning to Clara Otto said, "You were just a little girl when I left for the army. How old were you then? I remember you running around the yard in bare feet chasing Olga and Louie. I would not have recognized you."

Clara smiled and replied, "I remember you also but I would not have known who you were either. Welcome back, Otto. If you will excuse me now, I do have to go and serve the other guests."

Shortly after Clara had gone with her plate of sausage, Olga came by with some cheese, than Louie came by with some kuchen and not be outdone, Gustav made the rounds with his brand of refreshments. The November afternoon sun had warmed the sheltered yard sufficiently, for a short outdoor gathering, but as the sun began to near the horizon, the air soon cooled off and the outdoor guests began gravitating to the inside of the house.

Once inside, the guests were served with hot food from the oven. The guests helped themselves to roast pork, roast goose, mashed potatoes and gravy, turnips, dill pickles, cabbage rolls, thick slices of bread and butter and, of course, a generous helping of Gustav Jung's famous home brew. Everything that was served had been produced on the Jung property. After Oswald and Otto had their meal, they went into the yard for a smoke.

"Oswald, who made the sausage that is being served here today?" Asked Otto.

"I did," came the reply, "with the help of Clara, my future bride's father, Robert Laenger. He came from Lodz for a few days and showed me how to make this sausage. We are going to have to make some more because Clara and I are getting married in a few weeks from now. If you would like, you could come and help us butcher and make the sausage."

"Isn't the wedding going to be in Lodz?" questioned Otto.

"The wedding itself will be in Lodz, but mother and father are insisting that there be a celebration here as well. It will be a few weeks after our wedding," came the reply.

"Okay, Oswald. I would like very much to learn how to become a good sausage maker. Hugo and I do have some livestock so it would be good if I learned how to make kielbasa. I also like the taste of liver sausage, buckwheat sausage, pressed maggin and even blood sausage as well. Do you have the recipes for them?"

"Not all, but I will get them. Good! Now let's go in the house and do a little dancing. I hear the music has started," said Oswald.

It was hours past midnight by the time Otto and his brother Hugo began their two mile walk home. The night was crisp and frost was beginning to accumulate on the grass bordering the dirt road that lead them to their house. The moon gave off enough light for them to see the path that they would follow. Still feeling the effects of Gustav's home brew, they mumbled and stumbled along.

"How did you like the party?" Asked Hugo.

"I liked it a lot. Thanks for making me go. It was good to become reacquainted with many people that I haven't seen in years. There were some there that I did not even recognize. For example, Oswald's sisters, Clara and Olga. When I left for Russia, Clara could not have been more than nine years old and Olga was even younger. I danced with both of them and they were very pleasant. The whole Jung family seems to be a very nice family. They came through the war and the Spanish flu in good shape. Oswald told me that some of their houses are empty because of either the plague or because the men did not return from the war. Hugo, I am going to go back to the Jung place when Oswald is going to make sausage again. I want to learn how it is done," continued Otto.

CHAPTER 20

"Did you have a chance to dance with anyone interesting last night?" Olga quizzed Clara as they tidied up the kitchen from the festivities of the previous evening.

"Yes," replied Clara, "I danced a polka and a waltz with Otto Flath and I also danced with Hugo, but besides them, there really weren't many boys . . . . men, our ages to dance with, were there?"

"How do you like Otto and Hugo?" Continued Olga's questioning.

"It's odd, but Otto seems to be so much older. I think that he is too old for me . . . . and Hugo, well, he is fine, but I don't think he is interested in me," declared Clara.

"How about you? Did you have fun? It has been a long time since we have had so many people together at our place," continued Clara.

"Well," said Olga, "I had a really good time. I danced with many people also, but so far none have caught my eye. Besides I am still too young; you, however are eighteen and it is about time that you started looking for a husband."

Ida entered the kitchen and the conversation stopped.

Two weeks later, Oswald sent his younger brother, Louie to find Otto and relay the message that the butchering and the sausage making would take place the following morning.

Otto arrived on time the following morning to observe and to help in the process. Since he had not ever made sausage previously, he did more observing than helping. He watched how the animals were slaughtered and how they were either skinned or scraped. He watched and mentally took notes as the men carefully separated those parts of the animals that would be used from those that would be fed to the dogs and the pigs. He watched as the sausage makers cut up the flesh, ground it, mixed it, cooled it, stuffed it into the previously cleaned casings, and then boiled the sausages in large containers. Finally the sausages were hung where they would cool thoroughly, before being stored away in the cellars. The process took three men, besides Otto, all day and late into the night before the task was completed. Otto did not write down any notes but he mentally repeated each step over and over again and trusted that his memory would serve him well enough when it came time for him to make his own.

When the task was complete, all the butchers gathered around the Jung's kitchen table and sampled the fruits of their labor. Again, it was Ida, Clara and Olga who served the men their supper and Otto had another opportunity to speak with Clara. He decided later that he liked Clara and maybe a ten year difference was not too great a spread in age. He rationalized that now that he was back in Poland, he would not remain single for the rest of this life.

Clara and Otto's relationship was slow to materialize. They had known of each others existence for many years and it was only after Otto's return from Russia, that Clara had begun to view Otto as a possible partner and the decision to wed was not made in haste. For Otto, he had only returned to Poland for just over a year and still suffered from flashbacks and yearnings for those things he had held dear. He did not feel that he was quite ready to take on the responsibility of a wife and possibly rearing children. Clara, on the other hand, found that there were very few gentlemen near her age available for marriage. The war had killed off several boys that she had grown up with and the Spanish flu had taken the lives of several others. There weren't many men knocking on Ida and Gustav's door asking for their daughter's hand in marriage.

Over the course of the last few months of 1918 and the winter of 1919, there were many occasions where both Clara and Otto found themselves in attendance. Otto had been to the Jung's End of War celebration, he had been to the Jung's place to learn how to make sausage, he was then invited to Oswald and Clara's marriage celebration and they often found themselves attending church at the same time. They had talked casually and Clara knew that Otto's young sister Olga, was being raised by an aunt. She learned that Otto and Hugo were both working in the textile mills and at the same time, were attending to the plot of land that their father Martin, had left behind when he had emigrated to Radisson, Saskatchewan in Canada. Clara also learned that by the spring of 1919, no word had come from Canada, so there was no way of knowing whether Otto's and Hugo's letters to Saskatchewan ever reached their destination. There was no way of knowing whether Martin, Adolph and Teofil even knew of Paulina's death.

Clara and Otto spent much time together during the spring and early summer months. Otto often visited with Oswald and his new bride and Clara would often appear at her brother and sister-in-law's new home as well. Moszczenica did not have an abundance of entertainment, however, Piotrkow and even Lodz, was not too far away to go to partake in a variety of entertainment. The high speed railroad trains which ran between Piotrkow and Lodz passed through Moszczenica which made traveling to either place convenient.

"I see that a Charlie Chaplan moving picture show is playing in Piotrkow. Would you like to go?" Asked Otto of Clara.

Without hesitation, Clara consented. She and her siblings had often gone to the movie theaters before the war and Charlie Chaplin was for them all, their favorite actor. She had not been to a movie for a couple of years.

Clara and Otto would board the train early in the morning, then return later the same day. The ride to Piotrkow would take less than an hour so they would have plenty of time to stroll through the streets of Piotrkow and to enjoy a leisurely lunch before the movie started in the afternoon. Clara wore a light mid calf length, sleeveless floral dress, over which she wore a plain light blue wool sweater. She had curled her shoulder length hair and let the curls dangle loosely from her head. She then put on a small hat which was held in place by long hat pins. She carried a pair of dress gloves in her brown leather purse which matched her brown, low-healed leather shoes. Her only jewelry, which had been lent to her by her mother for the day, consisted of tiny gold hoops in her pierced ears. She then applied a few drops of perfume on herself, checked her finger nails, and then applied a couple of dabs of rouge. Clara decided that she would make herself as irresistible as was possible. After primping and fussing for over an hour, Clara looked at the image reflected form the mirror and offered a tiny smile of approval. Clara then, clasping her purse, which contained a few zlotys, her handkerchief and some make up, hurried out the door and walked briskly to the train station where she would meet Otto.

Otto was waiting for her arrival; he too, was looking forward to the day's outing. He had been going to work in Piotrkow daily but he had not spent much time there otherwise. The fare was only two zlotys each and after securing their seats, they settled down and chatted eagerly about the day's activities. Clara had not been to Piotrkow in a long while and as the train entered the city and wound its way to the city center where the station was located, she noted to Otto that it seemed to her like the city was going through a face lift. All around them, there was evidence of new construction, street improvement and building renovation. There was plenty of work available and since Poland became independent, the residents showed a renewed interest and optimism in their city.

The train, arriving on time, came to a stop and the passengers unloaded. Clara and Otto linked arms on the platform and strolled off, beginning their day together. After walking along streets leading to the center of the city, they decided to sit down and enjoy a cup of coffee. The cafe was situated in a small building facing the market square. Since it was Saturday, the square was busy with street vendors setting up their tables, which would be covered with fresh eggs, baking, and vegetables. Since Piotrkow housed a large Jewish population, many of the tables set up displayed kosher meat as well as many traditional baked goods. A small fountain graced the center of the square where several small children and several dogs chased each other around and round the fountain, barking and squealing as they pushed and wrestled with each other. Not many words were exchanged as Otto and Clara observed the hustle and bustle of the market square . . . . each thinking how different the scene would have been four years previous.

They finished their coffee and then linking arms again they began to leisurely stroll through the streets of Piotrkow. As they walked and talked, they passed many newly opened shops that were selling items that had not been available for several years, they passed reopened textile factories, they passed by several theaters and movie houses, each advertising the current activity. The whole city was buzzing with activity and a new found optimism. The optimism and feeling of happiness also captured Clara and Otto.

The doors to the theater opened at one o'clock, Otto purchased the tickets and the couple was ushered to their seats.

"It feels good to be back in here," stated Clara as they sat down in the red velvet stuffed chairs.

"I have been in this theater several times before the war," she went on to explain.

"Papa and Mama had brought us here to see some vaudeville shows, some plays and some moving pictures when we were smaller. It was closed as soon as the war broke out. It still looks the same though," continued Clara.

The show began and the audience laughed and clapped as Charlie went through his antics. Charlie Chaplin appealed to audiences of any language . . . . silent film did not need interpreters.

The couple had no intentions of returning to Gajkowice early and had several hours to explore the shops and cafes in central Piotrkow before the train back home was scheduled to leave.

"Are you hungry?" Otto asked as they both caught a whiff of food being cooked in the kitchen of a restaurant that they were passing by.

"It is almost four o'clock and our train is not leaving for two hours so we have time to eat."

Clara thought for a moment, then agreed that they should probably eat something before they returned for home. The restaurant that they chose to dine at had obviously been recently updated, boasting white linen table clothes and candles on the table. The waiters wore pressed black pants and long sleeved white shirts and carried printed menus with them. Otto and Clara were seated by the thirty some year old waiter and were promptly offered a pot of tea. Clara and Otto studied the menu while sipping their tea and Clara decided to order roast pork with potatoes and gravy, as Otto chose the pork chops.

The sun was disappearing over the horizon when they began their walk home from the Moszczenica train station. Otto would walk with Clara to her parent's home. They once again linked their arms as they made their way to the Jung's home, reaching the garden gate, just as darkness fell. When they reached the gate, they stopped, turned, faced one another, then spontaneously they put their arms around one another. Clara looked up at Otto offering her lips to him and he lowered his head to reach down to meet her. Following their embrace, Clara whispered,

"Ich liebe euch Otto." ("I love you Otto".)

"Ich liebe auch sie Clara," ("I love you too Clara",) replied Otto.

With those words, the match was made. Next would come the plans for the wedding and their plans for where they would live and not to forget Ida and Gustav's permission.

Otto had gone to Piotrkow by himself and had not told his brother Hugo why he was going and Hugo did not ask. It was a Saturday and really Otto should have stayed at home and helped Hugo with the weeding of the garden and the hilling of potatoes but Hugo thought,

"Otto must have something more important on his agenda than the unwelcome thought of weeding."

Hugo had had enough of weeding by the time his brother returned and was found sitting in the shade drinking a cold glass of water that he had just retrieved from the well. Otto appeared to be a little nervous when he approached Hugo, reached into his pocket and pulled out a small bag.

"Look what I bought in Piotrkow today," stated Otto.

"What is it?" Came the reply.

Carefully Otto untied the top of the little sack and slowly shook its contents into the palm of his left hand. Without a word, he carefully opened the tiny box and held it out so that Hugo could get a better look at it.

"Well, well, Otto! This is a very nice diamond ring! I was wondering when you would be coming home with one. I assume that it is for Clara and have you asked her yet if she will marry you?" Asked Hugo.

Otto went on to explain that, even though he had not presented Clara with the formal request, he felt sure that she would accept and that Ida and Gustav would be in agreement to the marriage proposal. He further explained that Clara and he would probably be buying or renting one of Gustav's properties and that he would continue working on the looms in the textile mill. He was just waiting for the appropriate situation to arise when he would present Clara with the ring and the proposal. Hugo nodded in understanding and then said,

"This is changing the subject Otto, but the postal clerk came by today and delivered this letter."

With that said, Hugo pulled a letter from the pocket of his overalls and handed it to Otto. Otto took the letter and immediately recognized the handwriting on the envelope. The return address on it identified the sender as their father, Martin, whose return address was Hafford, Saskatchewan, Canada. Otto removed the letter from the envelope and read:

> Dear Otto, Hugo and Olga;
>
> It is with a heavy heart that I write this letter to you. The news of my dear Paulina's death has deeply saddened, not only me, but it was also devastating for Adolph and Teofil. I pray for her soul and I pray for all back in Poland. I pray that your day to day life is easier for you than it has been for Adolph, Teofil and myself. It is not only your absence that saddens me, but also, I am saddened by my decision to immigrate to Canada and drag Adolph and Teofil with me. If I could scrape up enough money, I would like to return to you all.
>
> Life here has not been kind to us. The winters are dreadfully cold, the farm land is poor and the distance to any village or town makes traveling to them nearly impossible during the winter and very awkward in summer. Life is very lonely but I am most pleased that Adolph and Teofil are here with me: they are a great help to me. The worst of everything though, was not receiving any news

from Poland since the war began five years ago. It is a long time to live without knowing what has happened or is happening to your own family.

I must confess that upon reading of the battles fought in Galicia, Poland and Russia, I had given up complete hope of ever hearing from you again, especially Otto. You cannot imagine the surprise, relief and joy I felt when I received your letters. Now that we know that at least our Otto, Hugo and Olga are alive and well, will give us more reason to work towards bringing you over to Canada if we don't return to Poland.

I need to mention that I have bought a farm fourteen miles from the village of Radisson and thirteen miles from the village of Hafford. It is a long way to travel but we will do our best to make a life for us here. I have two oxen and a horse, a cow, some pigs and some chickens. I also have a good shotgun that I love to go hunting with. There are plenty of ducks and wild chickens so we do not go hungry. There was a house and barn already built and some of the land had been cleared so at least I can plant a garden and a crop. We do have some neighbors that live within a mile or two of our place. Some of them are German and some are Ukrainian. We are all poor but I *think that now that the war is over, things will improve.*

I should also tell you that during the war, we were never out of work but no one had any money so our wages were very, very poor and we could not save enough to buy a real good farm closer to a town but, God willing, we will survive. Now that the war is over and the mail is reaching Poland again, we will be able to write more often.

I will close by saying I love you all and miss you greatly. I especially miss seeing Olga grow up. Please pass this letter on to her.

Your father,
Martin

After reading Martin's letter a second time, both Otto and Hugo sat quietly, each immersed in his own thoughts and sorting out the messages contained in their father's letter. Finally, Hugo spoke,

"It seems that Canada is not exactly a place where everyone, who goes there, is assured of easy ownership of good farm land, nor does it appear to be a place where anybody can get rich quickly. Adolph is now twenty-two years old and has been in Canada for five years but he still has not been able to start out on his own."

"I was thinking the same thing Hugo," replied Otto. "I think that it is wise to stay here in Poland, now that it has its own government, and we'll see how things go for us here. We still have cousins, aunts and uncles living near by and we both have work. Not that we are earning a whole lot of money, but at least we are able to put a roof over our heads and are able to eat three meals a day. Papa didn't say much about Teofil and how he was doing. I wonder what he is doing? He is eighteen years old now so he must be working somewhere as well. No, Hugo, I don't think Canada is the paradise that it is made out to be. By the way, have you seen any advertisements for possible emigration to Canada? I have not yet seen any myself. I know that I will wait a while before I try to go and I think that we should make every effort to help Olga with whatever she would like to do; I don't know if our aunt Emilie is really that interested in raising Olga, she has had a lot to deal with herself," continued Otto.

"I agree," answered Hugo. "By the way, Otto, when do you plan to give Clara the ring that you just bought?"

"I will carry it with me when I see her and if the right moment presents itself, I will give it to her but first I have to ask Gustav and Ida if they will give their permission. We still have time today to go to see Olga and show her the letter, okay?"

A whole week went by before Otto finally gathered enough courage to march over to Ida and Gustav's place to seek their approval on asking for Clara's hand in marriage. He knew that Clara and her sisters would usually be found cleaning house, baking and ironing clothes on Saturdays. Otto thought that perhaps they would be too busy to see him arrive and he would be able to catch Ida and Gustav in the garden or somewhere outside of the house. He sharpened his straight razor on the leather strop, removed the shaving brush from its leather pouch and removed the cup of shaving cream that he stored in a cupboard holding the wash basin. He thought that for this duty, he would definitely have to look his best. Next, he went to the kitchen stove lifted the hot kettle of water from it and poured a generous measure into the wash basin. Taking a face cloth, he soaked it in the hot water and then placed the steaming hot cloth on his face. He kept the cloth on his face until the cloth felt cool. Then taking the shaving brush, dipped it into the hot water and then swirled it around inside the shaving cream mug. With an adequate supply of creamy foam, he applied it to his face using a circular motion. When the whiskers were sufficiently soft and warm, he began the careful task of shaving with his straight razor. He had carried out this act of shaving numerous times before so his only real concern was that he would not do any damage to his handlebar moustache of which he was very proud and which had become part of his persona years before. After shaving the whiskers and after removing the excess shaving cream, he examined the results and was pleased that he had not even nicked himself. Through the course of shaving, his moustache had lost its shape, so next came the task of trimming and waxing. With the aid of a pair of scissors he clipped some strands of whiskers shorter and evened out the length of beard on the handle bar. When he was satisfied that the ends were of the same length he rubbed some bees wax between thumb and finger of his right hand, looked in the mirror and began twisting the wax into the ends of the moustache. It took a few minutes to complete the task but the final results produced a moustache that started slightly below his nostrils and ended well short of covering his top lip. The ends reached half way between his nostril and the edge of his face. The waxed curls rose in graceful semi circles level with the bottom of each nostril. It was a piece of art. How could Gustav and Ida refuse a face like that! But Otto, not taking any chances of not yet garnering enough courage to ask, helped himself to a generous gulp of schnapps that he and Hugo, since associating with the Jungs, always kept on hand.

His mission turned out well. He did find Ida and Gustav together in their yard and upon seeing Otto dressed up and looking his best on a Saturday afternoon, they suspected accurately the reason for his visit. Ida and Gustav had a few questions for Otto which he had anticipated and prepared for. When do you expect the date for the wedding to be? Where do you plan to live? Do you make enough money to support a wife and family? In what church do you expect to be married? How many guests do you plan to invite? Finally, Gustav reached out, shook Otto's hand smiled and said,

"Yes, Otto, you have our permission."

Now that he had cleared that hurdle, he was faced with the dilemma of when and how to propose to Clara. Oswald and his wife Clara, were planning on a trip to Lodz to visit her parents and her brother Alphons, and after a few timely hints dropped by Otto, Oswald invited Otto and Clara to accompany them on this visit. The plan was to catch the early morning train, stay the night and return the following day.

Although Lodz was basically an industrial city comprised mainly of textile mills, it did show off some nicely groomed parks and walk ways. Piotrowska Avenue, which was Lodz's showcase street, stretching for several miles, was lined with shops, theaters, restaurants, apartments and government buildings. The railroad station lay only a block from Piotrowska Avenue and the Laengers lived within walking distance of the station.

Prior to knocking on Robert and Maria Laenger's door, the two couples spent the morning walking along Piotrowska Avenue and enjoying all the new items displayed in the shops and stores. Clara and Clara even spent some time trying on the latest dress and hat fashions. Following a lunch consisting of tea and crepes topped with strawberry jam, they made their way to the home of Oswald's in-laws.

Richard and Maria had been expecting them and welcomed their daughter, her husband Oswald and their friends with open arms. The afternoon was spent relating news about family members in Poland and now that the mail from overseas was getting through, from abroad as well. The men drifted off into conversation relating to making good sausage, work, and the usual topic, politics. Maria had prepared for an early supper so after the meal, Otto and Clara announced that they would like to go for walk before darkness fell. Alphons suggested a pathway that led to a small park. Alphons mentioned that the park was usually busy with people on Saturdays, as there was a good playground for the children and many new benches lined the path which surrounded a small pond.

Otto and Clara had no difficulty finding the park and upon entering, they automatically linked arms and continued their walk. As they strolled past an ice cream stand, Otto suggested that they stop and enjoy a dish of ice cream. They sat down on a park bench overlooking the pond and enjoyed the treat.

Otto checked to make certain that he had not lost the little pouch which housed the ring because he thought,

"Now is as good a time as any to ask Clara to marry me."

They finished their treat, returned the empty dishes and returned to the park bench to observe the ducks and geese in the pond. Otto fidgeted and nervously reached into his side pocket and retrieved the pouch. He turned to Clara, reached out and took both her hands in his. Clara said nothing but her big blue eyes opened wider and wider as she awaited the question that she surely thought was coming. Clara had been waiting for this moment for some time and she knew what her response would be.

Otto simply said, "Clara, will you be my wife?"

At the same time, he removed the diamond that he had been carrying with him for a few weeks, and began putting it on her ring finger. Clara felt a few tears trickle down her cheeks and replied,

"Yes, Otto, I want to be your wife."

CHAPTER 21

Autumn, following the completion of the harvest is always a good time for a wedding and for Ida and Gustav, hosting and planning the wedding for their eldest daughter, would be a special event. Plans for the occasion were started soon after the couple announced their engagement. The wedding would take place the first week in October of 1919.

The first item on the list to contend with for Clara and Otto, was to decide where they were going to live. Gustav, who owned several plots of land on which houses were already built, offered one possibility. Another possibility would be to move in with Otto's brother, Hugo, onto the Flath property. The third possibility would be to leave Gajkowice and rent a flat in Piotrkow where Otto worked. After holding court with Ida and Gustav and then with Hugo, it was decided that Hugo would remain in the Flath house and Otto and Clara would take up residence in one of Gustav's places in the Gajkowice community. Otto would take with him from the Flath home, only that which he had accumulated since his return from Russia.

Gajkowice was a small village bordering on the western side of Moszczenica. The properties all fronted onto a narrow dirt road and most measured not more than five acres, stretching like a long narrow ribbon behind the house and barn yard. Most of the houses were small, containing perhaps three rooms at most and were built either of plastered logs with a thatched roof or were built using cut lumber nailed on vertical support posts covered by hand split wood shakes. The house that was available to Clara and Otto was a wood frame house and was covered by wood shakes. The rest of the property consisted of a cow shed, a pig barn and a poultry shelter. A fence had been built around the yard and continued further on to contain the pastured animals. The property had been leased to the Fisker family but became available because the family had decided to move to Lodz where Mr. Fisker had found steady employment. The property had been vacant for some time which, upon first inspection, did not present itself very well, but with some work and the help of family, it would become home to Clara and Otto.

While Otto was concerned with getting the house ready, Ida, Clara and Olga were more concerned with organizing the wedding. Dresses had to be sewn, food had to be prepared, arrangements with the pastor had to be made, musicians had to be enlisted, the guest list had to be finalized and invitations had to be extended. A few trips to Piotrkow would be necessary to arrange for photographs, to purchase a wedding band for Otto, to shop for ear rings to grace Clara's pierced ear lobes, to buy decorations for the house . . . . the list seemed endless.

Preparations for the October 17 event, continued throughout the summer and into the final month. It had been a very busy summer and fall for the Jungs, as well as for Otto and Hugo. Ida, Clara and Olga along with the help of young Bertha and Wanda, were able to sew new dresses for all of them and had time to sew Gustav, Max and Louie new white shirts. Olga had gone to Piotrkow with Clara and there they chose a plain gold band for Otto, bought Clara a pair of plain gold hoop ear rings, new white shoes, white elbow length gloves and a gold chain. Ida had arranged for a photographer from Moszczenica to come to the Jung's home for the formal wedding photograph. Otto and Clara, with the help of Oswald and his Clara, had taken Gustav's team of horses and wagon to Piotrkow and brought back a bed, a table with four chairs, a kitchen stove, some pots and pans and a coal oil lamp . . . . all paid for by Gustav and Ida as part of Clara's dowry. In addition to the furniture, they would receive two pigs and a horse.

Not all of the planning and duties that was required to put on the wedding, was left to the women folk of the family; the menfolk had their obligations to fulfill in ensuring that the wedding was a success as well. The harvest was good and there was ample wheat for grinding, which would be baked into the wedding loaf, the kuchen and the poppy seed rolls. Gustav's bees also supplied the family with honey that would be used in combination with the poppy seeds in the baking of poppy seed rolls. The vegetable garden had produced bushels of potatoes, cabbage, carrots, beets and poppies; all of which would become part of the wedding feast. In readiness for the celebration, Gustav, Oswald, Max and Otto had butchered a pig and had readied smoked ham, bacon and sausage. The men had swept out the threshing shed, cleaned up the manure from the yard and cleaned and polished the wagon which would be the vehicle used to chauffeur the bride and groom. Extra seating had been brought in, in anticipation of the large number of guests that would be attending.

A few days prior to the wedding, the guest list was reviewed. Not all that had been invited had responded but it was common that even if there was no confirmation given, many would appear. Several members of the Laenger family would be attending. All of Clara's brothers and sisters, several of her neighborhood girl friends, several of Gustav and Ida's friends, neighbors and business associates would be attending as well. Otto's list included his brother Hugo, sister Olga, two of his uncles and all of their families. In all, the Jungs were prepared to host more than sixty guests.

Several guests who lived some distance away from Gajkowice arrived a few days prior to the wedding. Otto's father had four brothers and two of them had left for U.S.A. before the war but two had remained in Poland. Otto's uncle, Rudolf and his wife Emilie and children along with Olga, whom they were raising since Paulina's death, arrived from Pabianice. Robert and Alphons Laenger also arrived early from Piotrkow. Ida and Gustav had sufficient help during the days leading up to the wedding.

On the eve of the wedding, the men from both the Jung and the Flath families gathered at Hugo and Otto's place while the women were left to prepare the bride at the Jung's home. Gustav and Oswald, as usual brought with them an arm load of kielbasa sausage and homemade bread. Otto's uncle Rudolf had also brought a supply of his favorite beverage. The toasts to Otto began early in the afternoon and did not stop until the early hours of the day of the wedding. Otto though, found his bed early and had several hours of sleep. The remainder of the men found a comfortable corner in which to lay down and sleep as well.

The women had several duties to perform on the eve of the wedding and they were kept busy until late in the evening. One very important task undertaken was that of baking the wedding loaf of bread. Tradition specified, that the outcome of the baked bread would be a harbinger for the future success or failure of the marriage. Every detail and every precaution was taken to ensure that the braided loaf would rise and bake uniformly. The ingredients of wheat, flour, eggs, butter, salt and yeast were carefully measured. The dough which was kneaded by Ida and no one else, was left to rise, then kneaded again and left to rise once again, before it was braided into a long loaf. Care was taken to ensure that the loaf would not fall or crack because if either happened, the marriage would surely be in trouble. While the bread was prepared for baking, the sisters of the bride were busy creating a tiara for Clara. Stems of dried flowers were tied together to form the tiara, then bits of jewelry, flowers and various ornamental items were placed on it. When the girls were satisfied with their creation, they tried it on Clara to make sure that it would fit and would be sturdy enough to keep its contents intact; if any part should fall from it, bad luck would follow but if it held together, the marriage would last a long time. Clara was not permitted to help construct the tiara, nor was she allowed to help create the bouquet of flowers that she would carry with her on her wedding day. Her role was to sit back and enjoy the activities around her.

On the morning of October 17, 1919, Gustav made his way home, had breakfast, went out to the barnyard to prepare the team of horses and wagon which would transport Ida, Clara and Olga to the church. Ida and a host of other females fussed and prepared for the reception and meal which was to follow the wedding ceremony.

Sister Olga and sister-in-law Clara were in charge of doing Clara's hair and dressing her in her wedding gown.

The day had brought blue skies and warm sun. The braided bread browned nicely, kept its shape and was free of cracks . . . . all good omens. Everything was unfolding as it should, so the women and young girls joyfully and happily carried out their duties, while Clara enjoyed every bit of pampering while it was available because following the wedding, there would be very little more of that to come. Olga and Clara washed and curled her hair, then while waiting for Clara's hair to dry, they laid out all the clothing and jewelry that they and Clara would wear. Meanwhile in the kitchen, Ida along with other women who had come over to lend their assistance, were busy setting tables, peeling vegetables, cooking cabbage rolls and attending to, what seemed a hundred other tasks, in order to be ready for the afternoon.

At one o'clock Gustav opened the door and announced that the transportation to the church was ready to leave. He then went back to the wagon and waited for the bridal party to appear. Within a minute, the door opened to reveal Clara being held by each arm and led toward the wagon by her bridesmaids. Clara, symbolically resisting, and the bridesmaids symbolically dragging her to the altar. Following some giggling and coaxing, Clara stepped onto the wagon and took her place on the seat which had been added to the wagon especially for this occasion.

"You look lovely," said Gustav. "It is going to be a very beautiful wedding."

"Thank you, Papa, for everything," replied Clara, "I am a little frightened with the prospect of marriage but I know all will be well, once it is done."

Otto and his entourage would make certain that they would not appear at the church before the bride. His morning was spent in much the same manner as Clara's. He had bought a brand new formal jacket . . . . black, single breasted with a continuous narrow collar and lapel that narrowed down to a single button just above his trousers top but would show the cummerbund that he would be wearing. He also had bought a new pair of black wool slacks, a white shirt, a matching black vest and silver chain that linked his silver pocket watch in the right hand pocket to the button hole on the left side of the vest. His groomsmen were similarly attired.

By one o'clock and after partaking in a light lunch, he was ready to go to the altar. Several acquaintances from the neighborhood had arrived, some carrying an assortment of musical instruments, who would accompany the groom, on foot, to the church. Before the group of men had even reached the road that led to the church, their music and singing began. Some called out loud that Otto was going to be married, while others cheered, clapped and laughed. The procession moved quickly down the road and occasionally others who were going to attend the service, joined in the parade. The light hearted mood of the group suddenly became serious when they reached the door of the church. The wedding service, like every other service in church, was a serious matter, not to be taken lightly. Hymns were sung, prayers were given, a short sermon was included as well as holy communion. Following the exchange of vows and rings, the signing of the marriage certificate, and accepting well wishes at the receiving line, the whole group began to wend its way to the Jung's residence. This time though, Otto would ride on the wagon with his new bride and once again the music, the singing, the chatter and the throwing of rice accompanied the party along the three mile stretch leading to the reception.

Otto was first to step down from the wagon, gracefully lifted Clara and set her gently on the ground. The photographer was ready and waiting to take the formal wedding photograph and following that, with all the formalities complete, the guests began to visit and drink while waiting for the wedding meal to begin.

The bridal party along with Clara's parents were served first. Next to be served were the men, then the women and finally the young children. When all had had their fill of roast goose, roast pork, sliced ham, mashed potatoes with gravy, cooked cabbage and turnips, cabbage rolls and plum dumplings, it was time for the bride to break the braided wedding bread. As Clara broke off a small piece of the loaf, she fed Otto first, and then broke the loaf into bite size pieces. The guests, led by her father Gustav, would pass the table, take a piece of the loaf, wish the couple good fortune and some would even give Clara a kiss on her cheek and deposit a coin in a small basket. Everyone from oldest to the youngest shared in the loaf. Toasts were made and before the dinner had ended, three hours had passed.

The music started up again and the guests danced, sang and drank late into the night. Clara and Otto were chivaried all the way to their new home, but upon arriving at their home, the merry makers left. Otto then picked up Clara in his arms and carried her across the threshold. Clara Jung was now Clara Flath.

CHAPTER 22

Clara and Otto settled down quickly into a routine. Otto was kept busy with work at the loom, dabbling at agriculture and making sausage whenever he had the opportunity. The busy daily activity had the necessary therapeutic effect and many days would pass without him being reminded of his tenure in Russia.

Clara was content in her new role as wife and housekeeper. Her home was not large but it was comfortable. Her parents and all of her siblings lived near by, within walking distance to one another. Otto had been welcomed openly by all the Jungs and became one of the family. Economically, Otto and Clara were not wealthy, nor would they ever have the opportunity to become wealthy, given the work that Otto was engaged in and the level of wage he received for his labors. Otto too, was not eager to venture too far away from the security of his close association with the Jungs and with the job that he had. Socially, Clara and Otto often exchanged visitations with other family members, especially with Oswald and his wife Clara. Sundays saw Clara and Otto in church and quite often, following the service, the whole Jung clan gathered at Ida and Gustav's place, where they would partake in a big meal and trade stories of events that they experienced during the previous week. Talk often centered on domestic activities relating to the growing of crops, raising livestock, grinding grain and other farm activities. Gustav, of course, would elaborate on his expertise as a bee keeper, and what economic benefits could possibly be derived from the excess production of honey.

For the time being, the political scene had stabilized with Poland achieving independence and controlling its own affairs. Several of the boundaries between Poland, Russia, the Ukraine and Germany had not been finalized and sporadic local conflict arose but none of that had any impact on the area surrounding Lodz.

The cultural community in Lodz and Piotkow had reawakened and now offered a variety of entertainment.

Even though many members of the Flath family and some of the Jung family had left Poland for what they thought were 'greener pastures', Gustav and Ida, the Laenger family, Otto and Clara, as well as Hugo Flath, decided that they would remain where they were and should conditions change, they would then reconsider. They realized that, unlike twenty years previously, when they felt comfortable with their surroundings and felt to be a contributing part of society, now with the changing attitude towards German Protestants in Poland, they could sense that perhaps their security and well being could become compromised.

The news coming from Canada came mainly via Martin Flath's pen and since Martin was not a prolific correspondent, the letters received by Otto and Hugo were rare; but in those letters that did arrive, Martin continued to describe the pioneer life in Saskatchewan as difficult and at best, bordering on depressing. Martin explained that unless you had access to large mechanized equipment you were relegated to a subsistence level of farming, which he stated he had found himself in. He wrote that he, Adolph and Teofil would often have to find work away from their farm to acquire some cash. He stated that there were new branch railroads being constructed and new elevators were being built along these new rail lines and there, work could be found. The work was hard and the pay was marginal but was better than nothing. He stated that those who could afford to purchase a steam engine and threshing machine could do well because the price of grain was good; but, his own farmable acreage was small and he could not see himself working with a steam engine. He promised Otto and Hugo that he would keep working towards bringing young Olga to Canada and he was hoping that Otto, Clara and Hugo would be able to immigrate as well. After reading their father's letters, Otto and Hugo were more convinced than ever, that the pioneer life was not for them and that they would not leave unless they absolutely had to.

On a blustery cold March night, as Otto and Clara lay snuggled in their bed, Clara announced that she was pregnant and that they would have a baby in late fall. The baby arrived on October 28, 1920. It was a baby boy and they named him Oscar. Having a new baby in the household brought a new found joy to both Clara and Otto as well as the rest of the Jung clan. Clara and Otto found that since Oscar's arrival they were entertaining more visitors in their home and were going out less often. They were happy with the challenge of rearing a youngster and were looking forward to adding to the family. Three years later on April 8, 1923, another boy arrived and they named him Eugene. The addition of another mouth to feed did not actually place any additional burden on Otto's ability to support the family as he was able to work as many hours as he pleased. The textile mills in and around Lodz were going full steam to meet the demand for cloth.

Even though there was plenty of work, the harvests good and the new Polish constitution guaranteed minorities living in the new country of Poland their equal rights, several events occurred that signaled a change in the relationship between German Protestants and Polish Catholics. Despite relations between Germans and Poles in Lodz, Piotrkow and Moszczenica, having been positive for many years, there now existed an inherent suspicion and distrust of each other. Generally, Germans married Germans, Poles married Poles, Jews married Jews, and rarely would a German Protestant marry a Polish Catholic; but a Jew marrying either a German or a Pole was a very rare occurrence. The Poles had for many years been governed by foreign governments and now that the Poles were making the laws, many of the citizenry viewed the new situation as an opportunity to perhaps regain what they felt they were entitled to. Consequently negative sermons from the church pulpits and hostile articles directed at German speaking Protestants, written in newspapers, began circulating. The change in attitude toward the Germans in Gajkovice was not sudden and not as noticeable as it was in the northern city of Danzig where open hostilities and attacks were being carried out. The Jungs and other of their German friends concluded that it was a passing phase in the evolution of an establishing country and given a few years, relations would return to where they had been previous to 1914. However, as the months wore on, more blatantly hateful sermons were being preached and more hateful articles were being released. The campaign to demonize the German citizenry had its desired effect and eventually reached the Jung clan in Gajkowice as well.

The family talked. Otto talked about a boyhood friend whom he had associated with for years, looked the other way when he last met him on the street. Oswald, who had Polish customers for years, found that fewer and fewer were asking him to make their sausage. Gustav who ground grain and sold honey to many Polish families, found that fewer were knocking on his door for his services. Clara noted that some of the neighborhood children began calling Oscar names and sometimes threatened him. The school had changed so that only the Polish language could be taught at school and they heard that several German teachers were no longer allowed to teach German and some were replaced by Polish speaking teachers. They talked about how they couldn't understand how attitudes could change so quickly. They began to realize that the reasons for emigration from Poland were quickly changing and that their decision to stay would probably have to be reevaluated. They realized that when Martin Flath left with two of his sons, it was because of the hopes of a better economic life; now, it would be for a better social and political life. Their hopes, that time would heal the hatred and suspicion directed toward them, did not happen; but rather, the malicious preaching, the harassment of children, the biases shown by the authorities and the negative propaganda broadcast in newspapers and radio all increased in scope, making the day to day living not only uncomfortable but often dangerous.

Otto and Clara, Hugo, sister Olga and her guardians Rudolf and Emilie Flath, and Rudolf's brother Alfred, also met to discuss the deteriorating conditions and the possibility of leaving Poland before things became much worse. Rudolf informed the group that he and his family would sell everything as soon as possible and emigrate to whatever country was accepting immigrants. Alfred voiced the same decision. However, Otto and Hugo, knowing the situation in Canada, stated that they would wait and see.

In 1924, Rudolf Flath and his family, purchased a ticket for seventeen year old Olga to emigrate to Canada and reunite with her father Martin and brothers Adolph and Teofil. Rudolf was able to get permission to immigrate to Brazil and bought passage to Porto Alegre, Brazil. Alfred Flath went to the U.S.A. through Ellis Island, New York.

Gustav Jung, as usual, was found sitting at the head of the table and, as usual, the rest of the Jung clan had gathered for Sunday dinner. Oswald, Clara and their young son Arnold were present. Clara, her husband Otto and their two boys Oscar and Eugene were present. Nineteen year old Bertha was present, as was sixteen year old Wanda. The only member of the immediate family absent was twenty-three year old Olga.

Wanda piped up, "Where is Olga today . . . . she wasn't in church either?"

"I know where she is," replied Bertha, "she is with her boy friend Wiktor; she told me that they were going to Piotrkow for a few hours and that they should be returning later this afternoon."

This announcement did not come as a surprise to the others gathered as Wiktor and Olga had been friends for a long time.

"I don't know why they just don't get married . . . . they have been going together for more than two years," replied Louie.

No response came from Ida or Gustav . . . . everyone knew the reason why Wiktor and Olga had not yet announced their engagement or their intention to get married. Everyone was aware that a girl at age twenty-three was considered a spinster and surely there must be something amiss if she had not yet married. There had been some remarks directed toward Olga regarding her reluctance to get married but it was understandable, because Wiktor had joined the newly formed Polish army and had intermittently been away assisting in the establishment of the borders of Poland. Besides he was a Polish Catholic and Olga was a German Protestant. They would, as a married couple, find it difficult to be accepted into either community, especially now that there seemed to be a campaign to deliberately drive a wedge between Polish Catholics and German Protestants.

No one said anything for several moments and finally after tugging at his beard the whole while, Gustav philosophically spoke up,

"I am not a person who cares much for the Catholic church but I do have to admire those two. They just proved that once a good relationship is established, very few things can happen to break up that relationship. For example, I have many loyal customers at our mill who are not German. Many people who are renting land and houses from us are not German either. They still remain my friends and customers. Sure, some customers have gone elsewhere but we have all of our places full and have enough work to keep our mill grinding. We are still doing fine. One good thing is that the bees are neither Catholic or Protestant or Polish or German; they just keep on making honey. I am still hopeful that we will be able to get our citizenship papers here and then we will have the same rights as the Poles. As it is now, we are at the mercy of the government and have very little protection. We will see how things turn out."

No sooner had those words from Gustav been uttered, when Olga and Wiktor walked into the room, holding hands and with big smiles on their faces, announced simultaneously that they were engaged to be married. They hoped that everyone in the family would bless them and they hoped to get married in the following spring. Clara, who was not only Olga's older sister but also her best family friend, was the first to hand Eugene over to Otto and rush to give Olga a hug and offer her best wishes. The rest of the family followed Clara with Bertha and Wanda each demanding that she be chosen to be the bridesmaid.

Clara was once again pregnant when Wiktor and Olga were married and on May 27, in the year 1925, Clara and Otto became the proud parents of a baby daughter; they named her Lydia.

CHAPTER 23

"Ida, the time has come when we have to make a decision whether to leave Poland or not. It has been eight years since the war has ended and that we have been waiting for conditions to settle down. They have not, as you well know. We have seen family after family leaving Gajkowice so that now there are only a very few of our friends and neighbors left. Our church congregation is getting smaller all the time. It is obvious that the government has no interest in protecting the German people in Poland so we can be abused by neighbors, police and the law courts. We have no security here. I am going to call all of our family together and together, we will decide what we should do. Ida, it has to be done," affirmed Gustav.

Three weeks later, the whole Jung clan gathered as usual at Gustav's and Ida's home where the life changing decision would be made. Richard, Ida's brother and his son Alphons, had come from Lodz, Otto and Clara, Oswald and his Clara, Max and Louis, Olga and her husband Wiktor, Bertha and Wanda, were all in attendance. Everyone had known for some time that sooner or later a decision would have to be made and they came ready to speak their personal thoughts, telling of their experiences and conclusions that they were leaning toward. This whole matter was not one that was being taken lightly by anyone . . . . each one had been thinking about it for, not only weeks, but for years already. They were fully aware that the outcome of this meeting might scatter the members of the family like chaff in the wind and once their lives would be tossed into the air, there would be no predicting where the individuals would all end up. They were fully aware that the toil of their fathers and mothers and their ancestors and the results of that toil were in jeopardy. The decision to be made was a choice between attempting, as best they could, to preserve what they had, or to salvage what they could and with that, whatever it was, to leave and start all over again in the new world . . . . a monumental decision indeed.

Even though the sun shone brightly on the day of the gathering, the mood inside the Jung's home was not congruent with the bright sunshine outside. From oldest to youngest, they sat in silence and listened to the patriarch as he outlined their options and offered his opinions. As he spoke, those who had been born in that house and had spent their youth together, recalling the laughter, the joys, the tears, the scoldings and the work, were overcome with emotion and tears flowed from their eyes and down the cheeks of even the toughest men; their minds cluttered with the words spoken by Gustav, competing with their innermost images that his words were bringing forth.

"How could this be happening?" Reflected Bertha. "This is not supposed to be! What is papa asking me to do? Is he asking me to give up my Humel and go away somewhere? I know he will not leave Lodz to go to Canada and I know that I cannot leave without him. I have to talk the others into staying here in Poland!"

Otto and Clara had made up their minds. Their decision came easier for them than for many of the others. When they had discussed their future, they reasoned that with Martin, Adolph, Teofil and Olga already in Canada, they had a place to go to in Canada. In addition, just recently a thief had entered their yard, loaded up two pigs in broad daylight, was reported and caught, but the thief was not charged or convicted by the authorities, and not only that, the thief kept the pigs!

The members of the family talked for several hours and by evening, it was decided that those who were in favor of emigrating would put their properties up for sale immediately and that the application for emigration should be made as soon as the properties were disposed of. The consensus was that as many as possible would emigrate to the same location. It was to be done . . . . there would be no looking back now . . . . only ahead.

Gustav, Otto, Oswald and Wiktor paid a visit to the emigration office in Piotrkow and met with an immigration agent representing Canada and completed the required application for immigration. The immigration agent would, for a fee, arrange all the paper work; he would fill out the application forms, submit them to the Canadian Consul in Lodz and he would arrange for all connecting train and ship tickets from Piotrkow to their various destinations. The date of departure would depend on the disposal of the property. Otto was informed that the *Lutheran Immigration Board* in Winnipeg, Manitoba would be their sponsors but their train ticket would take them to their destination . . . . Hafford, Saskatchewan, Canada! They were told that all the paperwork would be ready and waiting for them within a few months and that when they were ready to go, it would be necessary to make an additional trip to the emigration office in Piotrkow to secure berths on the immigration ship. They were also told that every effort would be made to have them travel together but there was no guarantee, other than that the immediate family would definitely travel as a unit. The names, ages, relationships and occupation of each passenger was required at the time of application.

Otto discussed their plans to go to Canada at length with his brother Hugo, trying to persuade Hugo to go as well, but Otto soon discovered that Hugo had other plans. He informed Otto that he had met a woman and that he was determined to make her his bride. When asked for her name, Hugo replied, "Elsie Wahl."

Hugo would be the last of Martin Flath's immediate family left to reside in Poland.

For many of Gustav and Ida's family, the decision whether to emigrate or not was very difficult. In the end, all of their children and their spouses except for the two youngest members, Bertha and Wanda, who, after shedding many tears and agonizing over the decision, decided that life on the frozen expanse of Saskatchewan would not offer much opportunity for single girls. They decided to move to Lodz and move in with their uncle Richard. Richard had decided that he and his son Alphons would remain in Lodz. After all, he reasoned, Lodz was in the midst of an economic boom. People from all over the countryside were pouring into Lodz where there was ample work and opportunity for an education and employment in many and varied industries.

Once everyone had gotten over the emotional hurdle of leaving behind property, friends, acquaintances and keepsakes, the business of disposing of everything and converting the proceeds into cash, the thought of moving to a new country excited them and they were anxious and ready to do all that was necessary and as quickly as possible.

The buyers that came to place their offers to purchase the properties, livestock, machinery and household items that came up for sale, knew that the sellers were anxious to leave and their offers to purchase were only a fraction of what the properties were worth. However, Gustav thought that the properties in Canada were not very expensive either, so he accepted the offers to the highest bidders, for cash.

By February of 1927, everything of monetary value had been disposed of, and that which did not sell, was passed on to neighbors and other acquaintances. Gustav and all others affected made the return trip to Piotrkow to purchase tickets and obtain their berths on the ships. They were going to Canada.

Gustav, Ida and all others, except Otto and Clara, were booked with the *Baltic American* steamship line; the ship's name was the *S.S.Lithuania* which would be leaving from the port of Danzig on April 11, 1927, and their destination was Halifax, Nova Scotia. The intended docking date was April 23, 1927. Otto, Clara and their children were booked with the *Canadian Pacific* steamship line; the ship's name was the *Minnedosa* which would be leaving from the port of Liverpool, England on April 29, 1927, and was scheduled to arrive at the port of Quebec on May 6, 1927. They too, would travel by train to Danzig and from there, sail to Liverpool, England where they would board the *Minnedosa* and then on to Quebec City in Canada. Once there, they would be held in quarantine for a couple of days, then board the train for the week long train trip across a wide expanse of Canada.

The prospect of never seeing loved ones again is never met with any joy. Two weeks prior to their departure the Jung clan was given a memorable farewell party by the church congregation in Jarosty, then again by the community of Gajkowice. There were no farewell gifts, other than the gift of fond memory speeches and heartfelt parting praise for all that they had done for the church and for the community. Following the last person to speak on behalf of the community, Gustav stood before the well wishers and gave his farewell speech. Later he confided in Ida that his farewell speech was the most difficult thing that he had ever faced.

"Clara," Otto whispered as he and Clara, lay that night in their bed that they had shared for eight years, "this is our last night here in this house. Tomorrow, will be the start of a new life for us and I am worried about what the future has in store. This is going to be the third time in my life that I have faced major life changing events. First, it was staying in Russia when I didn't have to, then it was marrying you and living here, and now it is leaving everything behind and going to Canada. Clara, I am thirty-seven years old, married, have three children and one on the way and here I am, with barely enough money to pay for our passage to Canada and if, and when, we arrive, we don't have any place to live, nor do I have a job waiting for me. We are having to depend on my father to help us out and, God knows, he has enough trouble looking after himself and Olga and with all of us there, it will only add to his problems."

Clara responded, "Otto, don't worry, God will help us. We have made the right decision; we could not stay here much longer anyway. At least, we are leaving together and have someone at the other end waiting for us. I think too, that going to your father's place rather than going with mama and papa was the right decision. They don't even know the people that are going to meet them. What is the name of the place? . . . . Lintlaw, Saskatchewan . . . . that's it. My worst fears are the long ship voyage and the long train ride. I have no idea even where it is that we are going to and to what kind of land we are going. All that I hear is that there are thousands of miles of bush, full of Indians. I worry about Oscar, Eugene and Lydia catching a disease on the crowded immigrant ship and the train. I hope that I don't get too sick on the ship. You know how sick I get when I am pregnant. I know that I would like to be closer to mama and papa and my sister and maybe, after we get to Canada, we will be able to move close to one another. Hopefully, we will be able to visit back and forth. I hear that many people in Canada now have automobiles that can travel great distances quite quickly. Maybe we will be able to buy one and then we will be able to go and visit. Otto, let's get some sleep now because tomorrow is going to a long day. After tomorrow, the only family left here in Gajkowice will be your brother Hugo; mama and the rest left for Danzig ten days ago, and Bertha and Wanda are living in Lodz already."

"Clara, everything we now own is in those two suitcases sitting by the door. We could not take anything else with us but our blankets. You have your hands full with the children so all the lifting and carrying is up to me. Oscar and Eugene will help carry some small ruck sacks but that is it. I have the tickets and other papers folded carefully and are in my coat pocket already so tomorrow morning we take the tram to Lodz and from there we will travel by train to Danzig which will take a day. There we will board the ship that will take us to Liverpool, England, and that is where we will find the ship *Minnedosa* which leaves for Quebec, Canada on April 29. We have enough money to pay for food along the way and we will only have to stay overnight in Liverpool, if all goes well. Don't worry Clara, I have had lots of experience traveling by train so I am not afraid: we will get by."

The journey from Gajkowice, Poland to Hafford, Saskatchewan would take more than two weeks. The first leg of the journey from Gajkowice to Danzig did not present any problems. The children behaved themselves and the time passed quickly. The journey by boat from Danzig to Liverpool proved to be much more strenuous. The boat was not equipped to carry families but because of the large number of families emigrating from Poland, there were many more families crowded onto the boat than the original plans had outlined. The three day sail did not agree with Clara. The first part of the trip which took them across the calm waters of the Baltic Sea through the narrow channel that separated Denmark from Sweden was enjoyed by Clara . . . . the seas were calm. However, when the boat entered the large swells of water that characterize the North Sea, Clara began to feel ill and suffered from sea sickness the rest of the way to Liverpool. Fortunately, neither Otto nor the children were affected. Upon reaching Liverpool and setting foot on solid ground, Clara's stomach returned to normal and she was able to eat again.

"Otto," she said, "I don't know if I will be able to survive the seven day ocean voyage to Quebec. I nearly died just coming here. Not only was my stomach upset, but numerous others were in the same shape as I, and the smell of vomit, urine and human excrement, created because of the lack of bathrooms, nearly killed me. If this is what I have to look forward to, for the next seven days, I think I am going to die."

Holding Clara's hand and confronting her, Otto replied, "Clara, we can only hope that the sea going to Quebec won't be as rough as it was going around Scotland. Also, I am going to find some perfume which may help with the odor. I don't think that our quarters will be much more comfortable on the *Minnedosa* because it is an immigration ship which means that we have to share bathroom and cooking facilities with the other passengers."

"I know," chimed in Clara, "and what even makes things worse is that many of the people on the ship come from much poorer areas than us and their hygiene, to be frank, is terrible. Otto, I tell you, I am not looking forward to the coming days. I just hope that no epidemic breaks out, as has happened on many of the immigration ships. In these crowded conditions with very little fresh air and unsanitary conditions, anything can happen."

Fortunately, the two days in Liverpool were enough for Clara to regain most of her strength and she had gotten over the sea sickness.

On the morning of the sailing date, the passengers were directed to a large warehouse where each passenger would be processed prior to boarding. Passenger lists were checked, identification papers were scrutinized and berths were assigned. Following the initial screening, the passengers were given a medical check and were required to answer health and education questions. Their luggage and blankets would be taken with them and stored in the small space between the bunk beds. They were told that food would be supplied but that the passengers would be responsible for their own house keeping, such as making of the beds and keeping the area around their space clean. Night pots and vomit pots would be provided.

While waiting for their turn to be processed, it became obvious that some of the passengers could neither read nor write, so Otto being able to read and write several languages, soon found himself helping others who were having difficulty filling out forms and answering questions, which were in many cases foreign to them. Most of the emigrants were in very similar positions as Otto and Clara. Most of the group in the room were from the Ukraine, Russia or Poland with a scattering of Norwegians, Dutch and Swedes. Curiously enough, the majority of the passengers were adult males who listed their occupations as 'farm laborers' and most of them listed Winnipeg, Manitoba as their destination. The destination was determined by the terminal point of the Canadian Pacific Railway's responsibility for transporting the immigrants. Separate arrangements would have to be made individually for the passengers final destination.

Clara's prediction came true; the five day crossing of the Atlantic, was pure hell once the ship steamed into the open Atlantic. The hope that the living conditions on the *Minnedosa* would be an improvement over the boat coming from Danzig to Liverpool, were soon dashed. This ship had been outfitted by the C.P.R. to carry some first class passengers, but more than forty percent were relegated to the steerage sections of the ship. Passengers in steerage were not permitted on the upper decks of the ship and were provided with a very small area where they could get some fresh air and exercise. The bunks were jammed close together and the mattresses on the bunks had been used by many other previous passengers.

"Fortunately," Clara thought, as she looked at their assigned beds, "our mattresses have been disinfected."

Passengers had their own blankets. Clara also thanked God, that since she was a mother with children, they were given a cubicle where at least they had some privacy. Most of the single passengers did not share in that luxury. All passengers slept in their day clothing . . . . no pajamas.

Clara knew the minute the ship hit the first swells of the Atlantic. She immediately began vomiting and her nauseous stomach plagued her until the ship reached the calmer waters of the St. Lawrence River. She didn't eat for three days and only could manage to drink tea and hot water. However, Otto was not affected by motion sickness and neither were the children. There were only a few other children on the ship, so Oscar, Eugene and Lydia were given plenty of attention and did not seem to mind the rough seas at all.

Once the ship entered the St. Lawrence and the rocking motion of the ship ceased, Clara again was quick to regain her strength and was able to enjoy the passing scenery along the river banks.

"What kind of a country is this Canada?" She asked. "We have been traveling all day and all I see is trees and hills. There are no people here. How big is this land anyway?"

"It looks a lot like Russia to me," said Otto. "The area around St. Petersburg is much the same but it must change somewhere because the letters that we have received and the information on the pamphlets speaks of flat land with hardly any trees . . . . much like it is in the Galicia. It must change somewhere but we are yet a long ways from Saskatchewan. We still have at least a week of travel left."

"Oh my God. I wish we were back in Poland," whispered Clara . . . . a thought that Clara would find resurfacing many times in the days and years ahead.

"Come Clara, let's go up on the deck and look at the passing scenery. It is a nice sunny day and the warm late afternoon sun and fresh air will make you feel better," replied Otto.

Bundling up Lydia and taking Oscar and Eugene by their hands, Otto and Clara walked up the narrow stairway and on to the crowded third class deck to watch the passing scene and to wait for the sun to set.

As it was on most ships carrying passengers to the new world, some of the passengers carried their precious musical instruments with them and upon seeing and hearing the music being played on the deck, Otto harkened back to his own memories of his connection with his flute. Merely thinking about the satisfaction he felt years ago while playing the flute, momentarily brought tears to his eyes.

"Is something wrong, Otto?" Asked Clara who had looked up and noticed Otto's tear filled eyes. "You look sad. Are you also thinking that coming here was a mistake? Are you afraid of what awaits us at the end of this journey? Are you worried that you will not be able to feed ourselves and our children? You know Otto, we have no home to go to now and you have no work to go to either. All we have is a bit of money and your father to meet us when we arrive. I don't know how we are all going to live together in the house that he and your sister Olga are living in. I just hope that we will be able to find a place of our own quickly. Otto, I wish that we would be going to live with my side of the family. They left for Canada on April 11 and were able to sail from Danzig to Halifax, wherever that is, and they should be in Saskatchewan by now; I really miss them

Otto, and I have never been far away from them ever before. I just hope that Lintlaw is not too far away from Hafford so that we will be able to visit back and forth with them."

Clara, with tears running down her face and her thoughts turning into spoken words, looked up at Otto once again and repeated, "Otto, are you thinking the same things that I am thinking right now?"

With the three children looking on in bewilderment, Otto gathered Clara into his arms and said, "Clara, Clara, yes, I share many of your worries about what we will find when we get to Hafford but I don't think that it was a mistake to leave Poland."

Not wanting to divulge the real reason for his momentary sadness, he went on, "I felt sad because of how sick you have been and how you have suffered on this journey. Clara, look, there are white whales following the ship . . . . Oscar, Eugene, Lydia . . . . look, look! Clara, it is fine . . . . listen to the music." And they did.

During the crossing, Otto had taken charge of looking after the children: he dressed Lydia, fed her, combed her hair, and he kept track of Oscar and Eugene's whereabouts as well. He brought tea and bread for Clara . . . . he placed wet cloths on Clara's forehead . . . . whenever he could, he would take the blankets on to the deck to air them out . . . . he picked up discarded objects from around their sleeping area . . . . and in the dim light of the evening, he would read from the bible and say the family prayers. Serving in the army for many years, had taught him that fresh air, clean water and general cleanliness was the best way to avoid dysentery, lice, boils and a host of other ailments that could occur under unclean and crowded conditions. He made it his mission to take his children daily on to the open deck for fresh air and to let them mingle with other children and passengers. While his children ran around, he would engage in conversations with fellow passengers and even some of the crew.

The majority of deck hands were from the British Isles and, as in Canada, spoke either English or French, but some were from central Europe and Otto became acquainted with a seasoned deck hand who spoke German. The deck hand told Otto that he had been sailing for twenty-five years and that he began working for the C.P.R. ship, the S.S. Minnedosa, since it had been refitted in 1925. Otto learned the Minnedosa originally was built to accommodate 1,200 third class passengers and 550 cabin passengers, but since the refitting, it now had 206 cabins, 550 tourist class and only 590 third class passengers. On this voyage, the third class passengers numbered closer to 500. Otto also was given a detailed description of what to expect once the ship entered the St. Lawrence River area. He was told that if there was on outbreak of cholera or some other epidemic, the ship was required to fly a blue or yellow flag as a warning to all, that the ship was infected. Formerly, the ship would continue to Grosse Isle, Quebec, an island in the middle of the St. Lawrence, 48 kilometers upstream from Quebec City. There the passengers would have been inspected and those infected would be housed in quarantine sheds until they either recovered or died. Those who had died at sea were dumped into the sea and the bodies of those that died while the ship was in the river, were dumped into a hold where, later, they would be pulled out with hooks and stacked on shore and then buried in unmarked graves on Grosse Isle. However, he was told that the Minnedosa would be boarded by a pilot and a physician at Pointe-au Pere, near Rimouski, Quebec. They would then sail on to Quebec City where their luggage would be disinfected . . . . hopefully, they would avoid Grosse Isle. Fortunately, there had not been an outbreak on this crossing and there would not be any need to place the passengers in the immigrant quarantine sheds on Grosse Isle, but that the passengers would go directly to the immigration processing halls and the sick would be treated at the new immigrant hospital in Quebec City. Upon hearing the good news, Otto picked up Lydia and ushered the boys down to their sleeping area and relayed the news to Clara.

CHAPTER 24

Something didn't feel right . . . . something had changed. During the transition from sleep to full awareness, Clara realized that things were different. As she lay, shaking the cobwebs from her brain, she began to understand what it was that was different. The constant vibration of the ship had ceased. The monotonous chugging of the steam engine was silent. There was no obvious movement of the ship and there was also an unusual increase of activity among the passengers. She poked Otto and said,

"Otto, I think we have arrived at Quebec City. The ship has stopped."

Waking quickly, Otto agreed with Clara's assessment and automatically began waking their children and getting them ready to leave.

"We won't have to make the bed today, Clara!"

Within minutes, an announcement, in French, then in English, came over the ship's intercom, confirming the ship's arrival at Quebec. The date was May 6, 1927.

A few minutes later, word came down to the passengers that an official would be boarding the vessel following breakfast and he would determine who would be permitted to go ashore and who would not. The passengers, following breakfast were to return to their sleeping area and wait for the inspector's decision. This same procedure had been conducted when Otto and Clara arrived at Liverpool eight days before. They ate breakfast, then checked their baggage and papers . . . . then they sat and waited. Within an hour, they were called to report to the physician who would examine them.

Otto and Clara picked up their bags, gathered their children, making certain that their faces were clean and made their way to the eating area which was being used as the screening room. The lineup ahead of them was long but the screening process seemed to be going quickly. They watched closely as each person was told to sit on a stool, take off their shoes and socks and remove their outer garment and hat. A recording clerk then recorded the person's name and waited for the inspecting doctor's diagnosis, which was then recorded.

"Look, Otto, look what is happening to some of the families," gasped Clara.

"What is going to happen to them? Look, Otto, that little boy was taken away from his parents and they are all crying and screaming. What is happening?"

"Clara, the doctors are checking for diseases such as cholera, chicken pox, small pox, diphtheria, influenza and other diseases. Many ships carrying people like us had been plagued with outbreaks and the government does not allow people suffering from these diseases into the country," explained Otto.

"As for what is going to happen to these families," continued Otto, "the ones who show no sign of illness can go ashore and wait for those who are sick, to get better. Did you forget? I was told that if a child was sick, one of the parents had to remain on board the ship with the child, and if the sick person did not recover from their sickness and died, that person who had accompanied the sick person would have to go into quarantine either on the ship or in the immigrant sheds, until such time as they were cleared."

"God, Otto, I pray that we will all be accepted," whispered Clara.

Fortunately, the majority of passengers on the Minnedosa passed inspection without incident. There had not been an outbreak of any communicable disease on the trip across the ocean. They would be spared the horror of quarantine, separation and isolation. By noon of May 6, 1927, Otto, Clara, Oscar, Eugene and Lydia Flath, crossed the gangplank and stepped onto terra firma . . . . then, to stand in front of the immigration official who would record their entry into Canada. The immigration office required each immigrant to complete information in twenty-seven categories beginning with: name, relationship, sex, age, place of birth, nationality, country of birth, race, literate in what language(s), who paid the passage, occupation, destination, contact relatives in Europe, criminal record, health, amount of money brought, destination and other sundry items.

Those passengers who had listed Winnipeg as their destination were assembled and led by an immigration attendant to the immigration hall where they would be able to wash, have a bath, wash some clothing, and get a meal. The Otto Flath family would also stay there the night, and then buy their food for their journey to Winnipeg. They would then board the train for Winnipeg, where a volunteer with the Lutheran Immigration Board would meet them and direct Otto, Clara and their children to their final destination.

The next morning, even though the low hanging dark clouds drizzled rain on the columns of immigrants as they made their way to the awaiting train, there was a joyous feeling of optimism among them. They had on the previous day, been accepted as new members of a country that held a great deal of promise for them. The reasons for their optimism varied with the immigrants, depending on their place of origin; but, for all of them there existed many common reasons for their mood.

Canada, the new world, promised each one of the newcomers, freedom of speech, freedom of religion, freedom from persecution due to race or color, ample economic opportunities with few taxes and a democratically elected parliament. The tensions between races, religion, and language which dominated the European peoples for centuries would not exist. Together, those who came before, combined with those that continued to arrive at Canadian shores would build and develop a united country and society based on the contributions of every unique cultural group that set foot on Canadian territory . . . . free of prejudice and discrimination . . . . so the brochures advertised!

Otto and Clara shared the same optimistic mood. Their first impressions of Canada were indeed positive . . . . the immigration officials were courteous and professional . . . . the volunteers that helped with their first night of lodging after disembarking were helpful and friendly . . . . the first meal served to them was well prepared and tasty . . . . the beds were clean and comfortable . . . . things looked promising.

"Maybe I was wrong," declared Clara, "maybe we will prosper in this new land."

In 1927, Quebec City was a charming city displaying a combination of old world charm and a new world infrastructure in the middle of a rugged, virgin forest. The walk from the docks to the C.P.R. train station led through the usual hodgepodge of shops and old hotels and then opened onto newly paved wide streets. The green steeply sloped roofs of the train station were mounted on a mixture of red and white bricks and the main entrance to the station majestically depicted thirty-five foot windows. The station looked impressive, especially with the huge Chateau Frontenac looming high above the station forming a picturesque background for the station.

"Not as impressive as the Moscow station in St. Petersburg," mused Otto, "but certainly, I was not expecting anything this well built and this modern."

The cluster of immigrants was ushered into the station and the guide seated the group, then on the group's behalf, inquired about the train that would take them to Winnipeg.

In anticipation of new immigrants arriving following WWI, the C.P.R. had acquired many new large steam locomotives and hundreds of passenger cars built of steel rather than the rickety wooden ones which were used until the early 1920's.

Otto and Clara did not know what to expect in the way of comforts on the train, but Adolph had written a description of the one that he, Teofil and Martin had traveled on, thirteen years before. The journey by train that Adolph had described, was most uncomfortable. The seats in the passenger cars consisted of wooden slats with no cushions. There was no light or heat in the cars which held about 40 passengers each. The passengers slept on the wooden slats of the seat or else they could lower the same type of wooden slatted bunk which hung from the ceiling. Otto and Clara wondered if this train would be the same.

After having their tickets verified by a ticket agent, Otto was given the track number on which the train that would transport them on the last leg of their journey, awaited their arrival. With stamped tickets in hand, Otto and his family waded through the bustling crowd and on to the station platform which was even more crowded than the inside of the station. Hundreds of fellow immigrants could be seen scurrying around trying to make sense of the train numbering system and ensuring that they were boarding the intended train. The ticket agent told Otto that in the past, several immigrants had boarded trains whose destination was miles and miles from their intended destination. The train that Otto and his family were to board was easy to identify because it was clearly signed and because it would travel all the way to Winnipeg. It was one of the few newer and larger ones parked at the station. They could see that the maroon colored passenger cars, each displaying the Canadian Pacific Railway name, numbered seven in all, were designed to carry immigrants to the West. Some were designed for short haul passengers going to Montreal, Toronto and a host of smaller centers along the main line. Otto, spotting the assigned train number, steered his family to the back of the line that awaited approval for boarding. After a short wait, the conductor, leading several black porters, walked by the column and, never having seen a black person in their whole lives, a hushed murmur sprang up. Clara overheard someone in line behind them, say in polish, and in all innocence,

"Are these niggers?"

No one responded to the woman and the porters went about their duties unaware of the woman's comment.

The passenger cars were filled in an orderly fashion, starting with the lead immigrant car and then working their way towards the last car. The Flath family boarded the third car and were assigned two seats which faced each other. After storing their belongings under the seats and making themselves comfortable, numerous observations and questions entered Clara and Otto's minds.

"How many people are in this car?" Asked Oscar.

"Well, Oscar, you count the seats and then we will be able to estimate how many people will occupy them," came the response.

"I see that there is a cook stove at the back as well as dishes and some cupboards and wash tables. I know that we will have to cook our own food and wash our own dishes. The stove top is quite large so I guess two people could cook at the same time . . . . maybe I will be able to share some of the cooking with another family . . . . that would really help. We bought enough food at the immigration hall to last us for three days . . . . we have milk, eggs, ham, potatoes, cabbage, bread, butter, coffee, porridge and cheese . . . . at least now we know what we will be eating. I am just happy that the food we have will be better than what was served on the Minnedosa. I also wonder about the toilets . . . . oh, there's a door that looks like it might lead to a toilet," uttered Clara, thinking out loud.

Otto, not waiting for Oscar to count the number of seats in the car, shared his observations,

"I have counted thirty-six seats, so there will probably be about seventy-two people in this car. I also see that there is an electric light for each set of seats. This must be a newer train than the one described by Adolph because these seats are upholstered and are very comfortable. I see that the seats can be turned and the backs can be folded down to make a bed for the night. Also, I see that the bunks hanging above the seats can be brought down and made into a bed. I think that this journey will be comfortable and we will be able to enjoy the trip from here to Winnipeg."

"Otto, I know that we still have a great distance to travel and that we will have to buy our train tickets to get to Hafford; we also will spend some money on candy or some treats for our children, so the question I have for you, Otto, is how much money do you have and what will that money buy us?" Asked Clara.

Otto, brushing and stroking his unshaven beard, deliberated a few moments, then spoke,

"I have fifty-nine Canadian dollars in my pocket. I have no idea what that money will buy. I do not know how much things cost in Canada. I just don't know. I just hope that we will have enough to get us to father's place in Hafford. I know that we still have to change trains to get to Hafford or maybe we will have to walk . . . . I don't know. We will probably be told by the Lutheran Immigration Board volunteers in Winnipeg; hopefully, they will be able to help us."

And just as Otto words came to their conclusion, the 'All Aboard' call from the conductor was given and number 2046 steam engine began its preparation for the two thousand kilometre journey to Winnipeg. With huge columns of black smoke belching out of its stack, excess steam hissing from the pressure control valve, the final three long whistles signaling the engineer's intention to throw the forward lever into position and with the steam building up pressure in the piston chamber, the six huge drive wheels slowly began to rotate and drag along with them the more than four hundred passengers, taking them nearer to their destinations. As the train gathered speed, the 'click,' 'click,' sound made each time a steel wheel of the railroad car passed over the expansion gap of two adjoining rails, settled into a steady rhythm. The passengers too, began to settle into a routine that would be followed for the next three days.

The train followed the St. Lawrence River as it headed west to Montreal, passing by many small towns and villages each one dominated by church steeples. The only stops this train would make would be at larger stations, where the coal car and water tanks would be refilled and where some passengers would leave or board.

Clara, Otto and their children settled down and soon developed a routine which they would follow for their trip to the West. Cooking their food did not present a problem and the sleeping accommodations, though not luxurious, proved to be adequate, even for Clara who was six months pregnant. Their days were spent observing the passing scenery, amusing their children, cooking and visiting with fellow passengers. Usually all passengers in their car were curled up in their make shift beds by ten p.m., with only the occasional cough or snoring interrupting the sounds made by the moving train. Upon reaching Montreal, the passengers were informed that the train would make a three hour stop and that those who wanted could leave their coaches and explore the station. The train then began its second leg of the journey. There would be several stops between Montreal and Toronto. Passengers who had travelled the route from Quebec City to Toronto previously, informed Otto and Clara that the countryside would change quickly, once the train would leave Toronto.

As the train tracks followed the shores of Lake Superior, Oscar asked, "Is that the ocean?"

"No, Oscar," came the reply, "that is Lake Superior. It will take more than ten hours of travel before we reach the far end of the lake."

"It is very interesting to look at," said Clara, "but all that there is here is bush, rocks, and swamp. I would think there are many flies that would bite, if we were to be outside. I sure hope that Saskatchewan is not like this."

"Sooner or later, this kind of land will have to change because there is no way that anyone would be able to plant a crop in this barren looking ground," Otto said as the train began to slow down for a stop at a water tower from which fresh water would be taken on.

"Mama, look!" Cried Eugene. "Look at those people! What are they?"

Overhearing Eugene's excited question, a man sitting in the seat next to Eugene, spoke up.

"Those people are called Indians. They live in the forested area around here and they sometimes come, out of interest, to see the trains that stop here and also, to catch a glimpse of the people on the trains. I am sure that we look as different to them as they look different to you. There are many Indians in Canada. You may have heard that there was a rebellion in Saskatchewan, where we are going, and that some settlers had been killed. That was many years ago . . . . you don't have to worry, everything is peaceful now . . . . you probably will not come across them when you get to your destination. Most of them live separate from the settlers."

Eugene and Oscar heard, but did not understand.

As the train neared Winnipeg, the terrain began to change from rocky hills covered by forests, to flat low lying marsh land, and then finally to open flat prairie. This change in scenery evoked many comments from the passengers, most stating that they were grateful that they would not be forced into attempts at farming in the rocky bush that had surrounded them for days.

The immigration hall in Winnipeg was not as large as the one in Quebec but it stood two stories high and contained eating, washing and sleeping facilities, just like the one in Quebec but only on a smaller scale. It would be here that most of the individuals and families that had made the journey from Liverpool, would go their separate ways. It would be here that each person would be responsible for the purchase of their own ticket and be responsible for looking after themselves. Winnipeg was known as the 'Gateway to the West'—the portal to the land of unlimited opportunity and wealth.

Clara was not convinced . . . . she had her doubts, but she had promised herself that she would do whatever was necessary to provide a home for her children. Even though the huge surge of immigrants, of previous years, passing through Winnipeg had waned considerably, there were still many that continued to arrive. Officials and volunteers from a variety of organizations continued to greet the new immigrants whenever an immigrant train was scheduled to arrive. The volunteers assisted the new arrivals by helping them secure train tickets, directing them to the laundry facilities as well as the bath rooms. If the newcomers were unable to make rail connections to continue their journey, the volunteers would direct the newcomers to places where they would be able to spend the night and would be given food.

Clara and Otto's train pulled slowly into the railway yards, the brakes squealing as the iron wheels grated against the iron rails. After coming to a complete stop, a short whistle signaled to all on board that for this train, the trip was over . . . . it had done it's job . . . . now it was time for all to leave. Looking out the window, Otto and Clara could see that there were several people with signs standing on the station platform awaiting those that might require assistance. The signs were written in many different languages and it did not take much searching to spot one written in German that displayed 'Lutheran Immigration Board'. Upon seeing the sign, Clara and Otto breathed a sigh of relief knowing that there was someone available to help them and guide them to their destination.

Tired, haggard, weary, dirty and hungry, the Flath family stepped onto the station platform and made their way to the immigration assistant. Following their introductions, Helen, the comely immigrant assistant, said,

"If you have your documents with you, I would like to see them and make certain that we can put you on the right train to where it is that you are going."

Otto retrieved the documents from the inner pocket of his coat and handed them over to Helen, who carefully viewed them and then said,

"I see that your destination is Hafford, Saskatchewan."

"Yes," said Otto, "that is where my father lives and that is where we are going to go."

"I know that you all are tired and are looking for a place to clean up but come with me and let us sort out your train routes and tickets before we do anything else. Your children aren't fussing, so let's go and complete this. Once you know when your train will be leaving, you will be able to decide other things," said Helen. "Come, we have a table inside the immigrant house that has maps and other information which we need to plan the rest of your journey. I know that the C.P.R.

does not service that part of Saskatchewan that you are going to, so we have to take you to a different station to meet your train but there are people from the C.N.R. inside the immigrant house where you will be able to purchase your tickets."

With that news, the Flath family followed Helen into the immigrant house.

The ticket agent informed Otto and Clara that getting to Hafford by train would require changing to different trains at two locations, which would result in several more hours of travel time. They could however, travel directly to Radisson but that would mean a twenty mile trip by horse and wagon or by automobile.

Otto looked at Clara and following a brief discussion, decided to take the train to Hafford. Boarding time would be 9:00 a.m. the following morning.

Later that night, after been given a good meal, and having had a good bath, as well as given a private room for the family, Otto and Clara found themselves in a room that was occupied only by themselves.

"We haven't had a private time like this for three weeks now," declared Clara, "I am so relieved that our journey is coming to an end and that we have arrived safely and healthy. I was very concerned about our safety before we left and while we were on the ship. You know, Otto, Canada may not be so bad. There are many automobiles in Winnipeg and the city looks prosperous. Helen was encouraging and it seems like there is much work for people," continued Clara.

"We will see," replied Otto.

"Come Clara, let's get some sleep. Tomorrow will be another long day on the train and these trains do not have seats that make up into beds so they will not be as comfortable as those that we were on previously. I think that we will have enough money to buy some food on the train and maybe some candy for our children. I have fifteen dollars left. I wonder what we would have done if we had not been able to pay for these train tickets . . . . but, we don't have to worry about it now, do we? Let's go to bed; it looks very inviting."

It was late at night when the train from Winnipeg arrived in Saskatoon and their connecting train to Prince Albert would not leave until the following morning. Even at that late hour, the station was active with arriving passengers and much like the Flaths, they too were completing their journeys. Like the Flaths, many had very little money left and would spend the next few hours in the station waiting for their departing train. Some passengers were already bedded down on benches covered by the blankets they had brought with them. Otto and Clara found an empty bench on which they could place their sleeping children. Clara and Otto would take turns napping in an upright position.

When morning arrived and the early trains began to enter the station, the weary passengers once again, gathered their meagre belongings and made their way to the station platform.

For Oscar and Eugene, the journey from Gajkowice, Poland, to Saskatoon, Saskatchewan, had been an adventure. Every day brought something new for them to explore and experience.

They had not complained, but little Lydia, who did not yet see the world from the same perspective as her older brothers, showed signs of fatigue. The constant disruption of sleep and change in diet, along with the mental toll that travel imposes on the very young, had finally caught up with Lydia. As it was time to once again board the train and endure another day of discomfort and of endless monotonous scenery, Clara also, feeling the effect of lengthy travel, forced her six month pregnant body to stir and attend to Lydia. She placed her arm on Otto's shoulder, gripped it, then pulling with her arm and pushing with her legs, she stood up, smoothed her wrinkled dress, ran a comb through her hair, then began to search through the brown grocery bag for the piece of left over bread crust, which would serve as a pacifier for Lydia. Taking the crust of bread in her hand, Clara turned her attention to Lydia who, after crying herself to sleep the night before, lay motionless, wrapped cocoon-like in the grubby wool blanket that, since the journey began, had served as a bed quilt. Gazing down at the little bundle of innocence, tears began to roll down Clara's cheeks. The sight of her chubby cheeked baby, face smeared with a combination of yesterday's food, tears and dirt, whose curly blond hair lay spread half covering her face, whose pudgy soft fingers lay curled in little fists outside the blanket, and who lying there had no idea what was happening and who, like her mother, had no idea what the future would bring. Lovingly, Clara reached down, gathered her sleeping bundle up gently and hugging Lydia to her body, turned to Otto and said,

"Thank God that this is our last day of travel. Let's go meet our fate. We should be in Hafford later today."

"I sent my father a telegram when we left Winnipeg, so he will know when we are arriving. I hope that he will be there to meet us," said Otto. "We will buy something to eat on the train . . . . I still have a little money left."

The Flaths made their way to the station platform and waited to hear the, now familiar 'All Aboard' call, from the train conductor.

CHAPTER 25

Martin and his only daughter, Olga, had for months been looking forward for this day to arrive. They had received a letter from Poland in February that Otto, Clara and their children Oscar, Eugene and Lydia had made application to immigrate to Canada and that their application had been approved. Subsequent letters told Martin that Otto and his family would be arriving at Hafford sometime in May, 1927, depending on the time that it took for the immigrant ship to cross the Atlantic Ocean.

With the coming of spring, activity at the Hafford railroad station started early in the day. The station agent washed, shaved and ate breakfast before 7 a.m. and a few minutes before 8:00 a.m., he slipped on his black removable, shirt sleeves, fixed his C.N.R. station agent cap on his head and stepped from his living quarters, which were attached to the station, and into the station's work room. There he quickly made a list of jobs that needed attention for the day. The list was long and he would be very busy all day long. There was the outgoing mail bags to attend to and there were a number of packages that were being sent on the train. The cans of cream placed on the station platform by farmers required organizing, recording and placing on the station wagon. The station platform needed sweeping and he had to sell passenger tickets to travelers who would be boarding the train. He had to attend to the telegraph messages which needed sending and telegraph messages that needed converting into the written word. The station was the only depot for incoming passengers, merchandise and supplies which served the 400 people of Hafford, as well as the 2000 new settlers in the surrounding area.

The agent was busy sweeping the waiting room floor when he heard the telegraph keys start their clicking sounds. The initial sounds were meant to alert the agent that a telegram would soon follow. He propped his broom against a wall and sat down in front of the telegraph board and waited for the message to come through. He waited only a few minutes when the keys began to click again and he, pen in hand, began interpreting the series of short and long clicks into English. The telegram read:

Will arrive in Hafford on Tuesday, May 18.
Sender: Otto Flath
Receiver: Martin Flath

The agent looked at the telegram and rubbing his chin, wondered who Martin Flath was and where he could be found. The agent set the telegram aside and resumed sweeping the floor, thinking that perhaps someone would come to the station that would know how to contact Martin Flath. If not, he would go to the pool hall where surely someone would know of Martin Flath, or perhaps Viktor, his unofficial helper, would drop by and he would know how to contact Martin.

By mid morning, the agent had his answer. Martin Flath lived on his farm located one mile west and one mile north of Hafford. With that information, he dispatched Viktor to complete the delivery of the telegram. Viktor secured the telegram in his shirt breast pocket and set out on foot. Even though the distance from Hafford to Martin's farm was only two miles, the walk would not be easy. The road heading west and leading to Martin's farm had been recently upgraded but not graveled. Recent rains made the surface muddy and the wagon and automobile tracks left behind were filled with mud which made walking difficult. After about 30 minutes, Viktor left the road heading west and turned north. The road leading north was merely a double spoored trail worn into the virgin prairie. The road allowance on which the trail was created led through open prairie as well as pathways cut through the bluffs of poplar trees. For Viktor, walking the mile north on the trail would be easier than walking on the slippery muddy upgraded road. Here on the trail he could avoid the ruts by walking on the grass between the two spoors. On his walk, Viktor only passed by two homesteads and he knew immediately when he reached his destination for the trail ended abruptly on the road allowance and the trail led to Martin's yard.

As he approached, Viktor could see a small building which appeared to serve as a house. The building was constructed of unpainted lumber and the roof was covered by shingles. It had two single pane windows and a store bought door. The building sat on rocks which served as a foundation—a brick chimney protruded two feet above the roof line. Two other buildings came into Viktor's view. One was a hastily built log structure covered by straw, which, he thought, probably served as a shelter for Martin's large domestic animals. The other structure appeared to serve as a pig sty or possibly a chicken coop. The buildings had been situated in an open clearing of an otherwise bush covered countryside broken up only by sloughs, some small plots of open prairie grass and an open field which had been carved out of the bush. There was no white picket fence surrounding the house, no flower beds, no fenced in yard and no gate to open to enter the yard.

Viktor noticed two cows tethered to stakes, grazing on the young spring prairie grass. He noticed a plot of newly turned soil which, he surmised, would become the vegetable garden. Also, there were some farm implements sitting idle next to some bushes. Two dogs, barking and wagging their tails, rushed towards him in greeting. The barking dogs had obviously alerted whoever it was that occupied the home, because the door to the house opened and a young girl stepped out to investigate. She shielded her eyes with her hand and waited for Viktor to approach the house.

"Is this the home of Martin Flath?" asked Viktor.

"Yes, it is," replied Olga.

"I have a telegram for him." With those words, Viktor reached into his pocket, handed the telegram to Olga, turned around and began his walk back to Hafford.

Olga's hands trembled with excitement as she took the telegram from Viktor. She opened the envelope and read the message. Excitedly she ran as fast as she could to relay the message to her father, Martin, that indeed, later on this day, Otto, Clara and their three children would be arriving. A thousand thoughts raced through her mind as she scurried through the grass and on to the newly ploughed field where Martin was busy ploughing the plot of land and getting it ready for seeding. She had not seen her brother, Otto, and his family since she had left Poland for Canada three years previous. She was anxious and thrilled to be able to see them again. This made her happy. She had not seen her brother, Hugo, since she came to Canada either and for the time being, he would remain in Poland. This made her sad. Her other brothers, Adolph and Teofil, were a thousand miles away working in Vancouver so they would not be able to share in the joy of reuniting with most of the family. This made her sad. Her mother had died nearly ten years previous . . . . there was no hope of the whole family ever being reunited. This made her sad as well. The mixture of joy and sadness brought tears to her eyes but these feelings came to an abrupt end when she came running up to Martin and handed him the telegram.

Seeing Olga running across the newly ploughed field, Martin reigned in the horses and stepped off the plough's seat and waited for Olga to bring him some news. Without a word, he took the telegram from Olga and read its brief message. He, folding the telegram and replacing it in the envelope, looked down at his daughter and said,

"Olga, this is a happy day for me but also a very sad day. It has been thirteen years since I have last seen my son Otto, who I thought I might never see again and it's been thirteen years since I have seen my wife who I will never see again. I'll unhitch the horses and we will go to the house and get some things ready for Otto's arrival. I will get the wagon ready and you can do what you have to do to get bedding and beds ready for them to sleep on. Also they will need a good meal so we will go to the butcher shop and buy a nice roast for supper. You baked some fresh bread yesterday and the cows have freshened so we have milk and some fresh butter to put on the bread . . . . Olga, I even have a little schnapps. We will have a nice supper even though it is much too early for fresh garden vegetables."

Martin and Olga arrived at the train station a half hour before the arrival time of the train which was carrying Otto, Clara and family. Martin tied the team to the long hitching rail along side of several other teams of horses. The parking lot serving the station on this day was crowded with teams of horses, single horses pulling buggies, saddled horses, some automobiles and even a couple of bicycles. Many people milled around on the station platform awaiting the train's arrival.

Martin and Olga, joining the crowd on the platform, encountered several groups of people speaking several different languages. The people of Hafford and surrounding districts had all just recently arrived from various parts of the globe.

Fur traders, settlers, prospectors, missionaries, the Northwest Mounted police, among others had traveled along the Carlton trail which ran through the area since the mid 1850's, but only a few homesteads were offered prior to 1906. When the survey was completed in 1906, hundreds of settlers poured into the area . . . . the bulk coming between the years 1906 and 1911. As Martin and Olga made their way through the crowd, they heard Ukrainian, Russian, English, French and even German spoken by those waiting for the train to arrive.

"Why are there so many people here, papa?" Asked Olga.

"Olga," replied Martin, "everything and everybody coming and going to Hafford comes by train. There are hundreds of families just like ours who are waiting for relatives to arrive, waiting for things ordered from Eatons, waiting for mail and many come just to see who and what goes onto the train or who and what comes off."

During the long hours of train travel from Quebec City to Saskatoon, Otto and Clara would often doze off during the day to seemingly shorten the time spent in traveling but on this day, neither Otto nor Clara dozed off. Both were keenly interested in viewing first hand the nature of the countryside which was to become their new home. As the train made its way along, the conductor of the passenger car would call out the name of the next stop and when Otto and Clara heard that the next stop would be Blaine Lake, they became even more interested in the passing countryside.

"This land looks very similar to the land that we left," mused Otto, "except that there are more trees and sloughs. The farm buildings around here are certainly different from those that we saw between Winnipeg and Saskatoon. The houses and barns look very similar to those I saw in Galicia . . . . there must be many Ukrainians and Russians in this area."

"No, I don't see any large homes built from lumber, nor do I see any large barns with large roofs over them. I was expecting to see more prosperous looking farmsteads," interjected Clara. "I hope that your father has a bigger house than most that I see around here; I hope that he has room for us, at least until we find our own place to live."

The train stopped at Blaine Lake and then for a short while at Krydor and finally after several weeks of travel, the weary family heard the much anticipated call,

"Next stop—Hafford."

"Well Otto, we made it . . . . let's give thanks to God." With those words Clara gave a short prayer of thanksgiving and requested God's protection for what lay ahead.

After the now familiar squealing of brakes had ceased and after the sound of hissing steam came to an end, the conductor opened the passenger door, set his footstool on the station platform and then requested the detraining passengers to make their way off the car and onto the station platform. Otto, Clara and family waited as other passengers detrained. They immediately recognized Martin and Olga standing among the crowd of people. Clara's memory of Martin was hazy but Otto upon first glance, recognized the man that was his father but the man there before him had changed from the man that Otto last saw thirteen years earlier. The man before him still stood proudly erect but the years of loneliness and toil had obviously taken its toll. Martin's hair, which was thick, neatly trimmed and black in 1914 was now turning grey and in need of trimming. The beard and mustache which Martin had taken very good care of was now changed to only a mustache but Otto noted that it was still neatly trimmed. His tired threadbare clothes were evidence of Martin having worn these same clothes many times.

"He probably does not have enough money to buy a new suit of clothing," thought Otto.

As he looked out of the window, Otto's mind began to fill with images of past events and experiences. The events and circumstances flashing through his brain were the result of decisions and choices made . . . . some of which he had controlled, others which had been made for him.

Hid mind flashed back to the Poland of his youth . . . . a Poland where his family had lived and thrived for over a hundred years. It was a place where he felt comfortable and secure . . . . a place where he had learned to walk, to talk, to go to school, to go to church and eventually to work. As a young man he had never expected, nor dreamed that events and circumstances would force him to leave his home and uproot, not only his family, but thousands of other families as well. He never dreamed that at the age of nineteen he would be taken from his family and home to serve eight years in Tsar Nicholas II's cavalry. He never dreamed that his years in St. Petersburg would expose him to a way of life only a few could enjoy. The images of the extreme wealth of the privileged class and because of his association with Pokovnik Constantine, he was able to experience first hand. He saw images of himself attending concerts, ballets and theatre in the finest concert halls and theatres in St. Petersburg, and images of himself being bowed down to by many citizens of St. Petersburg as he drove the Pokovnik's beautiful horse drawn carriage which displayed the Romanov emblem, the double headed eagle. Flashing through his mind's eyes, he saw fancy parties, gala events, impressive military displays, art galleries, beautiful and willing ladies . . . . all images of the easy privileged way of life of an officer.

These mental pictures were quickly replaced by the images of the horrific battle scenes experienced in Galicia. In his mind, he heard the unforgettable combined sounds of screaming horses as they lay dying, and the moaning, hysterical screaming of wounded men as they lay waiting to die. These, mixed with the whistling screams of incoming artillery and the resulting boom of exploding shells created a sound so frightening that it drove many who experienced it for the first time, into complete shock and bordering insanity. Accompanying the sounds of war, came the odor of the battle field. The smell of seared hair and flesh, combined with the vomit, the horse and human feces, the pungent urine, the burning clothing and vegetation, and the smell of exploding gunpowder, like the visual images, would never be forgotten. The battlefield images were quickly replaced by his tenure in St, Petersburg following the battle of Gorlice-Tarnow. His renewed life with Anya and children and his daily routine, then the agony of his forced separation from all that he loved in St. Petersburg, shook his body as these images flashed by. His renewed life in Poland also flashed before him . . . . the gripping sadness as he watched his mother die before him . . . .

the meeting, courting and marriage to Clara . . . . his job in the textile mills . . . . then again for the third time in his life, a forced set of circumstances expelling him to where he sat, here, on the train gazing at a hastily constructed village in the middle of a hostile climate. This was a village, less than fifteen years old, of about 400 people, in an area where the broken farm land and breaking of new ground had yet to prove that agriculture would indeed thrive . . . . a village that lacked sidewalks, whose streets were muddy and rutted, where only a few of the clapboard buildings were painted . . . . where the few scrubby trees had yet to leaf out . . . . a village that lay a day's travel by train to a nearest place that qualified as a city. Looking out, Otto could only guess, but he reasoned that most of the services required by the community would be supplied by the businesses in the community . . . . he wondered if the village was in need of butcher shop.

Captured by the scene before him . . . . his father, his sister, the mingling crowd and the sight of the village . . . . Otto was not aware that the other detraining passengers had left the car and that only he and his family had not made any attempt to go. Clara, watching Otto intently, wondered if her husband, lost in his own thoughts was mentally resisting the social adjustments, the financial insecurity, and the responsibility that was required for him starting anew for the third time in his adult life.

Gently, she gripped his forearm in her hand and said, "Otto, we have arrived, your father and sister are waiting . . . . let's go meet them. You go ahead, I will look after the children and we'll follow you."

Reuniting after a long period of time for a family, where the family bonds are strong but where these bonds are rarely displayed openly with hugs and kisses, is always difficult. As Otto detrained, he wondered how he and his family would be received. Should he fall into Martin's arms? Should be cry? Should he hold out his hand in welcome? Otto, with Clara by his side and children in tow, stepped on to the station platform and began making their way through the crowd and towards Martin and Olga. When Martin's gaze met Otto's, Otto stopped and there on the platform, father and son stared at each other, never taking their eyes away from each other. Each stood, waiting for the other to make the first move. The stalemate was broken very quickly by Olga, who broke from Martin's side, ran and threw herself into Otto's arms, showering him with tears and kisses. Martin was quick to follow and embracing Clara, welcomed her and then the children with open arms. Not much was said. There was so need for words . . . . words could wait . . . . now was the time for a genuine outpouring of pent-up love. The years of uncertainty and absence, had built up a huge reservoir of emotions which now poured forth, expressing themselves in hugging, kissing and crying. All those witnessing the scene, understood exactly what was transpiring, for they too, had come thousands of miles, leaving family and friends behind, traveling through unfamiliar territory, facing known and unknown dangers. They understood that to arrive at your destination safely was a major accomplishment. They also understood that arriving safely at Hafford was no guarantee for an economically prosperous future; there was work available, but the work was hard and the pay was mediocre. Those, who like Martin, had tried and were still trying to wrest a good life from the earth, knew that the environment did not surrender easily and willingly to the pioneer's plow. Converting the mostly stoney, tree covered landscape to arable land was not easy. Many of those witnessing Otto and Clara's arrival looked at them sympathetically because they knew better than Otto and Clara what lay ahead for them. They had the experience of pulling stumps, picking rocks, fencing, haying, and then coping with six months of solid, frozen earth and very cold temperatures often accompanied by blowing snow. They knew of the heartbreak that happens when, after months of hard labor, their seeded crops were reduced to nothing after being hit by early frost or being destroyed by hoards of grasshoppers.

"Come, Otto, Clara, Olga, come children. Let us go home. You must be hungry and tired—Olga will cook us up a nice supper—then we can talk," implored Martin.

With those words, suitcases were picked up and the newly reunited family moved towards the means of transportation waiting to carry them to Martin's farm. The means of transportation consisted of a team of horses pulling a four wheeled wagon upon which a wagon box was placed. The wagon and wagon box appeared to be relatively new. The wagon was not painted but the box was painted green. Looking around the station parking area, Otto noticed the similarity among most of the wagons. Otto was soon to learn that thousands of these wagons were produced and were designed to meet the needs of the pioneering families of the prairies. The wagons were built to carry heavy loads and designed to be pulled by a team of two horses. These wagons could accommodate boxes of various lengths as well as hay racks. The high oak spoked wheels, turning on greased metal hubs, made the wagons quite easy to pull. The wagon boxes made for these wagons could carry forty or fifty bushels of grain or could carry a family of six or seven people.

On this day, Martin's wagon was pulled by two of his four work horses. The horses which had just recently survived the cold winter were in the final stages of shedding their winter coat of hair, making them look rather shabby to Otto. Looking at them, Otto knew that they were of mixed breeds . . . . probably crosses between Belgian and Percheron but he was not sure . . . . certainly they were not Clydesdales.

Martin had removed the tail gate from the wagon box to make getting into the wagon box easier than having to climb up the spokes of the wheels and then over the edge of the wagon box. He also had placed two narrow homemade benches in the box so that his family could sit as they made their way from Hafford.

The whole Otto Flath family from the youngest to the oldest member was eager to get a taste of their new way of life, and within a half hour, they had their sampling.

First of all, Clara, being short of stature and pregnant, looked at the wagon quizzically and said, "How am I supposed to get into that? I can't step up that high!"

Martin, giving her a sideways glance, retorted, "Okay. I will take one of the benches from the box and you can use the bench as a step."

Soon after the family and their belongings had been loaded, the rig began to make its way along the rutted dirt road. Martin allowed the horses to walk, but even going at a slow pace, the ride was very uncomfortable. Each time a wheel would strike a rock or rut in the road, the wagon would jolt, sending the seated passengers into the air and then landing them back down hard onto the unstable bench. Unfortunately, the road was full of rocks and ruts.

"My God," thought Clara, "what am I getting myself into? I feel like I am going to have my baby right now. This is almost as bad as being on the ship."

Clara kept her thoughts to herself. Her hopes to formulate a good first impression, were dealt another blow with the sight of Martin's farm yard.

During the lengthly journey by train from Montreal, she had seen many large well-built horse barns, painted outbuildings and large two story homes. Many of these farm yards were fenced in and many boasted painted picket fences. She had also seen many farmsteads at the opposite end of the scale. She had dreamed that Martin's place would at least be somewhere in between the two extremes. As Martin's yard came into view, she knew immediately into which category his yard fit. At first glance, she knew that her immediate future would be difficult, to say the least. She also knew that there was no turning back now . . . . she would have to make the best of it.

Martin stood at the front of the wagon box as he guided the horses homeward and Otto stood next to him, talking as they made their way home.

"Otto, when we get home, Olga will start supper for us and if you want to, you can help me with the evening chores. The horses have to be watered and put out to pasture. The cows need milking and their calves need feeding . . . . as well as the pigs and chickens. Also, the eggs need to be gathered and wood brought into the house. We will have them completed in not much longer than an hour, with both of us doing the work."

Following their first evening meal together, Martin said, "We have many things to talk about and we will talk, but first we need to have our evening devotions."

Evening devotions, a daily family tradition which had lasted for more than a hundred years, meant reading a passage from both the old and the new testament. The bible readings would be followed by the whole family bowing their heads, folding their hands together, then reciting traditional prayers and ending with the Lord's prayer. Following the devotions, tea would be made and those who wanted to, would continue to sit around the table, talk, read books or play some games. Card games were not allowed except on Sundays after church and only if other extended family members or friends were present.

On that first evening together, there would be no reading of books or playing of games. There would be no cards played. Instead, there would be much talk and there was much that Martin wanted to share with the newcomers.

CHAPTER 26

Martin rubbed his greying hair, twisted the ends of his famous handlebar mustache and began his story.

"Otto I want you to know how much I have missed you and how glad I am to see you again after fourteen years. It means so much to me to have you and your family here with me and Olga. Your children are the first grandchildren that I have and that makes me glad also. I just wish that Hugo could have come with you and that Adolph and Teofil would be here as well. Otto, when the war broke out and you were in Russia, I was convinced that I would never see you again, especially when Paulina wrote and told be that you were sent to Galicia to fight against the Austrians; but look, here you are. God must be looking after you. Let me go on. I know how disappointed you must be seeing how Olga and I are living here and I am sorry that I don't have a bigger and nicer home to welcome you to. I want to explain."

"First of all, I want you to know that it was with a heavy heart that I left Poland and came to Canada. Paulina and I had many long talks about whether or not to emigrate from Poland. We knew that we would be leaving family and friends behind and we knew that coming to Canada was no guarantee of riches. On the other hand, we knew that there was much unrest in Europe and war was a possibility. You, Otto, were already conscripted and serving in Russia. We were fearful of your safety and we thought that if war should break out and last for some time, Hugo, Adolph and Teofil could possibly be conscripted as well. We felt that we were in danger of losing all of our sons. So you see, one of the reasons for leaving with Adolph and Teofil was to keep them from being conscripted. It was a very difficult decision to make when deciding who should emigrate. We finally decided to leave Hugo behind because he was older and, at that time, more able to support and look after your mother and sister. We were desperately hoping that by the end of your second stint and when you would return, I would have been able to save enough money by working in Canada, for tickets to Canada for the rest of the family. But you know what happened . . . . within a few months of landing in Canada, Russia was at war and there was no hope of you being released from the army as long as the war lasted. Also, it became nearly impossible for people from Poland to emigrate. At the time when Paulina and I decided that I should take Adolph and Teofil to Canada, I became excited about the move and was determined to work hard and save money to bring everyone else over to Canada. However, when the war broke out, I worried about the family's safety and I began to lose my ambition. I thought the situation to be hopeless. Yes, I worked to keep food on the table for Adolph, Teofil and myself but I was not very anxious to begin farming. I was not a real farmer in Poland and farming in Canada is far different than farming in Poland. By the time I arrived here, all the good homestead land had been claimed. Had we come just a few years earlier, we could have gotten some fairly good land. Besides, to be a successful farmer, one needed money for livestock, machinery and buildings. I had very little. In addition, the larger the family, the greater the chances of succeeding. One person could not begin to successfully complete all the work required . . . . there simply were not enough hours in a day and some things had to be simply forgotten. For men living alone, it was the domestic duties that suffered. Housekeeping, cooking, washing and ironing, gardening, picking berries, preserving food, milking cows, feeding chickens, baking and many other household duties were a full time job . . . . let alone having to tend to the livestock, fence, put up firewood, gather fodder for the livestock's winter food, break new ground for crops and to sow and reap the grain . . . . all this work was just overwhelming. Nevertheless, I did buy a farm twelve miles north and two miles east of Radisson. Believe me, Adolph, Teofil and I did try hard to make a success of farming there, but eventually, Adolph and Teofil gave up on farming and decided to try their luck at doing something else. They went to Vancouver where Teofil found work at the Georgia Hotel and Adolph found work clearing bush and working construction on Lulu Island."

"When the war ended in Russia and I knew that you were safely back in Poland, my hopes and dreams of bringing everyone to Canada were rekindled. Again, just when I thought things would get better, my dear Paulina died. The news of her sudden death devastated me. The main reason for living was snatched from me and to make matters worse, your and Hugo's decision to stay in Poland did not help. You know, when a person loses his main purpose for living, a person loses interest in everything, including ambition. I knew that I had to carry on because I dearly wanted to bring Olga to Canada and by 1924, I had enough money saved for her ticket. That was only three years ago. When she came, I began to have a renewed reason for living and when the opportunity to sell my farm outside of Radisson and buy the 320 acres only two miles from Hafford, I took the opportunity. I was hoping that with more land, all my sons would come and we would work together as a family. I am very, very happy to have you here but I was dearly hoping that Hugo would have come with you. Without him, my family is still too scattered. I hope also that Adolph and Teofil will return home. Otto I wish that I had enough money to pay you to work for me but I don't. There is much work around and you can live here until you get on your feet. Okay?"

The talk continued late into the night. Martin telling his story. Otto telling his. Clara telling hers and Olga telling hers also. Finally Martin said,

"It is getting very late. I would like to show you around the farm tomorrow morning and maybe take you over to Whiteberry school where Oscar can start school.

The arrival of Otto and family made life on Martin's farm a lot easier. Clara was able to help Olga with the garden and other domestic chores and Otto, even though having found work on neighboring farms, was able to help Martin clear more acres, put up hay, build fences and generally assist wherever needed.

The tiny crowded shack, called home, became a little more crowded with the arrival of Clara's fourth child, Arnold. His arrival in late August of 1927, was a joy but also an inconvenience as it happened during the busy harvest time but since the crops were good and the price of wheat was high, no one complained. The whole family was optimistic about the future.

Following the harvest, Otto approached the butcher in Hafford and was hired on to help butcher, cut up meat, make sausage and work in the front end of the butcher shop. Oscar had started school in Whiteberry as soon as they arrived and by the fall of 1927, was able to speak English well enough to get along in school. He would walk the nearly two miles to school when the weather was good, but on cold days, either his grandfather Martin, or Otto would drive him to school in the morning and then pick him up again after school.

The winter passed quickly and so did the year 1928. The crop of 1928 was not as good as it had been in 1927 and the price of wheat had dropped; but, the whole community remained in good spirits and believed they had made the right choice by coming to Canada. Otto continued to find work in the area and was able to put a few dollars away with the aim of starting his own butcher shop somewhere.

Letters were received and sent to Adolph, Teofil, Hugo and, of course, Clara's family. The letters that were received from Clara's family informed them that her family had homesteaded on land near Lintlaw, Saskatchewan. Clara also learned that they too lived on land that needed clearing before a crop could be sown. She learned that her family had built a small log plastered home and by the description, was not any better than the one she presently shared with seven other people.

The news that came from Poland was that Hugo had gotten married in 1927 to a girl named Elsie. The following letters told them that Hugo and Elsie had had a son in the spring of 1929 and that they were planning to emigrate to Canada. For Otto and Clara, this meant moving out of Martin's home and finding a place of their own.

"Clara," Otto said, "I have found us a place to live in Hafford. It will be better for us to have our own place. It is time that we moved anyway. Mr. Bohun just sold the butcher shop to a new owner, and I know that he is going to need help with his business."

"Well, Otto, I know that you really would like to run a butcher shop. Maybe this is a way for you to get into the business and who knows . . . . maybe if things keep going the way they are, you will be able to have your own. There is always lots of work on the farm but there is little money in it. There is not enough money coming from the few acres that your father has cultivated to provide enough money for himself, Olga and all of us as well, nor to buy mechanized machinery. Besides, now that Hugo and Elsie are coming, they will need a place to live and get started as well so I am all for moving into town.

The children also, will not have far to go to school. What is the house like? You know that I am expecting another baby; this time though, I am not going to the hospital to have my baby like I did when Arnold was born. Never ever again am I going to the hospital . . . . you will have to be the midwife."

Otto said nothing. He just nodded.

CHAPTER 27

1937

It was January, 1937, and the thermometer outside read minus forty degrees Fahrenheit. It was dangerously cold. Inside the butcher shop, the lone customer and probably the last one for the day, was a woman. Otto had known her for several years as she was Otto's regular customer for as long as he had owned the butcher shop. On this extremely cold late afternoon, she came into the shop bundled up in layers of threadbare sweaters and shawls. Otto did not take notice of her attire nor of her demeanor as she approached the service counter.

"Dobry den, Mrs. Symchuk."

("Good afternoon, Mrs. Symchuk.")

Otto greeted her in the Ukrainian language as he did with the majority of his customers. Ukrainian, being the dominant language spoken in Hafford had made it imperative for Otto to learn to speak it. He had adapted to the language easily as he was fluent in Russian and Polish, both of which had many similarities to Ukrainian. The language that gave Otto the most difficulty was English. Many of the other business owners, grain buyers, the station agent, teachers, the doctor, the postmaster, rail road section workers and RCMP, all spoke English. In addition, the traveling sales representatives that serviced his shop, all his invoices, orders and records were conducted in English. It had been difficult, but by 1937, Otto was able to conduct meaningful conversations and business in five languages. He had not deliberately learned these languages; but rather, the circumstances in which he found himself, dictated the need to learn them.

The frozen door hinges creaked and groaned as Mrs. Symchuk closed the door to the shop. With frozen snow stuck to the bottom of her felt boots, making crackling noises with each step that she took, she approached the service counter. Otto gazed down at her as she proceeded to remove the layers of shawls and scarves that were wound around her head. The only part of her face that was visible were her eyes . . . . the remainder of her face was covered. The frozen moisture from her breath had attached itself to the shawl that covered her whole head; only one spot of brown appeared on the shawl . . . . that being located where her breath passed through and which immediately turned into icicles . . . . two inches in length that reached to the bottom of her chin. She removed her thick home knit mitts and then continued to take the wrapping from her head. Once they were removed, she shook her head and greeted Otto. She looked over the selection of meat that was available and being late in the afternoon, the selection was rather limited.

Finally, she said, "I would like a two pound pork roast."

Otto took the large piece of meat from the cooler, placed it on his butcher block, reached over to his selection of knives, took his favorite carving knife, removed the honing steel, then with the expertise that only years of repetition could provide, he flashed the blade of the knife along the steel, giving the knife the sharpness of a new razor blade. He sliced off a chunk from the large piece of pork, trimmed some excess fat from it, and weighed it. The toledo scale registered two pounds and three ounces. He wrapped it, then handed it over to Mrs. Symchuk. Otto, peering over the counter, looked at Mrs. Symchuk and said,

"The meat weighs just over two pounds and that will be thirty cents please."

Otto stood still waiting for Mrs. Symchuk to reach into her pocket and retrieve the money needed for the purchase. Looking up at Otto and with watery eyes, she said,

"Mr. Flath, every time I come to your shop for meat, you give it to me, whether or not I have money to pay for it and I feel so ashamed every time that I have to ask you to put the money owing on my account. Mr. Flath, I have no money, but you know that when I get some, I will be here to settle my bill and pay you the money that I owe you. My husband, who is away, will be coming home next week . . . . hopefully he will have earned some money so that I can pay my bills."

Otto just nodded. He had known what her response would be.

"Okay, Mrs. Symchuk, but you have quite a large bill owing now, so please, don't let it build up too high, where you won't be able to pay. I was hoping that you were coming in today to pay it off. You know Mrs. Symchuk, I have a large family to support and I too, need money to pay all my bills."

"I understand and I am so sorry," replied Mrs. Symchuk.

She took the package of meat, reached among the many folds of clothing and deposited the package somewhere in the depths of those folds. She rewrapped her head in her shawl, turned and slowly clomped her way to the door. Otto walked around the counter and followed her to the door. As he opened the door for her, the warning bell perched above the door rang, as it had done when Mrs. Symchuk had entered the shop. Otto stood in the open doorway and surveyed the scene on the main street of Hafford. His eyes followed Mrs. Symchuk until her small bent figure melted into the darkness of swirling snow. Turning his attention away from her, he peered through the darkness to see if any other of the businesses were still open. There was no activity on the street. It was deserted. Across the street, Lee Don's Cafe was dark, the O.K. economy store was dark, and the hotel right next door to his butcher shop, appeared to be deserted as well. The bitterly cold air began to burn his lungs as he breathed, so he quickly turned and went inside, using his apron to turn the knob on the door. He knew from experience that grabbing hold of the knob with his moist bare hand would result in it instantly freezing solid to the knob, and then to remove his hand, the skin would be ripped from the palm of his hand.

Reentering his shop, Otto immediately began to close up. His first job was to get a corn broom and sweep up the mixture of water and sawdust that had accumulated by the doorway. Looking at the floor, he decided that only some of the sawdust that he had spread throughout his shop required replacing. The sawdust on the floor, served two purposes: firstly, sawdust would soak up all kinds of spillage and in that way, would protect the floor; secondly, the combined smell of fresh sawdust and fresh meat gave the butcher shop a unique pleasant smell and Otto liked to give his shop a clean smell. Anyone entering the shop knew immediately that they were in a butcher shop. He picked up the rag that he used to prevent the cold and drifting snow to enter through the space between the bottom of the door and the door sill. He then tucked it firmly against the crack and finally turned off the lone bare electric light which illuminated the front end of his shop.

Since it was Saturday, Otto had thought that he would walk the two miles back to the farm where his family now lived but after being outside for just a few minutes, decided that he would not risk freezing to death along the way. He often would stay overnight in his shop . . . . especially on sausage making days or when the weather prevented his walking home. He had told Clara that if he thought it was too cold and stormy, he would sleep over and come home during the day light. He knew that Clara and their children would be safe at home without his presence.

His next duty was to put the displayed meat into the cooler and thoroughly wash his equipment. Daily, he would disassemble the meat grinder and the meat slicer, soak the parts in boiling hot water and then let them lie, exposed to the air, to dry.

The last major chore to be completed was to tally up the receipts for the day's business. He pushed the 'No sale' button on the National Cash register and removed the drawer that held the few dollars and coins, as well as the several credit bills that had been written up. Before he would begin the bookwork, he decided that he should have something to eat. Finding food in his butcher shop was easy. Over the years, he always kept a pot of hot water on his stove located in the back of his shop and each business morning, he would take a link or two of his garlic sausage and drop it into the pot. He always had a loaf of bread, some butter and a jar of mustard sitting on the table located in the same room as the stove. On the front counter in the shop, he kept a jar of pickled sausage and a jar of pickled eggs. Along with the bread and sausage, he would boil up a large pot of coffee. Every noon and afternoon, several men from the village and men from the surrounding district would stop by, buy a piece of sausage and a coffee for the sum of ten cents and sit around the table or stove and discuss the state of the village and the world. Occasionally, some entrepreneurial farmers would bring in a quart or two of home brew . . . . he thought the brew always made the lunch taste better.

On this night, Otto gazed into the pot and found a six inch long piece of sausage simmering in the water. The coffee was old and bitter but he decided to drink some anyway. He wished that someone had left behind an ounce or two of home brew but after examining the array of empty containers, there was none to be found. Tonight he was left with only a half full pot of the morning coffee. He picked up one of the used cups that he was sure was the one that he had drunk from and filled it to the brim. Taking his cup of coffee and his sausage sandwich, he went into his office and sat down to record the day's activity. He knew before he ever sat down that the results would not be encouraging. Every day was the same . . . . it had been the same for all the years that he owned the shop and even before. The optimism that he had felt when he first began to work in the shop had been soon dashed when the effects of the depression expanded to the northern reaches of pioneer settlements in Saskatchewan.

In order to save every penny possible, Otto would only turn on the low level light bulb in the room where he would be working, so when he sat down at his desk, only one small dim bulb illuminated his desk and the rest of the shop lay in darkness. Slowly, he first removed the paper money from the cash drawer. Then he sorted the coins into their various designated values and lastly, he removed all the charge slips. Shaking his head but to no surprise, after counting and recording the day's receipts, the total value of sales for the day came to twenty-eight dollars and fifty cents. Of that amount, eight dollars was cash and the remaining twenty dollars and fifty cents was recorded as money owing. Propping his elbows on the desk, and then cupping his cheeks in his hands, he gazed forlornly at the two tiny piles of money.

"How long can his last?" Otto asked himself.

"Every year since I took over this shop, I believed that things would return to the way they were when we first arrived in Canada but each year just gets worse and this is the worst year yet. At least, up until this year, the farmers could feed their livestock and reap some produce from their gardens, but this year there was no crop at all . . . . all the farmers are destitute. I had heard and read of how the depression and the drought were driving thousands of families out of their homes in southern Saskatchewan but now I know what effects that no rain has. It makes me sad to see farmers coming into town pulling their cars with horses because they have no money for gasoline. It makes me sad to see people lined up and waiting in front of a box car of dried salted cod fish, eager to get a few pieces of the cardboard fish sent to the west from the Atlantic provinces. It makes me sad that I cannot provide a better place for my family. How often over the last years have I been on the verge of just closing the doors to the shop behind me and walking away? I cry when I see the little children, including my own, running around town barefooted, dressed in clothing that has patch upon patch, looking hungrily and longingly at the candies displayed in Lee Don's Cafe. I honestly did not believe that we would survive the summer's heat. I was glad when fall came and things cooled down, but now, the cold has taken over from the heat. It is not over yet. I really don't know how we will survive, but survive we will . . . . we have to."

He shook his head to chase the depressing thoughts from his head and a voice inside of him said, "Otto, you have come so far, you cannot give up now."

His sausage and coffee had turned cold but he drank the coffee and ate the sausage anyway. He focused on completing his chores before climbing under the blankets of his cot. He had wood for the stoves and blankets on his cot . . . . all would be well. He crammed as many pieces of dried aspen as he could in both the front Quebec heater and the McClarey kitchen stove located in the back portion of his shop. The back of the shop was where he cut up the carcasses, made his sausage, kept his records and where he, when necessary, would sleep. Even though he banked the stoves as much as possible, he knew that he would have to get up during the night and replenish the supply of wood in the stoves.

After removing his outer garments and still wearing his suit of Stanfield underwear, he extinguished the last remaining lit bulb. He then climbed under the blankets of his cot, pulled the blankets up to his chin and there, lying on his back and staring into the darkness of the room, he tried to fall asleep. As he lay with eyes wide open, he became aware that the room was totally dark. There was no glimmer of light entering from anywhere.

"How symbolic," he thought, "this darkness is just like my financial life right now . . . . no glimmer of light that would brighten up the future . . . . only darkness through which my eyes cannot penetrate no matter how long and how hard I stare. I might as well try to sleep because I have run out of ideas and plans but even as bleak as the future looks, I will not give up. I am not a quitter. I have survived freezing cold before; I have survived the horror of battle, and I will survive this drought and depression. I am thankful that my family and I, have so far, escaped the other curses brought on by the drought and depression. Many other families are dealing with tuberculosis, polio, dust related lung infections, sleeping sickness, hordes of grasshoppers, army worms and mounds of Russian thistle. For some years now, I cursed the sloughs on our land but this year I am thankful for them; at least I was able to mow enough slough hay to feed the cows for the winter. Now, go to sleep, Otto."

As hard as he tried to dismiss them from his thoughts, the events that had occurred between the years 1929 and 1937 played over and over again in his mind. He recalled the joy that everyone felt with the arrival of Hugo, his wife Elsie and their son, Irwin, in July of 1929. Because of the arrival of Hugo and his family, Otto recalled how he, Clara and the children had moved out of Martin's home and into the village of Hafford. He recalled the collapse of the Stock Market and how he had no understanding how that would impact him. He recalled that it did not take long to feel the effects of the collapse when he shipped two hogs to the Meat Packers in Prince Albert and upon receiving his transaction statement, he recalled that he was credited $7.00 for the two hogs, the shipping costs amounted to $6.00, thereby receiving a cheque for $1.00. He recalled how the only Christmas gifts bought were a box of oranges and some Christmas ribbon candy. The birth of his fourth son, Rudy, flashed through his mind. Then he began to recall how in 1931, his brother Hugo, died suddenly, leaving a pregnant Elsie with two children, without a father and how a year later, Adolph returned from Vancouver because of the high unemployment even in Vancouver and how Adolph married Hugo's widow Elsie soon after his return. He reviewed all the jobs and work that he had been engaged in since arriving in Canada. He recalled that when he first arrived in 1927, the daily wage paid an average of $3.50 per day. That was a lot compared to the wage of $1.00 per day which he received on the last job he had as a laborer. However, even with such low daily wages, he was very proud of himself because he was able to put aside a little cash and how over the years, his little secret stash of cash grew to the point where he was able to make a deal with the previous owner of the butcher shop. He recalled how the owner had come to him one day in 1934, and said,

"Otto, I have had enough. I am giving up trying to make a living from this shop. The reasons are many but mostly, it is because I am alone and have to pay for any help that I need in running the shop. I can't be out buying butcher grade livestock, doing the butchering, making sausage, and serving customers all at the same time and I can't afford to pay for help anymore. Your sons are growing up and are able to help you. Also, you have your brother, Adolph, who you have told me, is willing to help. You could probably survive here. I am willing to sell this place to you real cheap. I have an opportunity to get work elsewhere and if you don't want it, I will simply close the doors and walk away like many other small business owners are doing."

The depression and the drought for Otto was a blessing as well as a curse. He admitted to himself that if the depression had not occurred, he would not have been able to purchase the butcher shop for the price that he paid; however, he also was aware that finding a good bargain does not necessarily mean success, as he was currently having to cope with extremely low prices, extremely cold winters, extremely dry summers and extremely poor people from whom he was trying to earn a living. His thoughts turned again to the large stack of unpaid accounts owed to him. He knew that he was caught in a place from which there was not escape. If he would no longer extend credit to his customers, the relatives and friends of those customers would probably not support him, and if he would continue to extend credit, he would continue to work for almost nothing and lose money in the process. He felt that the many who owed money, owed so much that it would take years for them to be able to pay their outstanding bills. He knew that his was not the only business that was owed a great deal of money. He rationalized though, that the genuinely honest customers would find a way to pay him . . . . like the customer who came to him and offered his Model T Ford as payment for monies owing. The beginnings of a smile came on his face as he thought about the offer. He took the offer and the car was currently sitting behind his house, waiting for spring. When the offer was made, he recalled that he was not very eager to accept it, but after realizing that a car would improve his and his family's life immensely, he accepted. Oscar was seventeen years old . . . . old enough to drive and Eugene was fifteen, so by the coming summer, he too, would be eligible to drive a car. Clara would be able to attend Zion Lutheran Church which was located sixteen miles away. It would also help him to haul the butchered carcasses from his slaughter house to the shop as well as enable him to scout the area for potential butcher grade livestock.

"Now," he grinned, "if only I knew how to drive a car and if only I could afford the gasoline for it."

As the wood in the stoves began to turn to ashes, the frigid air covering the countryside began to creep inside the shop through the various cracks around windows, the door and through the walls. The tingling of his nose was the signal for him to climb out from under the warm blankets, feel his way through the darkness, find the firewood and restoke both stoves. He welcomed this chore thinking that the interruption from his thoughts would clear his head of past experiences and allow him to get some sleep.

His second attempt at sleep was no more successful than his first, but instead of thinking about his business, he began to think about his family. His first thoughts were of the number of babies for whom he had played the role of midwife. After Clara had given birth to Arnold in August of 1927, Clara informed him, in no uncertain terms, that should another baby arrive, she would not go to the hospital. Smiling, Otto counted the number of times he was the midwife. Every three years, as regular as clockwork, another baby came along . . . . in 1930, Rudy was born . . . . in 1933 Vonda was born . . . . in 1936 Edward was born.

"Well," he thought, "at least I have two more years before another one will come along."

"Having babies was easy," he thought, "but feeding and clothing them now is not."

Thinking about his and Clara's situation, Adolph and Elsie's situation, as well as his sister Olga's situation, made him feel sorry for his father Martin, upon whom much of the burden for living space was placed.

"The past ten years have certainly not been kind to my father," reflected Otto.

"Almost ten years ago, Clara and I, along with our three children came to Hafford and even though the living space was very cramped, he welcomed us. Then two years later Hugo, Elsie and their son Irwin replaced us. Then following Hugo's death in 1932, Elsie, Irwin and Edith, having no means of support, returned to live with father. In a way, that was good for father because Olga had moved out and was working for a family in the Speer's area and the companionship would have been welcomed. However by 1933 father, I guess, overcome by the pressures of trying to remain financially solvent in the midst of the devastating depression and by other factors not explained to me, gave up and turned his land over to Adolph and myself. The land . . . . section 33, township 43, range 10, west of the 3rd meridian . . . . was not much of a gift though as father had not yet paid the C.P.R. for the land and the title was still held by the Canadian Pacific Railway. He had continued to live in the house. That period of time was not kind to any of us. We found ourselves moving several times from homes that had been deserted by families who had given up and had moved out of the district. Having been given the one hundred sixty acres was fine and we decided that we would try to manage the butcher shop, as well as try to do some farming. At least by having land, we could plant a garden, raise some chickens and pigs, and milk some cows."

The C.P.R. was in no hurry to foreclose on the property and the agent asked only that the taxes be paid until times improved and different arrangements could then be made. Otto, Clara and their children finally moved into the 26' X 12' house on Sec 33, Township 43, Range 10, West of the 3rd meridian, when Martin moved in with his daughter Olga and her young daughter, Hertha.

"I am worried about Olga and her ability to survive on the one quarter section of land that she acquired. I suppose one of father's reasons for giving up his land and going to live with his daughter Olga, was to be able to help Olga in any way that he could. At least, father will now qualify for government relief, such as it is! One good thing, is that her land is not even a mile south of Hafford and she can walk to town for those things that she needs and Adolph and I are close enough that we, with our boys, are able to help when she needs help."

"Last year, after struggling for years to make ends meet, prices started improving and people were beginning to be able to buy some things; but God must be very angry, because last summer was the driest summer yet, the average yield for grain was less than three bushels per acre. That is hardly enough grain to feed the chickens, let alone sell some. So here I am now; farmers desperate for livestock feed and giving their cattle and hogs away and here I am, a butcher, lots of meat . . . . no money. Monday morning, two hogs and a steer are being brought to the slaughter house so when I get up, I will fill the stoves with coal and then walk over to the slaughter house and start a fire in the stove out there and put some water on the stove . . . . maybe I will ask Adolph to help me with the butchering because butchering in the cold is very hard."

Finally after several sleepless hours, Otto began to drift off . . . . his last conscious images were those of the bitter cold in Galicia, the warmth of the fires in St. Petersburg, the unforgettable images of Anya and their children.

"Oh, so long ago," he thought.

CHAPTER 28

The sun, north of the fifty-second degree parallel of latitude, takes its time bringing daylight to the frozen land and in January it makes its appearance over the horizon after 7:00 a.m.

By the time the sun rose, Otto had risen, eaten a breakfast of fried gritzwurst and coffee, had replenished the wood box with fire wood, had brought in a day supply of coal for the fires and had checked his frozen meat supply. He then put on his ushanka hat, pulled down the flaps, slipped into his great coat, wrapped a scarf around his head and neck, picked up his sack containing herrings from the ever present herring barrel and some garlic sausage, closed the door to the shop and stepped outside to face the gripping cold and began making his way . . . . first to the slaughter house and then from there, home to his family. The blowing and drifting snow had erased all signs of human traffic of the previous day. The village showed no signs of outdoor activity . . . . the only signs of life came from the smoke that rose from every chimney in the village. Standing on a rock hard, wind blown snow bank, Otto deliberated the idea of walking to the slaughter house.

"Am I the only fool in town, to brave this weather?" He thought.

There were no hardened tracks in the snow that he could follow . . . . he would have to break trail wherever he went and if the snow would give way under each step that he took, then the walking would be most difficult and tiring. If he became exhausted there would be no other passers-by that could help. He knew that sitting down to rest under these conditions would result in freezing to death. Otto decided that he would start out and if he found walking too difficult, he would return to the safety of his shop. He had made this trek many times before and he knew that, given normal conditions, he could be home in less than two hours, but given the extreme cold and unknown walking conditions, he reasoned that he should give himself an extra hour at least. He knew that even though the extreme cold would urge him to walk faster than normal, he would instead have to slow down his pace . . . . breaking into a sweat, then resting, would be his death knell.

Securing his sack onto his back, Otto began making his way out of town. He soon learned that the wind driven crust of snow would bear his weight and walking was actually quite easy. The only places that he would have to walk through the ten inch snow depth, was in the sheltered area where the swirling winds had not been able to form a drift. A half hour later, he found himself opening the doors to his slaughter house.

The slaughter house which lay in a small opening surrounded by aspen trees, consisted of a building where the butchering took place, a small corral which held the animals awaiting slaughter, and an open pit where the offal would be dumped.

The corral which was attached to the building on one side, included a narrow chute only wide enough into which to squeeze an animal. A large trap door, hinged on top, was built so that when the animal to be butchered, was felled, either by a bullet into its brain or a whack on the forehead with a sledge hammer, would lean against the trap door. The weight of the animal would spring the door open and the carcass would fall onto the concrete slab inside the building where the skinning, eviscerating and quartering would take place. A wooden beam fifteen feet above the concrete slab held three block and tackles, each holding various lengths of rounded wood pieces. As quickly as possible after the beef had fallen, its throat would be cut, one of the block and tackles would be lowered, the skin between the main ligament at the back of the knee would be pierced, each end of the appropriate length of wood would then be inserted into the holes and then the carcass would be hoisted into the air. The skinning would take place as the animal was being hoisted upward. Once the carcass was completely suspended and the hide removed, a ten inch long blade would be used to slice the belly open from top to bottom. The entrails would fall onto a wheel barrow. All the internal organs would then be carefully removed; the head would be sawed off, and then the task of splitting the carcass took place using a combination of saws, axes, and knives. A large wooden work table sat in the middle of the slaughter house. This work table had a hole cut in its center. The contents of the wheel barrow would be placed on the table where the various stomachs, entrails and organs were separated. The entrails would then be emptied of their contents with the unwanted material shoved through the hole and into the waiting pails which were placed under the table. The hide would be salted, then folded and placed in a corner of the slaughter house . . . . later the hide would be sold and shipped to a tannery. There was very little waste and what was left would be either scattered in the surrounding woods for the wild animals or thrown into the open pit, and in the summer would be covered with unslaked lime.

A large cook stove sat close to the work table. This stove provided the heat in winter as well as the sole source for hot water. Butchering a beef did not require hot water but the butchering of a hog did. Rather than being skinned, the butchered hogs had the hair scraped off. The process required boiling hot water to soften the bristles which made scraping them off much easier.

Besides the table, stove and the block and tackles, the only other contents was a cupboard which housed the various butchering utensils, Otto's single shot 22 rifle which he used to fell the beef, his five pound sledge hammer which he used to stun the hogs, his one and a half inch wide double sharpened blade which he used to pierce a hog's jugular vein, his blood collecting basin and the blood stir pot, both used in the making of his delicious blood sausage. The cupboard also housed various saws and knives, sharpening stones and various cleaning supplies . . . . cleanliness was of utmost importance to Otto.

Upon entering the slaughter house, Otto took a quick look around, removed his mitts and immediately began lighting a fire in the large cook stove.

"It's no warmer in here than outside," reflected Otto. "I will light the stove and then I will fill the boilers with snow because I will need water tomorrow."

Gathering some wood chips from his wood supply, Otto soon had a blazing fire going. Once he was satisfied that the fire would not go out, he packed the two boilers which he had sitting on the stove, with snow, sharpened his butcher knives, sharpened his saws and brought in a couple of large lumps of coal.

"Hopefully," he thought, "the coal will last until I return in the morning. It should not take very long to do the butchering if Adolph is able to give me a hand. Oscar or Eugene will have to open the shop and I will need one of them to help here to skin, stir the blood and generally help wherever needed."

After being satisfied with his preparations in the slaughter house, Otto began his slow walk home.

Clara lay in her bed with baby Edward on one side of her and young Vonda on the other. Both pressed close against her body. Dawn had broken and she knew that Eddy would be awake soon and looking for his morning breakfast from her breasts. Eddy, over a year old, would breast feed for only a few more months.

"Good thing," she thought, "there isn't much else to eat in the house." She hated to disturb her babies, but she knew that the water in the water pail and everything else in the shack would freeze solid if she didn't get up and replenish the fire. She looked across the room to where her other boys and Lydia lay huddled under their blankets. They, like her, were not anxious to step onto the ice cold floor and get dressed into their day clothes.

"It's still early. I'll stay here a little while longer . . . . I just hope Otto will be able to come home today." Settling back under the thick feather filled comforter, Clara glanced at the small single glazed window above her bed to see what the weather was like but to no avail. The small window was completely engulfed with a thick layer of ice and frost. She then listened intently, wondering if the wind that had blown the snow around the previous day had died down. All was silent. The only sounds that she heard were the rhythmic breathing of her sleeping children and the occasional rustle that came from the shifting of positions by her children. Hearing nothing, she knew that doing the daily outdoor chores would be easier than they were the previous day even if it was much colder. She quickly made a mental list of all the things needing attention. She would stoke the fire and try to warm up the drafty shack. She would also cook up a large pot of rolled oats. She had thought that since it was Sunday, she could possibly make something different for breakfast. There were some options . . . . there were a couple of eggs, there was a large sack of white flour and after mentally surveying her supplies, realized that that was it. There was no fruit, no syrup, no bacon, no fresh vegetables. Porridge, it would be and only if the milk cow had not gone completely dry. Clara then shifted her thoughts to the dinner meal. She planned to have it ready by two o'clock in the afternoon. She reasoned that Otto would be home by then and they could all eat together. She would do a roast, bring up potatoes and carrots from the earth cellar as well as a two quart jar of rhubarb fruit. There still were pickled cucumbers in the pickle barrel. She would make gravy from the roast drippings. Then the meal would end with cups of black tea.

"We have no money to buy clothes or toys and other nice things for our children but at least, we have enough food to eat . . . . at least for now. Soon the cow will dry up completely and the chickens will stop laying. Hopefully, there will be some money left over from the business that we will be able to buy some condensed Carnation milk and some eggs."

Refocusing on the present, Clara thought, "Oscar will milk the cow, have breakfast, then he and Eugene can finish the morning outdoor chores. They will have to feed the chickens some of the little wheat that we have in the bin. They will have to take the horses and cows to the well for a drink of water. I am sure that the water trough is completely frozen over and they will need to chop out some of the ice and make an ice bowl so that they have something into which to pour the water. After watering the cows and horses, they will have to pull some hay off of the haystack and feed the animals. It's too cold to clean the stalls today so they will need only to scatter a little of the hay on the floor; the cows like to bed down in their stalls. The wood box is just about empty so they will have to dig through the snow drifts to get to the wood stack and then bring a few arm loads of cut wood into the house. They can take whatever food is left over from breakfast and feed it to the dogs, probably in the barn where it is quite warm, even if the barn can hardly be called a barn. It's Sunday but we can't get to church. We will have devotions right after we eat our dinner. It's too cold to send Arnold, Rudy and Vonda outside to play today, so they will have to think of things to do inside. I guess they will play checkers and they have their school readers and some other books from school; or they can take their jack knives and whittle, make schnoir katas, flying hand propellers, jumping jacks, sewing spool tractors or spin tops, but I know what they will do . . . . they will end up wrestling . . . . let them sleep!"

Clara reached out and lifted her day dress and stockings from the chair beside her bed and tucked them next to her body under the comforter. They would warm up somewhat which would make getting dressed easier. After Eddy had had his breakfast, Clara pulled the heavy home knit wool stockings onto her feet and swung her feet onto the ice cold floor and quickly slipped her dress over her head. Then standing, she pulled it down into position.

She quickly added fuel to the fire, broke the thin layer of ice in the water bucket, poured some into the tea kettle and then placed the tea kettle on the hottest part of the stove. Minutes later the children rose, dressed quickly and gathered around the stove. It would take over an hour to get the temperature up high enough to be comfortable in the shack.

"How cold is it outside?" Asked Eugene.

"You know we don't have a thermometer or a radio or even a telephone so we have no way of knowing how cold it. All I know is that the cold comes through the cracks around the windows and door and through the walls. Jump up and down if your feet are cold or you can pull up a chair and put it in front of the oven door. Open the oven door and put your feet on the open door," replied Clara.

She gave out a sigh, knowing that she would have to referee the squabbles that were sure to erupt over the limited space of the oven door. Protecting the rights of the smaller children was always difficult as was her access to the stove top with all the children hovering around the stove.

"I better check the reservoir to see if it needs filling," continued Clara. "If it does need replenishing, Eugene will have to bring in a couple of buckets of snow and pack it into the reservoir so that by the time Otto gets home there will be hot water for washing the dishes and the children's hands and faces. They all had a bath in the wash tub yesterday so I won't have to melt snow for that but I will tomorrow as I have to wash clothes. I hope it warms up outside because in this weather, my hands will freeze pinning the wet clothes onto the line. If it's too cold, I will wash only Eddy's diapers and hang them over the backs of chairs and on the string that Otto strung across the room."

Wearily, Clara picked up the whimpering Eddy, sat down on the edge of the bed and began to feed him. From the bedside, she surveyed the place they called home. Watching her six children as they went about their activities, made her wonder what the future held in store for them.

"Oh dear God, will things ever get better?" Thought Clara.

CHAPTER 29

1939

Twelve long and trying years had passed since she, her husband and their children came to Saskatchewan to seek a better life than they had in Poland. Twelve years ago, she had left, feeling torn between apprehension and hope. She felt apprehensive because it was very hard to leave the land and the country in which she was born . . . . a country, where up until World War I, was a happy and secure place for her. Leaving behind a childhood filled with many happy memories . . . . leaving behind two of her younger sisters was not easy. Coming to a new land, having very little money, three children, pregnant with a fourth child, having no home to go to. Her feelings of hope, stemmed from news coming from Saskatchewan that, even though the frontier lacked many amenities, there was much available work, reasonable pay and ample opportunity for those who were willing to work hard. She knew that her husband would succeed.

By 1939, the years of drought, coupled with the great depression, had taken away all hopes and dreams of a paradise in Canada.

"How did this happen?' Clara thought.

"Not many years ago, I would be lying in a comfortable bed but here I am . . . . no money, no comforts, no pretty clothes, no concerts, miles from church, seven children, no privacy, no space and no hope for a better life . . . . lying in this old bed, my body wracked by labour pains, sweat oozing out of every pore, waiting for another child to arrive."

On this day there were no sounds other than those of birds singing and calling to each other, cows mooing in the pasture, crows and magpies cawing and cackling. Grasshoppers could be heard as they flitted from grass blade to grass blade as well as the high pitched chirping of gophers as they played in the warm sun. Nature was all around. No speeding cars, no train whistles, no roaring of jet planes, no humming of a tractor or the whizzing of a lawn mower. No police sirens hastily speeding to trouble. No ambulance or fire engine sirens. No sounds of children playing. The farm was quiet.

After a bitterly long and cold winter, the spring sun once again blessed the earth with its warmth, causing life to spring forth from the seeds which had lay dormant in the frozen soil for many months. Robins, meadow larks, crows, magpies, wrens, orioles, swallows, hawks were awake early and eagerly building their nests which would offer warm cozy homes for their young. All around there was a renewed sense of optimism and hope. Even the cows in the pasture with their newly born calves, the chickens with their newly hatched chicks were happy and content.

Inside, the bare wood floors were covered with crumbs, bits of straw and grass and lumps of dirt which had fallen from shoes. In the centre of the room, the round oak table was graced with a half full jug of fresh milk and a tray loaded with freshly washed breakfast dishes. The beds which consisted of Winnipeg couches which doubled as beds, were pushed against the walls. There was no radio or television, no telephone, the kerosene lamp had been put away for the summer. The huge kitchen stove was still warm from the wood fire which had been made to cook the morning porridge . . . . the only breakfast food in the house. The walls, grey from the long winter's wood smoke, awaited washing.

It was Friday morning. Earlier there had been seven children crowded into this room, busily preparing themselves for the day that lay ahead. Oscar, the oldest, had left early to harness the team of horses and to hitch them to the breaking plow. Eugene was getting dressed to walk to Hafford, where he helped in the butcher shop. Lydia, Arnold, Rudy and Vonda were ushered out the door earlier than usual and were on their way to Whiteberry School. Only three year old Eddy remained at home.

Clara had awakened before dawn and had gently poked Otto and said, "Otto, you can't go to the butcher shop today.

Eugene will have to manage on his own. You must stay at home."

"Was in der Welt ich ist, hier tuend! Gott, bitte, bitte, was tat ich, um das zu verdienen? Was tat ich, um das zu verdienen? Wie coud, den Sie mich einem anderen Kind in diese Holle einer Welt bringen lassen!" ("What in the world am I doing here! God, please, please, what did I do to deserve this? How could you let me bring another child into this hell of a world!")

Coming to Canada was supposed to have been an escape from the threat of persecution and danger in Poland . . . . a chance for a better life. The posters, the literature and information held so much promise. It sounded so good, so promising . . . .

"Lieber Gott," ("Dear God,") . . . . another stab of pain.

Tears, agony, pain, fear, determination, love, hate, despair . . . . every emotion thrown together at a time when another unwanted child was about to enter the world.

"Clara, wilst du zu der Krankenhaus gehen?" ("Clara, do you want to go to the hospital?")

"Nein Otto! ich gehe nicht zu der Krankenhaus—vielleicht ist es besser, das ich werden sterben. Ich habe nicht kiene leben hier." ("No Otto! I am not going to the hospital . . . . perhaps it would be just as well that I died. I have no life here.")

"Clara, du must nicht so sprechen—wir werden besser zieten nur sehen." ("Clara, you must not speak like that; we will see better times soon.")

"Otto, Otto, ich habe das schon fur zehn jahre gehort. Nien Otto, es geht nicht besser." ("Otto, Otto, I have been hearing that for ten years. No Otto, It's not going to get better.")

Few words were exchanged. Otto knew what had to be done . . . . he had done this several times. Being a midwife held no surprises. Methodically, he prepared for the delivery . . . . heating water, arranging towels and blankets, bringing Clara drinking water . . . . all the while reflecting on her admonition . . . . maybe she was right . . . . maybe things will never really improve.

"However," he thought, "I have seen signs of better things to come . . . . more and more people are able to pay for their meat, the crops were a lot better than last year, the grasshoppers also were not as bad as in 1937. There is also no doubt that another war will erupt in Europe and who knows what will happen if Canada is dragged into it and . . . ."

"Otto hurry, the baby is coming."

"Eddie, go outside and play with the dogs and cats until I call you back into the house!"

Three year old Eddie did not understand what was about to occur.

The birth was not difficult. There were no complications. Friday, June 2, 1939, at 11:30 a.m., the eighth of nine children born to Clara and Otto Flath was brought into the world. The birth certificate reads: Male. Section 33, Township 43, Range 10, West of the 3rd Meridian, Canada. They named the child Harry Martin Flath. The actual location . . . . a converted grain bin on a piece of land one mile west and one half mile north of the village of Hafford, Saskatchewan.

With the first gurgle and howl from Harry's tiny body, Clara's feelings of despair, grief and hopelessness turned to joy. With the new life inside their place called home, along with the new life emerging in the woods, fields and gardens, Clara and Otto were one with their surroundings. New life brings new hope. Gone was the despair felt only a few minutes before and a new purpose for living enveloped Clara. Surely better things awaited . . . . just around the corner.

EPILOGUE

Like the phoenix that rose from the ashes, so too, prosperity arose from the drought and depression of the 1930's. The children, that were born during the time of the worst economic opportunities ever experienced by people on the prairies, became the benefactors of the best economic opportunities ever experienced by those people from the prairies. As in the words of Charles Dickens,

"It was the best of times. It was the worst of times."

The thousands of families that came from Russia, from Poland, from Galicia, from Scandinavia, from the United Kingdom and a myriad of other places . . . . all came to settle in a land where the most appealing thing the government offered was an opportunity to carve out a better life for themselves and their children. There were few institutions in place where these people could turn to for help. They were on their own and across the vast prairie, community after community immediately began to build schools, roads, hospitals, churches, and community halls. It did not matter what their mother tongue was . . . . the people were eager to shed their sheepskin coats and embrace a new culture. When the clock struck 9:00 a.m., the teacher and students in every one of the thousands of country schools across the Prairies, proudly raised the Union Jack, recited the Lord's prayer and sang God Save the King.

However, in their eagerness to shed their sheepskin coats, there became a reluctance to pass on old family traditions and language. Much of the rich family history was quickly forgotten, leaving the offspring to only wonder and imagine what their ancestor's life was like as they thumbed through old photographs with curiosity and interest. In their eagerness to concentrate on their present and future identity, many families did not appreciate or understand the importance of their past.

THE FLATHS

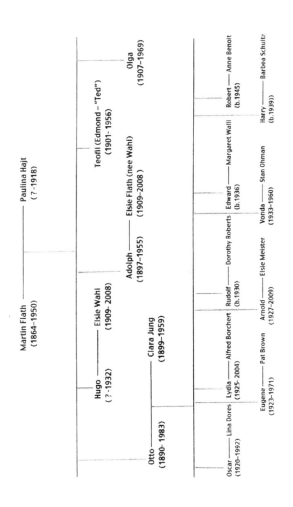

Martin Flath
(1864–1950)
———
Paulina Hajt
(? -1918)

Hugo
(? -1932)
———
Elsie Wahl
(1909- 2008)

Teofil (Edmond – "Ted")
(1901- 1956)
———
Olga
(1907–1969)

Otto
(1890- 1983)
———
Clara Jung
(1899–1959)

Adolph
(1897–1955)
———
Elsie Flath (nee Wahl)
(1909- 2008)

Oscar —— Lina Dores
(1920–1992)

Lydia —— Alfred Borchert
(1925- 2004)

Rudolf —— Dorothy Roberts
(b.1930)

Edward —— Margaret Walli
(b.1936)

Robert —— Anne Benoit
(b.1945)

Eugene —— Pat Brown
(1923–1971)

Arnold —— Elsie Meister
(1927–2009)

Vonda —— Stan Ohman
(1933–1960)

Harry —— Barbea Schultz
(b.1939)

337

THE JUNGS

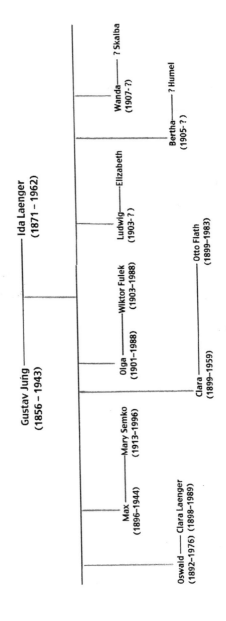

Gustav Jung (1856 – 1943) — Ida Laenger (1871 – 1962)

Max (1896–1944) — Mary Semko (1913–1996)

Oswald (1892–1976) — Clara Laenger (1898–1989)

Clara (1899–1959) — Otto Flath (1899–1983)

Olga (1901–1988) — Wiktor Fulek (1903–1988)

Ludwig (1903–?) — Elizabeth

Bertha (1905–?) — ? Humel

Wanda (1907–?) — ? Skalba

CPSIA information can be obtained at www.ICGtesting.com
Printed in the USA
LVOW13s1954131113

361176LV00001B/9/P